A REASON TO LIVE

A REASON TO LIVE

A Marty Singer Mystery

MATTHEW IDEN

THOMAS & MERCER

Text copyright © 2012 Matthew Iden
All rights reserved.

Published by Thomas & Mercer, Seattle
www.apub.com

Amazon, the Amazon logo, and Thomas & Mercer are trademarks of Amazon.com, Inc., or its affiliates.

ISBN-13: 9781477829417
ISBN-10: 1477829415

Printed in the United States of America

For Renee, who continues to make the whole thing possible.
For my family.
For my friends.

I.

I'll be leaving soon.

I've had time to think. So much time. I was lost for most of it. Scared that I didn't have purpose, not knowing what to do with the anger and the energy and the life that's left to me.

But I know now. I know how to put my life back together. What it will take. The sacrifices, the actions. I think you know, too.

It's what's kept me alive, you know. Not your interventions. Protecting the body is just half the equation. The spirit has to have a reason to go on, too. And now I have mine.

Please. Don't try to stop me. I need to do this.

CHAPTER ONE

"Detective Singer?"

"Not anymore," I said without thinking—and regretted it. The words stuck in my mouth after the sound was gone, rolling around like stones. Hard. Unwelcome. Bitter. I couldn't spit them out and couldn't swallow them.

I was killing time at a coffee shop, slouched in an overstuffed chair that had been beaten into submission years earlier. The café—I don't know the name, Middle Grounds or Mean Bean or something precious—was a grungy, brown stain of a place flanked by a failing Cajun restaurant on one side and a check-cashing store on the other. A crowd of Hispanic guys hung around out front looking simultaneously aimless and expectant, hoping their next job was about to pull up to the curb.

I looked up from my cup and stared at the girl who'd called me by name. She was slim, with delicate brown hair worn past the shoulders and intense, dark eyes set in a face so pale Poe would've written stories about it. She wore black tights and a long tunic the color of beach sand, with only a ragged jean-jacket to guard against the bite of early December. Her arms hugged two books to her chest and she toted a massive black backpack so heavy it had her hunched over like a miner.

My answer hung in the air and the silence stretched thin. The girl hesitated, floundering.

I let her. I was in a bad mood. A meaningless Thanksgiving was a week past and all morning I'd looked for something productive to do while my day dragged itself across the floor of my life. When the productivity failed to materialize and my thoughts started to crowd in, I'd come to the coffee shop to forget, not remember. And I'd almost done it, my mind gone gloriously blank until this girl had brought my thoughts tumbling around me like a midair collision. She opened her mouth to explain, maybe, or apologize. Her face was bright and full of enthusiasm. Energy and purpose radiated from her, wearying me. I waited to hear whatever it was she thought was important enough to reel me in from daydream land.

She never got to it. A shout from the street—a single, loud cry of frustration, rage, and raw emotion—shut her down and froze every person in the café. Cups stopped halfway to mouths, heads cocked like hunting dogs'. Anything the girl might've said—anything anyone was saying—took a backseat to that sound.

More shouts from the street swelled to envelop the first one and I found myself at the window with everyone else, the girl forgotten, peering through the glass, looking over shoulders, drawn to the potential of violence or drama. I wasn't alone. People reading Sartre and sipping no-foam lattes a second before now jostled each other, all asking, "What's happening?"

What's happening was unclear. The shout had come from the crowd of guys in front of the check-cashing store. They were dressed in the ubiquitous outfit of local Salvadoran or Guatemalan day laborers: tattered baseball caps, paint-spattered jeans, ripped sweatshirts. Two of the six were shouting at each other, their hands stabbing the air as they spoke, their jaws thrust forward. The body language didn't look good and I was on my way outside—forgetting that this wasn't my job anymore—when I heard someone from inside the café yell, "Holy shit!"

I was late. By the time I'd pushed the door open, the shorter one—stained gray sweatshirt, shoulders like a running back—had pulled a knife and was swinging at the other guy, his arm whipping back and forth. On the third arc, he connected, cutting the other guy open like he'd been unzipped from hip to belly button. A scream, high and long, split the air and the ring of onlookers melted away. The man who'd been cut glanced down at his own body with a look of disbelief, then staggered down the street, bouncing off parked cars and telephone poles, his arms hugging his stomach.

I kept my attention on the short guy who'd done the slicing. A wicked-looking linoleum knife—needlelike point, a forward curve, teeth at the base—dangled from his hand. His eyes were wide, the whites very white, the irises a bottomless dark brown. He hissed something in Spanish and waved the knife around like a conductor's baton. Common sense told me to run back into the coffee shop. Instead, I sidled closer, talking low and slow in terrible Spanish. I don't even know what I was saying to him. I was trying to ask him to calm down and give me the knife, but he erupted into tears the third time I asked, then came at me with wild, full-arm sweeps. The point of the knife winked in the flat December sun. It took no imagination to see it hooking into my gut and cutting clean through, making my other problems seem like small beans.

A trio of desperate twists got me out of range of one, two, three swipes, then I stepped forward, slipping inside his reach. He tried a quick backhanded slash, but I was too close for him to get any muscle behind it. With my chest to his back, I snaked my arm inside his elbow like I wanted to square-dance, then grabbed a handful of sweatshirt between his shoulder blades. With my other hand, I snatched at his free arm. Not a bad move, and the improvised armlock had neutralized the knife, but it wasn't going to last long. Teeth gnashed near my ear as he tried to bite me and when he started to flex those shoulders, my grip started to go, fast.

I didn't wait to see where that was going. I heaved one way, twisted my hips the other, and put him on the ground with an ankle sweep.

Desperation made me follow through harder than I meant to and—
without a hand to stop his fall—the guy's forehead hit the sidewalk with
the sound of a watermelon dropped on a kitchen floor. His grip on the
knife went slack, just like the rest of him.

Our scrap was over in seconds. Which was a good thing, since I
wasn't in much better shape than the guy with the knife. My bit of
pseudo-judo had taken me to the ground, too, and I lay there next
to him, arms still tangled with his, my chest heaving. I was dizzy and
would've fallen down if I hadn't already been lying on my back. My
breath rasped like an old steam engine trying to take a hill and my
elbow throbbed from where I'd banged it on the concrete. The bricks
were cold beneath me. Clouds passed across the sky. Sirens threaded
the air in the distance.

And the sound of footsteps scuffed close. I turned my head, hoping
it wasn't one of the guy's compadres coming to get in a free lick while I
was down. But the face that bent over me belonged to the girl from the
coffee shop. I seemed to remember she'd wanted to talk to me about a
million years ago. Her hair swung forward as she knelt down and she
reflexively tucked it behind one ear, only to have it fall back again. Her
eyes were dark with worry.

"Mr. Singer?" she asked. "Are you . . . are you okay?"

"I'm fine," I said from the ground. I closed my eyes. The sirens
that had sounded distant a second before now closed in, wailing like a
demented wolf pack on the run. "I just wish I was still getting paid to
do this."

It took me an hour to clear things up with the Arlington PD. It would've
taken longer, but a dozen people had watched the whole thing from
the safety of the coffee shop and vouched that my little dance might've
saved someone's life. Nice of them to say it, but I shrugged off the

accolades when I found out that the guy with the knife was an illegal immigrant from southern Mexico who'd learned this morning he was being deported back to Juárez. He'd drunk everything in his pocket, then gone off the deep end at something his amigos had said to him. The guy he'd cut had a fifty-fifty chance of making it. No winners here.

I gave my statement to the cops, the ambulances left, and the crowd faded away. A busboy came out from the Cajun restaurant and threw a bucket of soapy water on the blood from the first knife fight, creating a rust-colored puddle that pushed its way down the sidewalk. I watched it for a moment, then turned and headed back toward the coffee shop when I saw the jean-jacket girl standing to one side of the café door, looking uncomfortable. She'd waited through the entire escapade. Whatever it was she wanted to talk about must be important. She took a step forward, intercepting me as I reached the door.

"Mr. Singer, I'm really sorry to bother you," she said. "I know you're probably not in any shape to talk right now—"

"I can talk," I said, barely slowing down. "I might not want to."

She hesitated at my tone, then stuck her hand out. "Maybe we can start over. I'm Amanda Lane."

I stopped, shook, and waited for her to continue. When she didn't, I said, "Okay, Amanda Lane. What can I do for you?"

She looked stricken. "You don't—God, I'm sorry. I thought you'd remember right away. I'm Brenda Lane's daughter. You worked on my mom's case. Back in '96?"

"Oh. *Oh*," I said, straightening. My crabbiness dribbled away and I felt a flush creep up my neck. "What can I do for you, Ms. Lane? I'm not with the department anymore."

"It's just Amanda, Mr. Singer. My mom was Ms. Lane."

"All right, Amanda."

"I know you retired recently," she said. "I called the DC police and talked to someone in your squad. I mean, old squad. They told me you'd probably be here."

"You just called the MPDC and asked for me?" I said, surprised.

"No, I . . . I kept the card you gave me. That night. Your number didn't work, but it went over to someone else's extension."

"Jesus," I said. "You held on to that thing for twelve years?"

Her smile came back. "It's like a charm. The night you gave it to me, I put it in this little purse with a plastic shield and never took it out. Saved it from the wash more than once."

"I'm flattered," I said, then waited.

"Well," she said, faltering. "I know this is weird and I know you're not with the police anymore, but you seemed to be the only one I could call right now. The only one who might understand."

"Understand what?"

"I don't know if you're the right person, but I . . ." She trailed off.

My patience started to lift around the edges. "Look, Amanda, you came this far. You might as well tell me something."

Words tumbled out of her like kid's blocks from a box. "There hasn't been a crime, so I can't go to the police. In fact, nothing's actually happened, so there's nothing to even report, but my mom took too long and I'm afraid if I wait and see, then that's the dumbest thing I could possibly do. I don't want to end up as a story in the newspaper, I—"

"Hold on," I said. In just a few sentences, her voice had taken off, getting loud, rushed, and scared. "Start at the beginning. Keep it simple. Are you in danger?"

She swallowed. "Not right now."

"You said now. You think you will be soon?"

"Yes."

"From someone you know or a stranger?"

"Both," Amanda said.

"What does that mean?"

"It's Michael. Michael Wheeler, the man who killed my mom. He's back. And I think he's back for me."

CHAPTER TWO

"Let's take a walk," I said.

We left the coffee shop and headed down Wilson Boulevard past the new developments that had sucked the soul out of the neighborhood and toward the older homes—the ones with lawns and shutters and chimneys—that kept the community alive, even if it was on life support. It was cold. No snow had fallen yet but a crisp, white sun gave the impression that it was warmer than it was. I tucked my hands in my jacket and turtled my head into the collar.

I stole a glance at Amanda as we walked. She was taller than I'd first thought, a willowy five nine or ten. She tucked a lock of hair behind an ear as she walked, matching me stride for stride. "Thanks for agreeing to talk, Mr. Singer."

I waved a hand. "Just Marty. Mr. Singer makes me sound like a high school principal."

"Thanks, Marty," she said, and looked sideways at me. A shy smile slipped out.

"What?"

"You haven't changed much at all," she said. "Same black hair, same green eyes. I was afraid I'd be looking for an old guy with a gut and a comb-over."

"I'm glad I pass."

She kept up the appraisal. "You look tired, though. I thought retirement was supposed to be good for you."

Just like that, an iron band slipped around my heart and squeezed. "I don't want to talk about it."

The mask of the self-assured young woman fell away and, like the very first time I'd seen her, the face of a frightened girl peered back at me. "I'm sorry. I thought maybe it was a good thing, I—"

I grimaced. My voice had been raw, harsh. "Look, don't worry about it. Let's focus on you."

She smiled again, unsure. "All right."

We walked, letting our steps swallow the awkwardness. "So," I said after a second. "Michael Wheeler."

She nodded.

"That might be the first mistake," I said. "Assuming it's him. Let's start with what's got you worried and work towards a conclusion, instead of starting with the person first."

"The what and the who are linked," she said. "That's what's got me scared."

I didn't say anything. She took a deep breath.

"I guess you have to understand a few things to see the whole thing clearly. You may notice I call him Michael. Not Wheeler, not 'that guy' or 'the killer' or anything like that."

"I noticed."

"And you remember my mom's case?"

I nodded. I'd blanked on her name at first—it had been twelve years—but I could remember all my cases if given enough time. And I would've remembered the Lane murder regardless. It's kind of tough to forget a homicide involving a cop on your own police force.

"Back . . . then, before my mom was killed, Michael would come by the house, all the time. I mean, constantly. That's what creeped Mom out so much. It was stalking before anyone even used the word. But what made it worse is that it all started out so nice. Oh," she said with a pained look on her face, perhaps thinking I was bored by her tale. "You already know this."

"Relax. This is the expression I wear all the time," I said. "Just tell me how you remember things."

She paused, gathering her thoughts. "My mom and I lived alone. Dad was gone, killed in the Gulf. She hadn't started dating again and was working hard, so it was just the two of us. One night, before anything bad had actually happened, we heard a crash downstairs. We found out later it was the cat knocking things over, but we were terrified. I was scared like a little kid is scared, but the first thought in my mom's head was that she was a single woman with a twelve-year-old in a wealthy neighborhood. She called the police."

A woman with a small white dog walked toward us, then the dog abruptly stopped and squatted. We all pretended that he wasn't doing what he was doing. The dog looked embarrassed. "And Wheeler showed up."

"In a heartbeat. Later, when he started acting strange, Mom thought he might've made the noise himself that first night. He arrived so quickly, like he was sitting right around the corner. I don't think that was the case, but pretty soon we didn't need to dream up excuses for being scared of him."

"That was later, though," I said. "At first, he was the knight in shining armor."

"He was so nice, so . . . God, I hate to say it. I understand the concept, but . . . I despise the thought emotionally. It doesn't make me weak, but he was so—"

"Manly?" I offered.

"Yes," she said, scrubbing her face with a hand. "In the right way. I mean, I barely remembered my father. My mom was all I knew. I was a kid. The only males I ever saw were boys who grabbed themselves and the principal at school who smelled bad and here's this *policeman*, this big, hunky guy with a badge and a gun and a mustache . . ."

"I remember the mustache."

"I fell in love with him and maybe Mom did, too. She was lonely and working hard. Trying to maintain appearances and provide for me. Too busy to meet anyone, too tired to go out and try. Then chance dropped a man at our door. It's not a complicated scenario."

"And he picked up on that. Or at least tried to take advantage of it."

"No doubt."

"Was she sleeping with him?"

Amanda hesitated. "No."

I didn't say anything.

"I'm not deluding myself, Marty. I think it would've come to that, sure. But Michael turned weird too fast. The first few visits were sweet, like he was our guardian angel, you know? Then he started coming around three or four times a week."

I closed my eyes, trying to remember the details. "I looked at the complaints. I thought your mom reported him right away."

She shook her head. "My mom told the cops that she'd asked him to leave the second or third time he came around, but she hadn't. She said it after the fact to reinforce the complaint. He must've shown up a dozen times before she called it in."

"How long before your mom told him to leave the two of you alone?"

"A month, maybe? Then a week or two more before she made a complaint."

"Why wait?"

"She wasn't sure what to do. I mean, you report a cop to the cops and what happens? If you're lucky, they blow it off. If you're not, he hears about it and takes it out on you, right? But a friend convinced her that filing a complaint was what she had to do."

"So he had six weeks around you and your mom and your house before anyone even thought of slapping his hand."

"Yes."

"He ever come by when it was just you?"

"Yes."

"Alone?"

"His partner was with him most of the time, but sometimes he came by himself."

"Who was his partner?"

She thought about it. "You know, I can barely recall. A real tall guy. He'd always stay with the car, leaning against the door." She shook her head. "That's it. I only ever paid attention to Michael."

A December breeze kicked up and slipped an icy hand inside my collar. I hunched my shoulders and shoved my fists deeper into my pockets. "It was my case, after all, so I already know, or think I know, but I have to ask."

"He didn't molest me."

"And the next question is?"

"Yes, I'm sure. And, no, I'm not suppressing. I've been in therapy since I was twelve, Marty. It would've come out. All I remember was Michael being kind, being good. He made me a local celebrity with the other kids, coming to the house in his uniform, or bringing other cops around to show off. There always seemed to be a police car outside our place. No, if I blocked anything out, it was later, when Mom yelled at him, telling him to stay away. I hated her for that. I wanted her to like him. In retrospect, I know he was using me to get to her, but at the time I thought she was being a bitch."

"So how does this bring us to what's going on now?"

She sighed. "Michael came by a lot more often than Mom knew, since she was at work all the time. After he started scaring her, she sent me straight to the Jansens', next door. Even the night she was . . . she was killed, I was at the Jansens'. But for weeks before that he would come by after school."

I blinked, surprised, but didn't say anything. She continued, staring ahead but looking into the past.

"He would leave me these white flowers, tiny things. I would find them on the porch or stuck in the front gate. I thought they were roses. What did I know? They were just carnations. He probably bought them at a grocery store or something, ten for a dollar."

"What did you do with them?"

"I was careful to hide or trash most of them, but I kept one or two in my room. Mom found them and asked me where they'd come from, but I was embarrassed. I lied and told her they were from a boy at school. She thought it was cute."

"What about after your mom reported him?"

She made a face. "He came by a few times before Mom got really paranoid, then I didn't see him for . . . well, never. But even after she chased him off, I'd find flowers on the back porch or one in the basket of my bike. He got sneaky and would spread the petals on the sidewalk. The worst was when I found one on my pillow, a few days before . . . before it happened."

Even twelve years later, I felt sick. Brenda Lane's complaints should've been enough to save her life. They hadn't because they'd been dismissed with a shrug and a *so what?* But if you add obsessive pedophiliac tendencies to Wheeler's profile, *somebody* at MPDC would've paid attention. The hammer would've been dropped on him, hard. Maybe Brenda Lane would be alive. If anyone had known about it. My blood pressure spiked. "Why the hell didn't you tell someone?"

"I was twelve years old," she said, her anger flaring to match mine. "I barely knew what the hell happened the night my mom was shot. I was in Child and Family Services for two days before anyone even told me she was dead. And I still didn't believe it was Michael, not even after he was arrested. It took me a long time to accept that, and what happened at the trial didn't help."

I rubbed a hand over my jaw. "Sorry. It's just a hell of a thing to miss when you're trying to nail a guy for murder. And he walks."

We were both quiet. I stared down at the sidewalk under my feet. I counted five cracks before I said, "That fills in some gaps but doesn't change the past. What's going on now?"

She stopped abruptly and dropped her backpack to the ground. She unzipped a small pocket, fished around, and removed a Ziploc bag. Then, from the plastic bag, she pulled out exactly what I didn't want to see.

A small white carnation.

CHAPTER THREE

"I found it in front of my door two nights ago."

"Couldn't be an accident? Roommate, boyfriend, secret admirer?"

She shook her head. "No roommates. Too long since the last boyfriend. And it's an odd gift for a secret admirer, wouldn't you say?"

"Where do you work?"

"I'm a graduate student at George Washington University. Women's Studies."

I looked at her. "Students, rival grads, angry professors?"

"How would they know? What significance does it have if it's not from Michael?"

I took the flower from her and twirled it by the stem. A few petals fell off, littering the ground. It was a shoddy way to treat evidence, but the thing had been squashed in her backpack for two nights, destroying any integrity it might've had. Oh, and I wasn't a cop anymore. "So," I said, handing it back. "Why now?"

"I know. I asked myself, why should he come looking for me? It sounds stupid when I say it out loud."

"No, the why isn't stupid," I said. "There could be a hundred reasons why. The question is why *now*? Where's he been? And wherever that is, what's happened to trigger contact after so many years?"

"I did some digging around," she said. "You know, the kind of things you can do on the web."

"Sure," I said, like I knew. "What'd you find?"

"Nothing," she said. She hauled her backpack over a shoulder and we started walking again. We'd covered some serious ground and I was starting to feel it. "Not a damn thing. It's as if Michael was locked up for a decade, then walked out and decided to find me."

I grimaced and said, "We both know that didn't happen. The being locked-up part, I mean."

"I know. But it really is as if he vanished."

"It's not that hard to disappear," I said. "Especially for an ex-cop who knows the ropes. And, especially—no offense—to someone not trained to find people."

"I didn't just Google him," she said. "I've got friends at the university that can look into some sophisticated stuff. Not NSA level, sure, but access to credit reports, arrest records, job applications, stuff like that."

That got my attention. "Really?"

"GW has programs for journalists, law enforcement officers, lawyers, poli-sci analysts, most of whom intern at government agencies or high-powered law firms. They've got juice."

I snorted. "Juice?"

A blush started under her chin. "I heard it on TV."

"Don't worry about it," I said. "What did you find?"

"Everything I got was from the initial search. There was big press about my mom's murder when it happened, then a resurgence when Michael got off, then nothing. It became old news, fast. It was the Wild West in the mayor's office. He was making enough headlines to bump anybody off the front page."

"Tell me about it. I worked for the guy. Then what?"

"Then nothing," she said. "There were some follow-up articles about him moving out of the city, but they never said where he went. After that, it's as if he ceased to exist."

"We should be so lucky," I said. My breath steamed in the air and the sky was getting gray. "All right, we've got a couple possibilities. One, Wheeler's lived a quiet life raising pigs in Idaho and one day decides twelve years later is as good a time as any to risk jail time by coming back and throwing carnations at you."

"Or, he's wanted to stalk me this whole time, but been stuck somewhere else for twelve years."

"Like where?" I asked.

"I don't know. Overseas? The military?"

A bus passed us, drowning out conversation. Bored-looking passengers stared out of the windows. I waited until it got to the end of the street. "First one, no. You can get a plane any day of the week from most countries and it didn't take him twelve years to save money for a flight to DC. Second one, no. Unless we're talking the French Foreign Legion, soldiers still get leave, still get time off. It isn't prison, even if it feels like it."

"You said there were a couple of possibilities."

"Two. It's someone else entirely."

"It has to be Michael. I never told anyone about the flowers," she said. "You didn't even know."

"Sure, you never told anyone. But what if he did? He was such a smug prick, it's hard to believe he didn't confide in a buddy, a girlfriend, a coworker. This thing with the flowers didn't surface during the investigation or trial, so he knew we never found out about them. It would've been a tiny victory for him. Like he pulled one over on all of us. Guys like him would brag about something like that."

Her shoulders slumped. "So where does that leave me? It might be Michael or it might not. My life might be in danger or it might be a prank by some copycat sicko that wants to torture me about my mom's death."

I hesitated, then reached out and patted her shoulder. I'm not good at comforting people, but I've seen it done before. "First things first. You still at your apartment?"

She shook her head. "No. I freaked out as soon as I saw the flower. I packed a bag and spent the night at a friend's place."

"You've been there since?" I asked.

"Yes."

"All right, find another friend. Don't go there directly. Catch the Metro, grab a cab, whatever. Even better, switch a couple times. Don't just walk there. All right?"

She looked unhappy, but nodded.

"Next, can you take a break from classes?"

"Not really. And I have office hours, too."

I shook my head. "Show up for class late. Cancel a few, if you can. Don't move around alone, don't go anywhere after dark by yourself. Don't do office hours. Ask people to call if they need you. Posting the hours you'll actually be somewhere is, well, putting out a sign telling him where you're going to be."

Amanda was pale, but her narrow jaw jutted forward. "I can't stop everything I'm doing. I won't stop living. I refused to do that after Mom died and I'm not going to do it now."

I held up a hand. "You're not. We're just going to take some precautions."

She paused, then said, "We?"

"We. For now. Retirement is turning out to be pretty lousy and this gives me an excuse to leave the house. There are some things I can do, folks I can call. This is no accident. Someone is doing it. Therefore, we can make them stop." I smiled. "I still have a little juice."

"I . . . can't pay you much—" she began.

I stopped her. "Let's let my pension cover this. I think we owe you one. The least I can do is ask a couple questions, give you some advice. If you need me to break somebody's arm, then we'll talk price."

"I hope your rates are low," she said, her smile tentative. "What's your first move?"

"We've narrowed it down to Michael Wheeler or the rest of humanity," I said. "So let's start with Wheeler."

II.

There were points in life, he'd come to realize, that offered moments of absolute choice. The proverbial fork in the road. Either you did this thing or you didn't. Life would be this way . . . or that way. Compressed intervals of time that, before they turned up, meant you lived and acted and suffered in one way and—after them?—in a completely different way. If you were lucky enough to survive, you popped out the other side utterly changed. With a different set of values. And a different set of goals.

He'd had his moment already. It had taken him time to realize that it had even occurred because he hadn't suffered right away. He'd paid later—fuck, yes, he'd been put through the wringer—but at the time, he thought he'd ducked and dodged his way out of the consequences. In the end, fate had caught up with him and he'd learned the hard way what value and power those moments of change possessed.

But who said you couldn't have another moment? To make one for yourself? That you couldn't grab the edges of your destiny and pinch them when you wanted to, bring the moments of your life together and force the world to give you another chance? To undo the worst that had happened and return to the beginning.

Maybe, given enough time, it would simply happen on its own. But he wasn't willing to wait to find out if the universe was ready to open a door for him. He was going to grab his past, pull it into the present, and carve out a new future.

II

CHAPTER FOUR

I told Amanda to call campus security and fill them in on her situation, then made her promise to call me on the nines—once in the morning, once at night—to let me know she was okay. Like my other suggestions for her safety, they made her bristle, but I asked her if she wanted my help or not and that ended the protest. She took off and I headed home at a brisk walk, trying not to think about how little it took to put the jump back in my step these days. Back in the coffee shop, I'd been ready to tell Amanda to take a hike. Now, for the first time in weeks, I was looking forward to going home and doing something meaningful.

My slice of heaven is a three-bedroom Cape Cod with a decent-sized front porch, a backyard I can mow in thirty-two minutes, and neighbors to either side that change every few months. The furniture is decent and the decorations minimal. I'm cheap and unimaginative and generally buy things as IKEA sales dictate. It's five blocks from coffee shops, stores, and restaurants and not far from the major highways in the area, though given the Washington, DC, area's ubiquitous traffic snarl, that just means you get caught in a line of cars faster and closer to home.

When I got home, I headed straight for the kitchen, cracked open a can of food for my cat, Pierre, and stepped back. He's large and has a temper. The smell coming from the food bowl was enough to put off even a healthy adult human, but he attacked it like it was his last meal, grunting and yowling while he ate.

"Easy, killer," I said. Pierre looked up at me like I was next. When he'd licked the last morsel out of the bowl, he ran his tongue around his teeth, then bounded out the swinging inside-outside door to commit atrocities on the local squirrel population.

Holding my breath, I rinsed his bowl out, then headed upstairs to my office. My house, built in the slapdash optimism of the postwar forties, was small and probably meant to shelter a family of four, all of them apparently of smaller than average proportions and not put off by sharing bedroom or bathroom space. My office had been the kids' bedroom, with the slanted ceiling of the dormer interrupted by a solitary window overlooking the porch roof. I have to be careful I don't stand up too fast or I'll brain myself on the ceiling.

The room is austere. No computer. Just a typewriter, a stack of legal pads, and a Mason jar full of black pens sitting on a dented steel desk I rescued from a salvage pile. The desk is gunship gray, with a sticky vinyl bumper going around the lip of a slab top that would've looked more at home in a coroner's lab. Completing the décor is a battered office chair I filched from MPDC HQ and a filing cabinet. Five drawers are devoted to case files, one to personal items. Making it, I suppose, emblematic of my life.

We weren't supposed to do it, but I'd always made personal copies of all my work files when I was on the force. I never regretted it, at least not from a professional standpoint. Of all the cases I'd broken open in my career, I'd come up with the answers for half of them sitting in this office at three in the morning, leaning back in my scuzzy chair, my hands laced behind my head, staring at the ceiling.

After I'd retired, I hadn't been able to bring myself to throw the files out. I didn't know when I was going to do it; I just felt each day that *today* wasn't the right time. And now I was glad I hadn't been able to cross that bridge. I rummaged through the drawers, looking for the right folder. Since I filed cases under the victim's name, not the perpetrator's, Wheeler's well-thumbed file was in the fourth drawer under L for *Lane, Brenda.* The case file was an inch thick. Not the best sign. Most of my cases took two hands to pick up.

I threw the file on the desk and plopped down in the chair. A wave of irritation and depression hit me, catching me off guard. Old feelings of failure and lost opportunity welled up like the case was twelve hours, not years, old. I sat there and rolled the feelings around like they were flavors, savoring and tasting them again after the long hiatus. There was a lot of bitter and very little sweet. Things hadn't gone the way I thought they would, or should. Maybe this was my chance to make a difference.

Or maybe nothing could change what had happened.

I tamped down the surge of emotions and started flipping pages on the Lane case. The way I remembered it.

CHAPTER FIVE

In the mid-nineties, Mike Wheeler was a patrolman with three years in and a soft beat in the Palisades, a moderately wealthy suburb hugging the Potomac River in northwest Washington, DC. It's an overlooked corner of the city, full of leafy oaks and broad lanes, all within spitting distance of the more posh and accessible neighborhood of Georgetown. Not that anyone would ever spit there. That would've been the worst crime ever reported in the history of the neighborhood.

Until, that is, Wheeler met Brenda Lane, a good-looking thirty-something with a daughter and a cat in a nice, three-bedroom Tudor. Modest for the Palisades, a wealthy home anywhere else, it said that the Lanes were solidly well-to-do. The missing piece was Brenda's husband, who had been killed in the Persian Gulf five years before. Single-parent homes weren't the norm in the community, but a life insurance payout and Brenda's job as a team leader for a technology company on the cusp of the dot-com revolution kept the tiny family of two comfortable.

As Amanda had recounted, one evening after midnight Brenda thought she heard something downstairs and triggered the alarm using a bedside keypad. Inside eight minutes, Wheeler showed up like the cavalry, lights flashing and gun drawn. Crack investigative work revealed that the noise was caused by the cat doing cartwheels in the living room. All was well and the day was saved. Shaky laughter all around. Brenda Lane was justifiably grateful for the timely, heroic response of young

Officer Wheeler and likely tripped over herself thanking him, her voice filled with equal parts relief and embarrassment.

She was less pleased when Wheeler showed up the next night. And the night after that. And continued to do so several times a week. He haunted their neighborhood, often staked out front sitting in the cruiser or walking up the drive and ringing the bell at dinnertime. To check on them, naturally.

As the days and weeks progressed, she lodged complaints, trying to get the watch captain to take him off the beat, but it doesn't take a rocket scientist to figure out what kind of priority it was for the MPDC. When I interviewed some cops at the station, I found out that Wheeler was talking a big game, telling everyone how he was nailing Brenda every other night. She was a cop chaser, he said, crazy about uniforms. And now she was trying to get back at him because she'd found out he had a girlfriend. That kind of talk gets around, trickles both up and down the ladder. They blew her off, nodding and doodling aimlessly when she called. A few of the cops even warned him to watch out she didn't start stalking *him*.

But the complaints kept rolling in, with Brenda getting more upset and more demanding. She mentioned she was going to hire lawyers and contact newspapers. Her ward representative got involved and began making waves. The brass was being pressured to do something and the word was on its way down to get Wheeler reassigned to another squad before something happened to embarrass the department.

But the next squad that he dealt with was Homicide.

A few months after Wheeler's first response, late on a weeknight, he called in that he was checking out another possible break-in at the Lanes'. Dispatch asked for details since they hadn't received a 911. Wheeler didn't respond. Three minutes later, the switchboard got a frantic call from Brenda Lane that someone was at her front door, trying to break in. The woman was so frightened the operator could barely understand her. I listened to the tape many times. The garbled recording cut off with her high-pitched voice screaming "*You?*" and then "Don't, don't, don't" followed by gunshots.

Ten seconds after making the call, Brenda Lane was dead.

It took me half an hour to get across town from wrapping up another homicide. When I got to the Palisades, the Lanes' property was lit up like the president's tree at Christmastime. There were four MPDC cruisers with lights on, an ambulance, and a forensics team van, all of them pulled up to the curb in front of the house or on the lawn itself. Had it been a street corner downtown, it would've been routine. For the Palisades, it was a circus. Neighbors in bathrobes and wrong-buttoned shirts were crowded on the sidewalk, hugging their arms to their chest and standing on tiptoes, trying to see into the house.

I pushed my way through, looking for someone who knew what was going on, then did a double take. My partner, Jim Kransky, stood next to a cruiser, his arms at his sides and his stance awkward, as though he'd been stopped in mid-stride on his way to somewhere important. His eyes were glued to the front door like he expected the devil to walk out.

"Jim, what are you doing here?" I asked, walking up to him. "I thought you knocked off early after that Logan Circle thing this afternoon. The stabbing."

He turned to me, looking pale and worn out, but wired. He was a thin man and his features had always been sharp, but tonight his face was all planes and points, like there were knives underneath the angles of his cheeks, jaw, and chin. Normally, his eyes would be moving, scanning, taking in the environment, the people, the situation, but right now he looked blank and hollowed out. It was obvious he didn't know who was talking to him.

He blinked and took a breath, as if coming to. "Hey, Marty. Yeah, I went home for a little while, tried to get some sleep, couldn't. I heard this thing come over the wire and thought I'd check it out."

I raised my eyebrows, but said nothing. When I took the rest of the day off, I stayed off. I looked toward the house. "What do we know?"

"White female, single, thirty-three. Her name is—was, Brenda. Brenda Lane. Shot three times. One in the head and two in the chest."

"Where?"

"Bedroom, second floor."

"Anyone else?"

His face was pained. "A daughter. Ten, twelve years old. Amanda. She was at a sleepover at a neighbor's."

"God," I said, glancing at the house, then back at him. "Who called it in?"

"Mike Wheeler. Over there."

I turned. A knot of four cops stood in the driveway, arms folded or thumbs in their belts. The closest to me I recognized, but couldn't place the name. Simon? Simeon? He was thick like an engine block. You could draw a straight line from his shoulders to his shoes. Standing close enough to Simon to brush shoulders was a bald guy in his forties, with the fit look of a runner or biker. The third cop, leaning against the fender of one of the cruisers, was tall and greyhound-thin and sported a buzz cut so close that the bones and muscles in his skull stood out in shadowed relief. The last was my height, but paunchy, with brown hair brushed straight back. He had a comb-shaped mustache that didn't do much for him. He was smiling or laughing at something the tall one had said.

"Who're the badges?" I asked. "I know Simon."

"Tim Delaney is Mr. Fitness. Lawrence Ferrin is the walking stick."

"Ferrin? Really?"

He nodded.

I groaned inwardly. Jim Ferrin was the assistant chief of police. Lawrence was his son. The father had a reputation for keeping close tabs on departments, sticking his nose randomly into cases. Worse, there were whispers that he was on the take, crooked as the day is long, though no one had ever pinned anything on him. If his son were sniffing around this investigation, or involved, it could be anything from a pain in the ass to a major crisis.

"That's just great," I said. "Who's the one with the gut?"

"Mike Wheeler," he said, his voice steely.

I looked at him. "Problem?"

He glared at the group. "We've had our run-ins."

"Which is why you're over here and he's over there."

"Yeah," he said, then glanced back at the house. He reached up and rubbed his eyes until I thought they were going to pop out. "God."

"You okay?"

He sniffed loudly and shook his head. "The little girl. Reminds me of Lacey. They're almost the same age, go to the same school."

"She's starting . . . sixth grade this year, right?"

"Yeah. I met the mother at school events a few times. She's—she was a nice lady."

"That's lousy."

"Yeah."

I waited. "How's Beth?"

His lips straightened into a taut line. "I wouldn't know."

I looked away, uncomfortable. We stood for a second, looking at the front of the house, at the flash of lights playing on the windows. My own divorce was a year gone, but that didn't empower me with any special insight. Even if I'd had any, I'm not sure I would've shared; my partner was a private person. I would barely have known he had a wife except for the holiday parties. I turned to go talk to the badges when Jim grabbed my arm.

"Marty," he said, then stopped.

"What?"

"Wheeler called it in because Wheeler did it."

That got my attention. "*Wheeler* was the shooter?"

"Yeah."

"Christ," I said. My stomach started to churn. "Did no one think to tell me that before I got here?"

Jim was silent. The answer was obvious. You don't say that kind of thing over the radio.

"Anyone call Internal? And Comms? And the union?"

"On their way."

"Any other surprises I should know about before I step in them?"

Kransky hesitated. "I . . . no."

"You want to walk it with me?"

He waved me on. "Already been."

I pinched the bridge of my nose with a thumb and forefinger, trying to hold off a headache that was on its way. I opened my eyes and headed for the front door. Suddenly, I wasn't so eager to talk to Wheeler. Priorities shift when the shooter is standing right there. Better for me if I got a look at the crime scene first. But Wheeler had other ideas.

"Detective?" he called. I stopped and turned. He walked across the lawn from the driveway and met me on the herringbone-patterned brick walk leading to the house.

"Mike Wheeler," he said as he came up, holding his hand out. His eyes were glittering and a little too wide open. I shook his hand without enthusiasm.

"Marty Singer."

"Thanks for coming so quickly, Detective."

"It's what I do."

A smile split his face like I'd told a joke. He stroked his mustache, then his hand strayed to his gun belt and started playing with one of the loops. "Do you have any questions for me? Or maybe I could take you through the scene? It's confusing."

I glanced around, wanting him to go away. "I think I can handle it."

"It all went down in the bedroom. She had a nine, loaded and ready. Don't know where she got it, but she sure as shit had it pointed right at me the second I came through the door."

"I don't think you should—"

He plowed ahead as though I hadn't said anything. "I thought I was going to take a round right then and there, the way she had that thing aimed at me."

I stopped him. "Wheeler, look. First, you should be more concerned about the fact that you shot someone tonight. Second, you and I aren't on the same team right now, so keep your distance. Third, you better start thinking about what you're going to say to Internal. You'll have to take admin leave, go through the interviews, and pass the review board. There's going to be press everywhere and people calling you day and night. You worry about that and I'll handle my end."

"I know, but I thought if you saw how it happened. You know, where I was and how she was going to shoot—"

"I said I don't want to hear it."

"I think my side of things is crucial, Detective—"

I stepped up to him, stopping six inches from that mustache. "Wheeler, this is a homicide investigation. And since the Palisades isn't exactly crack country, there's going to be a shitload of explaining to do about how and why an MPDC cop happened to shoot a civilian dead in her bedroom at eleven o'clock on a Wednesday night. I don't know if this is a justified shooting. As far as I'm concerned, you're innocent until proven guilty. I'll get your story in time. But the more we talk before I put in a report—the more it looks like my investigation is tainted by me chatting with the guy who pulled the trigger—the more likely it is that the whole fucking thing will be balled up and thrown in the trash. And I don't like doing busywork. Now, would you please get the hell away from me? Or do I need to get Detective Kransky to come over here to put you down?"

Wheeler looked at me for a second, his face going through a couple of interesting shades of red and purple, then he closed his mouth with a snap and stalked away. I shook my head as I walked to the house, trying to clear my mind.

The front door hung from a single hinge; the lock had been ripped out of the wall and the brass safety chain snapped. I took my time looking around. The decorating was tasteful, if uninspired. The wall color was beige, the paintings were neutral, impersonal, the furniture likewise. It was as if the owner had wanted to decorate, then tired of the idea and asked someone else to do it for them. I moved down the hall. The conversations of the neighbors and the sound of running engines faded to a murmur.

There were stairs ahead of me, a parlor to the right, and a living room to the left. A neighbor and a badge were in the living room with a little girl. She was enveloped by one of those generic blue blankets that all cop cars and ambulances stock. Only her face was showing and it made me stop. Her skin was white, translucent, like the petals of an orchid. Doe's eyes peered out of a face that was both blank and slightly expectant, as though waiting for someone to tell her that everything that had happened was staged. A stunt, a big put-on. I'd seen that same face more times than I care to remember—it was the face that all survivors have. She stared at me as though trying to memorize my features, but I knew she wasn't seeing me.

I walked over and introduced myself. The neighbor hugged the girl protectively and glared at me, but I ignored her and knelt down. The girl watched me the whole way. I asked for her name and she told me. It was Amanda.

I fished out a card and gave it to her. "Amanda, this is for you. Things are going to be crazy for a while, and these people will take care of you, but I want you to call me if you need anything, okay?"

She looked at me with those eyes for a while, then a tiny white hand snuck out from under the blanket and took the card. There was a little glass figurine of a unicorn in the same hand. She hadn't said anything but her name. I smiled awkwardly. At the time I put her silence down to shock. It didn't occur to me until later that Amanda had no reason to trust anyone with a badge.

I left them and went upstairs to take in the scene, nodding to the rookie who was standing guard at the top of the steps. The bedroom was at the back of the hall, its light bright and penetrating. The lab techs were finishing their work, so I peeked in the other rooms while I waited for them to wrap up. Things seemed neat, orderly, and undisturbed. A few minutes later, the techs snapped their cases shut and clicked the latches. The pictures were done, measurements taken, posture described and noted. They picked up their gear, gave me a nod, and scooched past me. I stopped one of them.

"The light on like this when you got here?" I asked.

"Just like that," the tech said. "Bright as day."

"No mistake about that?"

He shrugged. "It's how we found it."

"All right, thanks."

They left. I squinted at the room from the hall, but a heavy oak dresser with a stereo on top blocked my view, so I moved into the room. I touched nothing, leaving it *in situ*, as the textbooks like to say. There were more thoughtless appointments on the walls. Framed pictures of sailboats and things like that. Facing the door and with my back to the hall, the queen-sized bed was against the left wall, arranged under a large window. Brenda Lane's body was sprawled on the far side of the bed. Some clothes had been flung over the chair. A pair of sandals rested on the floor at the foot of the bed, one lying over the other.

I studied the body. Two shots to the chest, one in the head, like Kransky had told me. The impact of the third shot had flung her back and she lay wound-side down so that her head disguised the exit. Long, dark hair fanned across the pillow. I moved closer and looked at her face. The bullet's entry made any kind of judgment suspect, but she seemed to have been a good-looking woman, with a heart-shaped face. Her right arm had flopped across her chest, almost covering the other two bullet holes. If you ignored the blood, you could've mistaken her for someone sleeping off a hard night. She wore baby-blue cotton pj's with a pattern of miniature lambs jumping over tiny fences.

On the floor by the side of the bed, a foot or so from her outstretched left hand, was a Browning BDM. I bent down to take a closer look. The BDM is a squared-off, ugly thing. It's not the biggest handgun in the world, but it's a real macho-looking piece. Residual powder flecked the trigger, guard, and barrel from where the lab team had dusted them. The safety was off. I plucked a handkerchief from my pocket and flicked the safety on, then slid the magazine out. It was a modified, fifteen round magazine not normally available to civilians. I counted fourteen still there. No one had said anything about Brenda Lane getting a shot off, so if the gun was fully loaded, there was one in the chamber. It's a procedural no-no, but live weapons at a crime scene make me nervous, so I wracked the slide to confirm my suspicion. A solo round ejected, and I put it and the magazine beside the gun where I'd found it.

I stood. Something was bothering me. I returned to the hall and paused outside the door. I made a pistol with my finger and thumb, aiming it at the body sprawled on the bed. Or tried to. With the angle I had, I couldn't even see it: the dresser was in the way. Keeping my arm outstretched, I shuffled by the half-step into the room until I was sure I had a clear shot. Not until I was five feet into the room did I feel I could've gotten even a one-handed snap shot off. Eight feet if I wanted to be sure of my aim.

I let my arm drop and soaked it all in. I didn't like what I saw. Or felt. I went back downstairs. The girl was gone, probably whisked away to a hospital. I walked outside, tired and with a crawling feeling in my gut. Wheeler and the clump of cops were still there, talking. Kransky was gone.

I was about to go over to Wheeler to talk to him when my pager went off. The number was a general extension for the MPDC HQ. Not a number to ignore. I veered toward the old Buick I was driving that year and called in from my car phone.

A firm, clipped voice answered. "Ferrin."

I took a breath. "Marty Singer, Chief. You paged me?"

"Singer. I heard you've got a real cluster fuck on your hands."

"I just walked the scene, Chief. I haven't talked to the shooter yet. It's an MPDC cop named Wheeler."

"I know who it is," Jim Ferrin said. "That's why I'm calling. The press is going to be riding our ass on this and we don't need any screwups in the field."

"I wasn't planning on dropping the ball," I said.

His voice was brittle. "Make sure you don't, Singer. We have a shitty reputation in this town as it is. If we gloss over any part of this case, it'll look like we're covering for Wheeler. And we can't suffer a black eye of that magnitude. Got it?"

I bit back a smart-ass reply. "Got it."

"Then get back to work, Detective," he said, and hung up.

I sat there, digesting what the assistant chief of police had just said, then shrugged. I hadn't planned on either hiding evidence or fabricating it. If a cop killing a civilian was a media relations nightmare, it wasn't my problem. I got out of the car, pissed off, and looked around for Wheeler. I caught his eye and motioned for him to come talk to me. He said something out of the side of his mouth to the other cops. Ferrin and Delaney laughed. Wheeler walked over to me with his thumbs hooked in his belt like a gunslinger, except his sidearm was missing, already turned in as evidence.

I asked him to give me the short version. He told me he had spotted someone creeping through backyards in the direction of the Lanes' house and had believed there was a break-in in progress. He called it in, then proceeded to enter the home, believing the Lanes' lives were in danger.

"Looks like you were right," I said. Wheeler flushed. "What happened then?"

"I ran upstairs assuming Ms. Lane and her daughter were asleep and in possible danger. I had my service weapon drawn. I approached Ms. Lane's bedroom to investigate and saw she had a pistol pointed at me. Fearing for my life, I reacted instinctively and shot her."

"From the hall?"

"Yes, sir. Just outside the doorway."

"Not in the room itself?"

"No, sir."

"Because then there would've been too much time for her to point the gun and you to react without thinking."

"Detective?"

"If you'd gone all the way into the room, it would've given her enough time to realize that you were a cop and not a burglar."

He hesitated, then said, "I don't know, sir. All I know is that she was about to shoot."

"You believe Ms. Lane thought you were a burglar?"

"Yes, sir."

"And did you find any evidence of the burglar you thought you saw earlier?"

"No, sir. Officer Ferrin and I searched the area, but didn't find anyone."

I stared at him, waiting for him to say more, but he simply looked back at me, expressionless. Finally, I said, "Okay, I got what I need. Keep yourself available. I'll need to talk to you in the next day or two."

He turned to go, stopped, and looked back at me. And said something that set my skin crawling. He said, "Thank you, Detective, for making the right decision in this justifiable and defensible shooting."

I stared at him as he walked to his cruiser, got in, and pulled away.

◆ ◆ ◆

I've thought a lot about that night.

Cops say and do strange things after they shoot someone. There might be tears, or anger, or silence. They might talk it out or they might take it in stride. Some guys act flippant, make jokes. Others pray. Whatever the reaction, they're all trying to keep themselves from thinking about the terrifying, momentous thing they've done. None of them will ever be the same cop they were when they started. Some aren't ever the same, period, and they turn in their badge a month later.

But rarely do they sound victorious. Smug. Certain. And that's how Michael Wheeler sounded that night. Like he'd gotten away with murder.

Which he had.

CHAPTER SIX

I was bent over the file, my nose almost touching the page, when my cell phone rang. Habit made me pick it up and glance at the number without thinking. The bottom dropped out of my gut when I saw who it was, but I answered anyway. The receptionist introduced herself and said, "Mr. Singer, Dr. Demitri had a cancellation this morning. Can you come in for your exam today?"

"What time?"

"As soon as you can get here," she said. "Three o'clock at the latest."

I glanced at the stack of papers spilling out of the Lane case folder. "Do we have to do this right away?"

"I think in this case, Mr. Singer," she said, "everything's always as soon as possible."

"See you by three," I said, and hung up.

I showered, then put on some comfortable clothes. For all I knew, the doctor was going to be performing some fairly intrusive tests and I'd rather cinch the drawstring on a pair of sweatpants than put on a pair of jeans afterward. I straightened up the office, checked the stove, and did a few other things until it was obvious I was stalling, then left.

Demitri's practice was tucked away in a cozy, two-story colonial brownstone in historic Old Town Alexandria, a small burg on the Virginia side of the Potomac. Where Arlington struggles to find itself amongst the chain stores and twenty-something bars and its live music, Old Town is smirkily certain of its identity. It has cobblestone streets that suck to drive on and period taverns where the staff tart themselves up in colonial-era costumes. You can almost believe George Washington left a minute ago to take his carriage back to Mount Vernon. It's so cute it almost can't stand itself. Almost.

The office was on the second floor. I signed in, exchanged my insurance card for a clipboard and pen, then took a seat. The waiting room was like doctors' waiting rooms everywhere. Chairs were strategically placed to allow people to sit in ones or twos with an empty in between. One other person occupied the room, an older black woman who was asleep or pretended to be. The tables were littered with magazines that satisfied the standard spread of interests: golf, finance, current events. Nothing on vacations or travel, I noticed. Too optimistic. Or cigar smoking. That seemed prudent. One table had a plastic holder for a bunch of pamphlets entitled "Your Illness and You." The top one was tattered and seemed to have been read and put back more than once. I guess most people would prefer not to take one, as though putting it in your pocket would confirm the diagnosis.

I'd flipped through two magazines and was starting in on a third when a young Asian nurse in pink scrubs and a name tag that said "Leah" opened the magic door and called my name. She led me through a maze of desks, scales, and racks of sterile supplies, past laminated cutaway diagrams of the human body, around strange beeping machines on rollers. We stopped at an examining room with the temperature of a meat locker, where Leah told me to undress and put on something she called a gown, but seemed to me like a large piece of toilet paper with drinking straw wrappers for strings. The gown ended at mid-thigh. If it were meant to hide anything, it would've been more effective if I wadded it up and wore it like a diaper. Then again, there was less of me to hide since most of my body parts were shrinking inward at an alarming rate.

After I'd changed, I glanced around. All the surfaces were smooth, shiny, and freezing except for the examining table, which had a roll of butcher paper drawn down its length. They'd want me up there anyway, so I hopped up and tried to tug the giant paper bag over the important parts.

Then I waited for someone to show up and tell me about my cancer.

◆ ◆ ◆

I think I knew when I saw the blood. There was a lot of it.

Not flung on the walls or pooling in an alley doorway. Not the result of a late-night, urban squabble or a meth deal gone instantly and terrifically wrong. Not the consequence of an accidental shove or revenge thirty years in the making or a love triangle violently reduced from three to two. These were all things I'd seen after thirty years with DC Homicide. But that was blood where I'd been expecting it, situations I'd almost come to consider normal.

This blood was mine. It was in my toilet.

Seeing it was embarrassing, horrifying. I tried to clean it up, forget about it, move on. I took a shower and washed myself a half-dozen times, running the cold water until the spray had teeth. I scrubbed the bathroom, then examined myself in the mirror, looking for outward signs of sickness or weakness, not sure how I felt when I couldn't find any. I made some coffee and stared at a wall.

I thought. I thought about the consequences of what had happened and what it would mean. About the fact that an hour ago, I didn't have this problem and now I did. That I didn't smoke, barely drank, had hardly had a cold in the last year. I was as healthy as an ox. All of it, irrelevant.

Inane things my father used to say—for almost any occasion, good or bad, happy or tragic—popped into my head. Like, *Well, there you go.* Or, *It is what it is.* And, *Well, what can you do?* I suppose these one-offs are less idiotic than they seem on the surface. They're all a way of saying the same thing, that shit happens and you have to deal with it. You can try to ignore it, wait for it to go away. Maybe that works, but sometimes the knot won't untie itself and your attention is required. A thing you never expected, could not have predicted, suddenly becomes the foremost event in your life and no amount of wishing it away will work. In some cases, the event is small and the ramifications manageable.

In my case, it affected everything. Forever.

In thirty-one years on the MPDC, I'd clawed my way up from beat cop to detective. I received honorable mentions and awards. Straight police work was something I liked and was good at, passing on opportunities to work in Vice, Internal, even SWAT when I was still in shape. Like a lot of places, if you're good at what you do for long enough, they eventually try to kick you upstairs, where you won't do any good at all. I refused and my indifference was noted: the promotions and invitations slowed to a trickle, then ceased altogether. The fast track to the top slid over the horizon. Which was fine with me, tucked away as I was in the recesses of Homicide, where I took each case as it came along, did my best, then moved on to the next one.

I was a typical cop and got the typical cop divorce. It was tough at the time, but it made my life easier in the long run. I could go about my job guilt-free. I could talk and drink with people who understood the life. Have casual relationships and one-night stands. Go home at night and feed my cat. The troubles in my life stayed with me and were only as big as I chose to make them. The rest I could ignore. Until I found blood in the toilet bowl.

I didn't get bounced off the force, exactly, but with thirty-one years in and a diagnosis of localized colorectal cancer hanging around my neck—a situation soon known to everyone around you—options were limited.

Maybe I was ready to get out anyway. Three decades is a long time to poke around people who have been beaten, stabbed, shot, poisoned, run over with a car. That kind of thing rubs off on you. And I like the idea of escaping the daily grind as much as the next guy. But I would've appreciated controlling the how, why, and when of it instead of having the terms handed to me. It was sudden and impersonal, like getting fired by telegram or having a note slipped under the door.

I didn't have to retire. I considered staying in, fighting the cancer all the way. But I read up on the symptoms. Nausea, fatigue, weakness, vomiting. Then I read up on the side effects of chemotherapy. Nausea, fatigue, weakness, vomiting. Is that how I wanted to show up to work every day? Did I want to back up the other guys on the squad, not knowing when I might keel over or give up chasing some crook down the street because I was too *tired*? In the end, I called it and walked out. I pretended not to notice the relief on everyone's face when I told them.

There were a lot of unanswered questions, like how long I could've kept going or what more I could've accomplished. Cases literally lying open on my desk had to be closed and handed off to someone else on the squad. And there were the unsolved, the pending, and the soon-to-be-committed crimes that I would never get to tackle.

The transition was sudden and disorienting. From diagnosis to resignation took four weeks. Ten days after that, I was walking down the steps of the MPDC building on Indiana Avenue, hugging the clichéd cardboard box. There was a nice departmental bash with cake and soda, almost comically subdued as people carefully avoided toasting to my health in their we'll-miss-you speeches. Some of my buddies wanted to go out to a bar afterward, but I could see them wondering if it was kosher to take a guy with cancer out boozing. In the end, I was the one that dragged them to Morrison's steakhouse and got everybody bombed. The waitresses didn't quite know what to do with a dozen armed, drunk cops raising their glasses to "Marty's ass cancer." It was swell.

And then the ride really took off. I saw my personal doctor, who sent me to a gastrointestinal specialist, who shuffled me off to a surgeon, who in turn referred me to an oncologist. It was a confusing, intimidating process. I was awash in professionally flavored understanding and sympathy, but no guidance through the system, per se. Each doctor simply did their part, pointed me in a new direction, and shoved.

I filled out more paperwork than I'd ever seen in my life and for a cop with thirty years in, that's saying something. I had insurance forms, releases, waivers, living wills, real wills, surveys, pension forms. I exchanged my service weapon and badge for comfortable clothing with drawstrings and elastic waistbands. Clothes I could sit around in. Clothes I could get out of in a hurry if I had the uncontrollable and unstoppable need to crap.

One doctor disapproved of my diet, so I bought a lot of bananas and orange juice. I cut out donuts and bacon. The steakhouse binge was the last red meat I ate for a while and the last bottle of booze I drank, though it seemed a futile gesture. As if what I put in my mouth would have any effect on cancer fifty-three years in the making. Like it would shoo it out of me. *Bad cancer! Go away!* I suppose it made people feel better if they thought they were doing something positive. That's fine. It couldn't hurt and might do some good in other ways. Imagine the irony if you keeled over from a high-cholesterol heart attack in your oncologist's waiting room.

I was surgically fitted with a Mediport near my collarbone, a handy device that lets the medical staff hook you up to the right machines without wearing out a vein from constant injections. It itched and got snagged on my shirts.

Then I was told to sit around and wait. There were batteries of tests to be conducted, samples still to be taken. Chemo was probably on the docket. Maybe surgery, maybe multiple surgeries. That's if the prognosis was good.

If it was bad, well, at least I had a new pair of sweatpants.

◆ ◆ ◆

Demitri was a solid-looking guy in his late fifties with an olive-oil cast to his features and thick mason's hands. After introducing himself and glancing over my chart, he put on his doctor's face and started talking.

"The purpose of this visit, Marty," he said, "is to give you an idea of your staging and how we're going to treat it. Some people think of cancer as an all-or-nothing proposition, but like most diseases, there are certain milestones we pass that help us determine what kind of treatment you should be getting, how aggressive we can afford to be, how aggressive we have to be. You may have recently had cell replication start or you might've lived with cancer for twenty years."

I nodded.

"The pathology of the biopsy taken from you a few weeks ago shows that you're in early stage two. While the cancer has spread to your lymph nodes, it's not terribly advanced."

"That's great," I said. "What the hell does that mean?"

"Well, we have options, and that's the good thing. If this were a later stage—if you'd waited a year, perhaps, or the cancer were more aggressive—we'd have to schedule surgery immediately. These kinds of surgeries can be extensive and often end up with the patient requiring a full colostomy."

"And in my case?"

"We have options, as I said. We don't need to rush into surgery, so we'll begin with chemotherapy."

"Chemo?"

"Not the full-blown variety you're probably thinking of. The idea here is to remove the cancer using chemo, but even if it isn't entirely effective, it may reduce the size of the tumors before we would have to surgically remove them. It's a simple equation: if the tumors are smaller, we have to remove less tissue, both good and bad. Removing less tissue is a good thing. There's a higher likelihood of preserving the sphincter that way."

"By all means," I said, feeling light-headed, "preserve the sphincter."

He smiled. "We'll do our best. There'll be some adjustment as your body gets used to the drugs. We're attacking some of the body's cells, after all. Poisoning them, if you will. But we're well aware of the side effects and can help you get through them. Any questions?"

I took a breath. "Just the big one."

He looked at me for a moment before answering. "Marty, I know you want a number, but I don't hand out percentages here. If I did, you'd be weighing things in your mind, trying to figure out what it would take to beat the odds. What I want you to do, instead, is concentrate on doing what we tell you, on getting better, on living. You do that, and your chances are great."

With that he clapped me on the back and left. It had been a pep talk and I wanted to call bullshit, but he had a point. I was sitting there, still digesting what Demitri had said, when there was a rapid knock and Nurse Leah came back in. I stared at her like she was part of the door frame.

She studied me for a second. "Hard to wrap your head around, huh?" she said.

"Yeah," I said. "I always thought I'd get my ticket punched on the job, not in a hospital bed."

"Don't be so down," she said. "You're in better shape than a lot of our patients."

"Okay, I never thought I'd say, 'I'd like to schedule my chemo appointment.'"

She picked up a chart and fussed with it. "Chemo isn't what it used to be. Most wonder what the big deal is afterwards. People have reactions, sure, but it's probably nothing worse than you had after a long night out or a bout of iffy Mexican food."

"Great."

"Look at it this way," she said, putting a hand on one hip. "What's the worst thing that ever happened to you? Physically, I mean."

"I was shot."

That stopped her for a second, but she pushed on. "Would you rather be shot again or feel like you had the flu for a couple weeks?"

"I'd rather have neither."

She shook her head. "Sorry, it doesn't work that way."

"Then I don't want to get shot."

"Right. So chemo is something that may save your life and it won't even be close to the worst thing that's ever happened to you."

"You got a funny way of looking at things," I said.

She smiled. "It's cancer. You take the good news when you can get it."

CHAPTER SEVEN

Heading home was out. I'd only sit around and mope. I toyed with the idea of going to the gym, but my energy level had been holding steady at somewhere between zero and one lately. I imagined myself having to be revived by an attendant after passing out on the treadmill. And, anyway, what was I doing, thinking about the gym? I said I'd help Amanda and that's what I should be doing. The obvious answer was: I was stalling. I didn't want to take the logical next step toward getting some answers on the case, which was to talk to the person who—next to me and Amanda—knew the most about it.

With a sinking feeling, I pointed the car downtown. Traffic was bad, but luckily for me all the bad mojo was going in the other direction as people tried to beat it out of town at the end of the workday. You'd think there was a bomb scare, the way the cars were jammed together on the highways out of the city. I zipped along against traffic, making it to Dupont Circle in twenty minutes, though it took twenty more to find parking. This wasn't something I was used to; for the last thirty years, I'd just parked on the sidewalk if I wanted.

I finally found a spot a couple blocks from the Circle and strolled up Nineteenth Street, noting the businesses and restaurants that had already closed or changed hands in the short time since I'd quit the force. I realized with a shock that it was already a few months since I'd been here. The streets were packed with people, all hustling somewhere.

Some had just knocked off work and were heading home for the night. Others were on their way out for a dinner or a drink with friends. People took long, purposeful strides, chatting as they walked, wrapped up in their personal dramas. I missed it. Despite the cold, there was energy in the air, a feeling of *doing*, a sense of expectation. The faces looked young and well scrubbed. I felt old and crummy.

The flow of foot traffic took me northward to the Circle. Clumps of people waited at the crosswalks, stamping their feet and leaning into a chill wind that swept down the street and pushed against all of us. I turned my collar up and jammed my hands in my pockets as I crossed the street, then paced the perimeter of the Circle, taking in the local color.

Die-hard chess players sat at the stone tables on the east side, blowing on their hands to keep their fingers warm between moves. A couple of budding documentarians from one of the local colleges interviewed homeless guys, offering sandwiches and coffee in return for answering questions. Nonprofit case workers and admin assistants chatted or sipped from Starbucks cups, somehow managing to look chic and modern on wages hovering a smidge above poverty level.

I needed to kill some time, so I picked a bench near the top of the Circle, slouching down to keep warm. A girl Amanda's age sat at the opposite end, eating some French fries. She gave me the wary, oblique glance of a city dweller, trying to check me out for potential danger and attraction simultaneously. After a pause, she went back to eating, indicating that I was apparently both harmless and sexless.

At five thirty, I got up and walked across to the east side, skirting the marble fountain in the center, with its eyeless sylphs forever looking to the sea, the stars, and the wind. Most of the chess players had packed it in, but one table was still going at it. A few of the guys, with their portable sets tucked under their arms, had formed a small crowd around the table, smoking and watching the two men duke it out. I took up a position behind one player, an old black guy with a white beard who looked like he'd learned chess when it had been invented. His moves were precise, economical. He never touched a piece until he was ready to move, considering the whole board before ever raising his hand.

The other had changed remarkably little since I'd last seen him. His black suit, blue shirt, and red tie said he was dressed to take on all the bureaucracy the city could throw at him, though the permanently down-turned mouth registered how much he liked having to do so. His face had the same ascetic, knife's-edge features I remembered, though he'd acquired deep lines straight down each cheek and a permanent trench dug along his brow. He was whip thin, having fought off the paunchiness that seemed to be the legacy of all cops over twenty-five. Then again, Vice kept most of its cops simultaneously busy, nervous, and depressed, which might explain the lack of weight gain.

"He got you, Desmond," one of the players said to the old black guy.

"Shut up, man. He's trying to think," said another.

Desmond took a long look at the board as we all watched the clock next to them. I'm not a chess player, so I couldn't have told you who was winning or losing. I knew black was one side and white the other and they had to make their move before the alarm went off on the clock. A few spectators whispered, heads together, pointing out what they would've done or where one of the players had gone wrong. Finally, Desmond let out a long breath that steamed the air.

"Not this time, man," he said and moved a piece shaped like a saltshaker across the board. The crowd erupted with groans and hoots and a couple of laughs. I stared at the board, lost.

"Stalemate, Des?" his opponent said, the shade of a grin coming across his face. "I'm shocked."

"Gotta do what you gotta do," the other said. He didn't look happy about it.

They shook hands across the board and the one named Des started putting the pieces in a box as the crowd melted away, heading for home, or dinner, or a drink. His opponent got up from the table and walked alone toward the north end of the Circle, hands shoved in his pockets and shoulders hunched against the cold.

"Kransky," I called after him. "Jim."

He stopped in his tracks and turned around. He peered at me like he was looking through a fog, though I was standing fifteen feet away. The small grin he'd given his chess partner was gone and the severe frown was back in its place. He gazed at me for a long moment with the blank, noncommittal gaze of a lizard looking at a fly.

"Singer," he said, finally. "What the hell do you want?"

◆ ◆ ◆

"Hi, Jim," I said, lamely. I hadn't given much thought to how I was going to approach this.

Kransky stared at me.

I took a step closer, stopped. "I figured I'd find you here. This is where you always went at five to chase the day away."

He got an impatient look on his face. "I know why I'm here. What do you want?"

"I need to talk. Have a sec?"

"No," he said and turned to walk away.

"Amanda Lane," I said.

He stopped and turned back again. "What?"

"Amanda Lane," I said. "Brenda Lane's daughter."

"I know who she is. What about her?"

"She's grown up, back in town, and in trouble," I said.

His face had all the warmth of one of the statues in the fountain. "Singer, it's cold, I'm on duty tonight, and—most important—I don't want to talk to you. You got something to say, I need to hear it. Now."

"It's complicated," I said. "I need a minute. That's all."

He stared at me, considering. We hadn't bumped into each other much over the years, despite both having careers in the MPDC. Having a couple thousand bodies on the force helped with that. It was probably a good thing, since we hadn't parted under the best terms. I could see him thinking those same things. He didn't owe me anything and had probably only stopped—and would only help me—out of curiosity. Whether that curiosity would win out over his feelings for me was a big gamble. I waited him out.

He jerked his head to one side. "Let's walk."

I fell into step beside him as we chased the loop out of the Circle and headed toward Eighteenth Street. I was several inches taller than him, but we matched our pace, walking slowly, uncomfortable with each other and thinking carefully about what we wanted to say. The narrow sidewalk, crowded with outdoor seating, fences, and trees, made it hard to maintain a safe distance.

Kransky broke the ice after half a block. "All right. You came looking for me. What do you want?"

I ran a hand through my hair, composing my thoughts, then described my meeting with Amanda. I told him about her fears and what she'd told me about Wheeler's clandestine friendship: the flowers, the visits. I gave him my first impressions, which weren't good. Kransky was quiet during my monologue, only breaking the silence to swear once or twice and glower up the street. A couple walking toward us took a step into the street to get out of our way.

"You need to find Wheeler."

"Yep," I said. "Sooner rather than later."

"She should've called it in," he said. "And you should've bagged the flower."

"She'd already handled it, tossed it in her backpack. As for calling it in, what's she supposed to say? The guy acquitted of murdering her mom twelve years ago might be back for her? Or maybe somebody likes leaving flowers at her door?"

"It'd still be a place to start," he said.

"I hear what you're saying, but I know how I would've answered the call and you do, too. You'd take her name and a number and wait for something to happen. Except that might be too late."

We walked another half block in silence. A stab of pain lanced its way through my abdomen and I winced. It didn't hurt that much, but I couldn't help but wonder. Gas? Or cancer? I put it in the back of my head to deal with later.

Kransky, deep in thought, hadn't noticed. "Why me?"

I stepped carefully over the broken remnants of a cement sidewalk slab, victim of the roots of a large, sidewalk-bound oak tree. "Because you've been mad about this for twelve years. Because you felt like we let this girl down when Wheeler walked out of that courtroom."

"Because you need my help," he said.

"That, too."

"Why don't you ask Dods?" he asked, talking about my last partner, Kransky's replacement after he left Homicide to get away from me.

"Dods is a great guy, but he doesn't have the motivation you or I do to see Wheeler put away. He might do it as a favor to me, but the Lane case was just a headline to him when it happened. For us, it's something we lived through."

"Dods is Homicide. I'm Vice. He'd be in a better position."

"Maybe. I'll ask if I have to, but I thought you'd want a piece of this."

Kransky put his head down, his chin almost touching his chest as he walked, then shuddered. "Wheeler should've never gotten off in the first place."

"I agree," I said. "But it's ancient history. We have to focus on what's happening now."

"You can't talk about the one without the other," he said. "We had that son of a bitch nailed to the wall and he walked. If that hadn't happened, we wouldn't be talking now."

"I can't think about that."

"You'd better. If he's really after the girl, you better look in the mirror damn hard and ask yourself how he got off that time and how it's not going to happen again. He strolled right out of the courtroom and now he's back in her life like nothing ever happened."

"I was there, Jim," I said. "You don't have to remind me."

"So show some fucking remorse, then."

My jaw worked as I tried to keep my temper. "Don't tell me what I did or didn't feel. I wanted Wheeler as badly as you did. I wasn't exactly handing out cigars when he got off scot-free. You're not the only one who was invested in it."

"But you were the only one in charge of the case, *Marty*," he said, stopping and jabbing a finger in my chest. "The rest of us got to stand by and watch it go down the tubes. A good woman died, a girl got orphaned, and we got to watch Wheeler walk out with a smile on his face because you screwed up."

My temper flared and I resisted the urge to take a swing. In the time it took to walk a few city blocks, Kransky had managed to peel back the layers, exposing all of the anger and disgust and self-recrimination I'd buried over the last twelve years. It didn't matter that his accusations were blown out of proportion. I hadn't been working solo on the case, for Christ's sake; there was plenty of lapsed responsibility to go around, from the beat cops to the prosecutor. But blame and guilt don't get used up by sharing; we all have an inexhaustible supply in our emotional wells. The sense of unfairness and rage I'd felt the day of the trial boiled right back up from the depths where I'd buried it, almost scaring me with how close to the surface, how raw and immediate, it was. I pointed a finger at him.

"First, you can go to hell. I did everything I could to put Wheeler away and, yeah, it didn't happen. Sometimes that's the way it goes. It sucks and I hate it but you move on if you don't want to end up going crazy. Second, who the hell are you to lay the blame on me? You were there every step of the way, pal, and while I might've been the one in charge of the case, it was the prosecution that dropped the ball and you know it. Last, what's past is past. Amanda Lane came to me for help *today*. You can stay stuck in the nineties if you want to, but whatever happened then is going to have to stay there, because she needs my help now."

I turned and walked away, cursing. I'd have to go to Dods now, something I didn't want to do. He was in charge of Homicide and had a thousand things to take care of every day, none of them named Amanda Lane. He didn't need to be running searches and sifting through MPDC records for me or babysitting someone who might or might not become a victim of a lunatic who might or might not be stalking her.

"Singer," Kransky shouted. I kept walking.

"Marty, goddamn it," he called, and I heard quick footsteps behind me. I turned to face him. He had a hand outstretched, as though to grab my arm and stop me, or offer it in help. I looked at him, not saying anything. He scowled, looked down the street, then put his hands back in his pockets as the wind whipped the coattails on his blazer. We stood that way for half a minute.

"Look," he said. "I'm mad as hell. Still. You'd think after twelve years it'd be gone and forgotten, but it's not. Wheeler's always been at the top of my list. We didn't nail him when we had the chance and it kills me. I blame you, I blame the system, I blame myself. I guess it's a lot easier to unload on you than it is to face the fact that we all screwed up."

I took a breath and willed my muscles to relax. "Amanda needs our help now, Jim."

He scowled some more, then nodded. He was a dedicated, hardheaded, angry cop and this was the closest thing to an apology I was going to get from him. I was still seething myself, but at least I could understand his anger. It was the same as mine, a fury that should've been directed at Michael Wheeler. But since Wheeler wasn't around, I'd been a good substitute.

I said, "Truce?"

He nodded. "Truce."

"Then let's get a beer. I'm freezing my ass off."

◆　◆　◆

We pulled into the first place we could find, some Pan-Asian restaurant that played bad Japanese samurai movies on the walls and served drinks with names like Bloody Mao and For Goodness Sake. We took a booth by a window and ordered beers. The shogun-styled dining room smelled of charred vegetables, soy sauce, and fried food, all of which made my gorge rise. I clamped down on the feeling and concentrated on the task ahead.

Kransky took a pull from his beer, then set it down carefully on a red paper napkin. "First steps?"

I turned my pint glass in small circles. "Find him. Make him stop. Maybe even build a case that sticks this time. It won't be murder one, but maybe something we can slap him with."

"Harassment, stalking, intent to injure?"

"Something like that," I said.

"Weak."

I shrugged, admitting it. "It's not much, but whatever jail time we can squeeze him into would make me disproportionately happy."

"How about shot while resisting arrest?"

"One can only hope. But that's going to have to be your call, if the time comes."

"You carrying?"

"Naturally."

"Registered?"

"Of course."

Kransky went silent for a moment, tracing the grain on the wood table. "You got a drop?"

I stopped spinning my glass. "Let's not go there."

Kransky shrugged. "So what happens when you find him?"

"I don't know," I said. "I know what we both *want* to do, but I'm not ready to serve twenty to life for a minute's satisfaction. That'd be too much irony for me. He doesn't serve a day in jail and I die in prison? No, I have to know where he is, what his situation is first. Then we can talk about how to move on it."

"How's that going to happen?"

"You. I don't have access now. To anything. If I dig something up, I can't chase it down, can't follow it until I get something out of it."

"You want me to dig up anyone from that posse he always had around him?"

"Who?" I asked. "Lawrence Ferrin? Delaney?"

He nodded. "Those assholes always stuck together. Ferrin especially, thinking he was the cat's ass because his old man would get him out of a bind if he needed it."

I shrugged. "If you don't turn something up on Wheeler, sure. It would tickle me to no end to find out that we could nail Ferrin or Delaney on something related to Wheeler. 'Til then, though, make Wheeler number one."

We were quiet for a minute. My beer sat, untouched. Kransky took another sip of his, staring outside. All around us, the place clattered and banged with the delivery of sushi boards and rice dishes.

"You know," he said slowly. "After the trial, I made it a hobby to keep track of him."

I didn't say anything.

"I was ready to bust him on anything. Littering, jaywalking, whatever it took to reel him in. I was . . . a little out of my head. I wanted to make his life hell. If I'd found him, I was ready to plant something on him. Drugs, a gun, anything to put him away. I've never done that in my life."

"And?"

"A month or two after the trial, he was gone. I checked his plates, ran his record, but he just floated away."

"When's the last time you checked?"

"Years," he admitted.

"So, nothing recent? LexisNexis?"

He shook his head. "Nothing in the modern age."

"So, it's been a while, but Wheeler didn't just cease to exist. Maybe something's been digitized since the last time you checked. Run the records again. If you dig something up, I can chase down the leads. And keep Amanda safe."

"I can do that. What are you going to do while I look around?"

"Something I don't want to do," I said with a sour look.

His eyebrows shot upward. "Atwater?"

"She might know something. Hell, maybe they've stayed in touch this whole time. Crooks have been known to fall in love with their defense attorneys for getting them off. Maybe all I have to do is peek in her bedroom window."

He watched the kooky samurai movie for a second. I could sense a wave of discomfort coming from him. "I heard about the . . ."

I gave him a second, then said, "Cancer, Jim. You can say it."

He nodded, discomfort on his face. "You up for this?"

I took a sip of beer, put my glass down. "I'd better be. She doesn't have anybody else. She's not long out of college, probably doesn't have two nickels to rub together. Who am I to turn her down?"

"What if you can't take care of it?"

I said nothing, though a muscle in my cheek ticced involuntarily. I watched his face as he figured it out.

"That's why you came to me," he said. "You were afraid if you didn't make it . . ."

"She needs somebody on her side, Jim. As long as I'm it, I'll do what I can. But if I'm out of the picture, I know there's only one other person who cares enough to take over. You and I don't have to hold hands over this, but it would be good to know you'll be there if she needs you. Like I said, we both owe it to her. You in?"

"I'm in," he said. "I always have been."

III.

The old man coughed into his fist. His nurse, out of earshot but watching him closely, moved forward. The old man waved him away and spoke into the phone.

"You can't find him?"

"He's in DC, that's all we know," the voice on the other end said. "Used a credit card in Logan Circle. We squeezed the number out of the shitbird that gave it to him."

"Dead end?"

"Single use, then he ditched the card."

"Keep on it. Did you find the girl?"

"She's a professor or something at GW. There's something, though. She made a trip to Arlington."

"And?"

The man paused. "I saw her talking with Marty Singer."

The old man closed his eyes out of disgust instead of pain. "She met with Marty fucking Singer?"

The man said nothing.

"Goddamn it," the old man said, then suddenly his face clenched and rippled in pain. He squeezed his eyes shut to keep from yelling. Without opening them, he put a hand up to stop the nurse he knew had taken a step toward him again. "Put Jackson on Singer and tell him to report back to me. You keep following the girl. Try not to bump into each other if they meet again."

"What should I do if I see our target around the girl?"

"Christ, don't do anything," the old man said. "Just call me. We screwed this up twelve years ago. We can't afford to do it again."

He hung up the phone and stared at nothing for a moment, thinking. Another sharp pain brought him back to reality and, wearily, he nodded for the nurse to approach.

CHAPTER EIGHT

Breakfast is the only meal I know how to cook, but I'm pretty good at it. Well, I'm enthusiastic. I throw a lot of stuff in a pan and let it go to work. This morning's version was a diner-style extravaganza of four eggs, two pieces of toast, and a quarter pound of bacon. I hadn't exactly jumped out of bed that morning and was hoping that a thousand-calorie pick-me-up would do the trick.

I frowned, though, the second the bacon hit the pan. The smell of pork fat sizzling away should've made my mouth water. Instead, my stomach clenched like I was expecting to take a punch. The feeling was so strong that I took a step back from the stove and glared at the pan like it was poisonous.

"Jesus, what's wrong with you?" I said out loud. Pierre meowed from the corner, wondering the same thing. I took a deep breath and shrugged it off, forcing my mind back to the previous day's conversation with Kransky. And then I made myself think about yet another distasteful task I'd have to do today if I truly wanted to start off on the right foot.

It worked. I stirred the contents of the pan mechanically and was staring off into space when I realized that the smoke I was seeing was coming from the eggs I was supposed to be cooking. I snapped the heat off, forked them onto a plate with the other gourmet items, then sat down to polish it all off.

I'd taken three bites when the bottom of my stomach tried to introduce itself to the back of my tongue. I jackknifed to my feet, slamming the chair against the wall, and lurched to the sink where I spat out the mouthful with a barking cough. There was a terrible pause and then I vomited down the drain. I fumbled for the cold water tap, opening it up full blast. Long minutes passed as I stood there, dribbling and coughing into the swirling water. Tears formed around my eyes from the pressure of vomiting and I felt light-headed. I splashed my face a dozen times. When the spasms finally stopped, I risked a sip of water.

I leaned against the counter for a long, long time, then turned the water off and stood up. I avoided looking at the plate like it was a corpse at a crime scene. The smell of bacon fat hung in the air and I had to breathe through my shirt to keep my stomach under control. Despite the cold, I opened the windows and left them that way. I warmed a cup of cold coffee—for holding on to, not drinking—and retreated to my office, feeling frail, brittle, and old. If I didn't have breakfast, at least I had work.

Julie Atwater had been Michael Wheeler's defense attorney. She'd been a surprise choice at the time because Wheeler's case was such a sensational one—murderous cop, unrequited love, and so forth—and she'd tried few cases before his. She'd been a prosecutor for several years before the switch to defense attorney, so she wasn't entirely without experience, but eyebrows had been raised at the time. Only to be raised again ever higher when the verdict rolled in.

I was hoping that as Wheeler's lawyer she would know what he'd done and where he'd gone after the trial. The news would be twelve years old, but it would be more information than I had now. Or, maybe I'd get lucky and find out they'd been pen pals this whole time and she could hand over his address without breaking a sweat.

Unfortunately, the real question was whether Atwater would even talk to me. We didn't have a personal beef, exactly, but she wouldn't have forgotten I'd been the prosecuting officer in Wheeler's case. Plus minor run-ins involving other cases over the last decade or so. Then add the normal antipathy that exists between cops that nabbed the crooks and the attorneys that did their best to get them off. I'd say that the relationship was like the one between cats and dogs, but that's a conflict created by nature. And there's nothing natural about defense lawyers.

I found the number for her practice in the phone book and called, waiting through five or six buzzes. No receptionist. I hung up before voice mail kicked in; no sense in giving her advance warning. Ten minutes later I tried again. Same deal. I went downstairs, drank a glass of water straight down while standing at the sink, ignoring the cold plate of bacon and eggs on the table. I gazed out my back window instead, where my neighbor was wrestling about a million oak leaves into a plastic garbage bag. I smirked with a slight twinge of guilt. The oak tree that had dropped all those leaves was in my yard.

I went back upstairs and hit redial. I figured no defense attorney in the world was going to ignore three calls in an hour from an unknown number. Not if they wanted to stay employed. I was right. The phone picked up after two rings.

"Atwater." Her voice was as terse as I remembered it.

"Ms. Atwater, this is Marty Singer. I used to be with the MPDC—"

"I know who you are."

Huh. "I was wondering if you had some time to talk about a past case, one we both worked on in the mid-nineties."

"Are you asking me as a potential client, Mr. Singer?"

Mister, not *Detective.* She was up to speed on my situation. "No. I just need to ask you a few questions."

"And I need paying clients, Mr. Singer. If you aren't being arraigned in the next few days on a criminal charge, I'm not prepared to sacrifice any of my time for you."

"It wouldn't be much of a sacrifice," I said. "I've got a situation where the daughter of a victim of someone you represented is in danger and you might have information—"

"Do you have a license, Mr. Singer?" she asked, her voice sweet now. "If you're taking on clients whose lives might be in danger, I certainly hope you're qualified—and registered—to do so."

"I don't need a license to ask questions, which is all I'm doing at the moment," I said, trying to stay calm. It helped if I imagined her head being squeezed beneath the foot of a circus elephant.

"Sorry, can't help you." I heard a rustling, as if she were pulling the phone away from her ear.

"Michael Wheeler," I shouted into the phone, hoping to catch her before I heard the click.

A pause. Then, "What did you say?"

"Michael Wheeler," I said. "I need ten minutes. That's it."

I heard her take a deep, ragged breath. Then, in a guttural voice, she said, "Go to hell, Singer."

A beep signaled the end of the call. The whole exchange had taken less than a minute. I stared at my phone for a while, couldn't come up with anything useful, then called someone who might actually talk to me.

Dods was short for David O. Davidovitch. In Ukrainian, it meant David, son of David. You'd think they could just tack "Jr." on the end. Dods was a short, wide, smart homicide detective who couldn't keep a shirt tucked in or a tie knotted to save his life. Most of the time he had the air of a tired cabbie coming off a Friday-night shift. He'd been my partner for eleven years, right up until the end.

"Davidovitch," he answered on the fourth ring.

"Hey, Junior," I said.

"Marty," he said, real pleasure in his voice, though you wouldn't know it from the sound. His voice was like a bucket full of rocks being rolled around. "How the hell are you?"

"Hanging in there."

"How's . . . everything? You need anything? You want to have dinner with Margie and me?"

"I'm good, Dods," I said, trying not to think about breakfast. "I'll swing by soon. Not tonight."

"She's asking about you. Rides my case all the time." His voice became high and nasal. "'Did you see Marty today? Why doesn't he come over? Why haven't you *called* him?'"

I smiled. "I can hear her voice now."

"How could you not? She sounds like Edith Bunker. Anyway, what's on your mind?"

"What do you know about Julie Atwater?"

"Atwater?" he asked. "As in, the prosecutor?"

"Yeah."

"What do you mean? You know as much as I do about that—I mean, about her."

"Act like I don't know anything. Talk it out with me."

"She started in the prosecutor's office," he said slowly. "But didn't like the money or the hours, so she sold out and went private. She'll defend anything that drags itself to her door."

"So nothing's changed?"

"Status quo," Dods said. "Why? What's your interest?"

"You remember Mike Wheeler? That whole thing?"

"That piece of shit?" he asked. "Naturally. I mean, I wasn't in Homicide yet, but I followed it like everybody else."

"She was his defense attorney."

"Yeah," he said, drawing the word out like he'd just discovered it. "How could I forget?"

"Age," I said, trying to be helpful. "Substance abuse. Falling down the steps as a kid."

"Right. Thanks."

"Wheeler was one of her first cases after she went private, right?"

"Maybe, I dunno. The timing is right. She was a PD for maybe three or four years before the money called her away."

"Then she got the break of the century when the case on Wheeler went to hell," I said.

"Yeah and fell off the map. I mean, she's in court all the time, but it's always for low-level dealers, repeat cons, busted pimps. Getting Wheeler off should've given her career an atomic boost. She ought to be defending CEOs and senators, not creeps. Well, same thing, maybe. You know what I mean. Why is it you care, again?"

I hesitated, then gave him a sanitized version, trying to downplay the situation. It wasn't that I didn't trust Dods. I did, and with my life. But I knew he'd overdo it. He would've stood up and walked out of the precinct right then if he thought he could help. I didn't need that. Not yet. I had Kransky on it, sure, but there was something else. Call it pride or maybe discretion—if things got too hot later, I'd holler for him—but I didn't want to call in my ace yet. I wanted to do this myself.

He seemed to understand instinctively, reminding me why we'd been such good partners. "So you want to get to Wheeler through her."

"Yeah."

"Long shot," he said.

"Tell me about it. Something's bugging her, though." I told him about my call with Atwater. "Has she changed since I was there?"

"Marty, you been gone like two, three months. You think she's developed a limp or something? Wears an eye patch, now?"

"Humor me, will you? Start at zero. Like I never saw her before, never knew her."

"Well, she's got this pitchfork, see—"

"Dods."

He sighed. "She's foxy, but mean and kind of, I don't know, bland. Same black suit. At least, it was black in the nineties. Same beat-up briefcase. Wears the same clothes every time I see her. Stomps around like she wants to stick her foot up someone's ass."

I closed my eyes, thought back to the last time I'd seen Julie Atwater in court. It had been, what, two months since I'd retired? Four or five since I'd even passed her in a hall or outside a courtroom. Like Dods said, she probably hadn't changed much. She was a good-looking woman—petite, black hair, late thirties—but worn out, weary, bitter. "How about emotionally? Mentally?"

"Hell, Marty. I don't know. She was always a class-A bitch. Chip on her shoulder. You ask me, hanging up on you is standard operating procedure. If she didn't serve papers on you, I'd say you must've gotten on her good side somehow."

"She's a pissed-off lady with a bad wardrobe? That's it?"

"Yeah. Speaking of pissed off, that's what I'm gonna be if I have to work late tonight. You want her number or something?"

"I got it. Give me her address."

"Home? Office?"

"Both, if you got them."

I heard the slicking of computer keys. He rattled off the information I needed, then asked, "What are you going to do, you find Wheeler?"

"Why does everybody keep asking me that? Let me find the guy first."

"Okay, okay. But no cowboy shit from you, all right? You learn something, you share. Something happens to the girl, you share. I hear you going Lone Ranger on us and I'm going to have to drag you in."

"Jeez, Dods," I said, impressed. "You sound like you mean it."

I heard a clatter as the phone was dropped and then a small scuffing sound as Dods picked it up again. "That punk Henderson was walking by," he whispered. "I had to give him something. I say, if you find Wheeler—whether he's doing this stuff to the girl or not—you waste him and dump him in the Potomac."

CHAPTER NINE

After I hung up with Dods, I thought about the call with Atwater.

The excessive hostility was no surprise. It's probably how I would've answered the phone if she'd called me and asked for a freebie. Nothing new there. But the quality of her voice when I'd mentioned Wheeler's case . . . that I hadn't planned on. In a few, short, breathy words she'd sounded shocked. Angry. Frightened. It was a remarkable reaction for a case twelve years old from a lady who was normally hard as flint. And remarkable reactions in unshakable people trigger the bloodhound in me. I picked up the scrap of paper where I'd scribbled down Atwater's address, thinking. I drew a line through the office address. Then circled her home address.

It took me twenty minutes to get there. It would've taken less than ten if I'd had a siren and a gumball on the roof. Her house was off George Mason Drive in what developers like to describe without irony as a community. No one knows anyone else's name—though the places are close enough to pass the barbeque sauce from one deck to the other—and the sidewalks end at bridge abutments or freeway entrances. The conceit extended to the thin, boxy homes that were meant to invoke the feel of Bostonian brownstones, but the faux wrought-iron railings were rusting and the finely pointed red brick was only on the front. Cheap vinyl siding—once white, now yellowing—covered the backs and the sides of the end units. All of the cookie-cutter dumps looked exactly like the others, so I slowed to a sedate ten miles an hour and crawled up and around the rows, looking for Atwater's place.

I found it fronting Pershing Avenue in one of the nicer sections of the development, across the street from a long run of 1950s-era single-family homes. The serene pastel houses with their short porches and prim, postage-stamp gardens gave the town houses facing them a kind of borrowed class. Enough that you could forget that, around the corner, the rest of the development sat cheek-by-jowl with a convenience store, a Laundromat, and a gas station. Route 50 growled a block or two away; I could feel the rumble of traffic sitting in my car.

I did a U-turn in front of the nice houses, where I parked, got out, and stretched. I crossed the street and walked up the row like I was out for a Sunday stroll. One town house had a "For Sale" sign in the front and a plastic dispenser full of flyers. In the unlikely event anyone was watching, I pulled one out and looked like I was interested, which couldn't have been further from the truth when I saw what they were asking for it. I sauntered down the sidewalk as if assessing the neighborhood, holding the flyer like a road map.

The front of Atwater's place was as nondescript as the others, with a red-brick façade, one medium-size window, and a standard door with a corroded brass knocker. In lieu of grass, the lawn had some white stones, some of which had dribbled onto the sidewalk. The only landscaping consisted of two small shrubs, brown and nearly dead.

The one standout detail was a small sign on a post jammed into the soil of the front yard. It tilted at a crazy angle, like it had been a while since it had been put there. Printed on the sign in authoritative capital letters were the words, "THIS HOUSE PROTECTED BY SECURETREX." In a smaller font below the warning message was a phone number to call in case of emergencies or natural disasters.

I stared at it for a second, an idea taking shape. I liked what I came up with and pulled out my phone, punching in the phone number from the sign. A woman with a British accent, firm and cultured, answered. "SecureTrex. How can I help you?"

I made my voice shaky. "Hi, SecureTrex? Yeah, I was walking down the street and saw a guy go into one of the properties you protect." I gave her the address.

"We don't have an alarm coming from that address," the woman said. "Are you sure, sir?"

"You're damn right, I'm sure," I said, sounding offended. *How dare they?* "The guy jimmied the door open and went right in."

"Is this . . ." A pause. "Mr. Atwater?"

"Who? No, I was walking by and saw the guy go in. And your sign in the front yard, that's why I called."

"May I have your name, please, sir?"

I hung up on the nice lady and walked back to my car. I had five or ten minutes, depending on whether they had roving patrols or a dispatch station and garage nearby. I was leaning against the hood, still marveling at the flyer, when I heard screeching tires. A glance at my watch made it almost fifteen minutes. SecureTrex seemed a poor choice for any home protection needs.

A black Navigator—tinted windows, no logo, license plate SECTREX1—pulled up fast, but under control. I smiled at the choice of vehicle. The big SUV looked imposing and sinister, exactly like it was meant to, but every federal security force in the area used black SUVs with tinted windows, too. They could probably do a hundred miles an hour in the streets of DC, Virginia, or Maryland and most cops would just assume they were from the FBI, CIA, Secret Service, or one of a hundred other federal departments. The lack of a government plate would give it away, but even if the cop noticed, he'd shrug and move on to easier pickings.

The SUV bucked to a stop at an angle to the curb, blocking half the street. Two guys in matching khakis and black polo shirts jumped out. They had big arms, small waists, and legs thick from twenty-rep sets.

Both had dark hair cut close so that the scalp showed through and each had one of those wireless earplugs for their cell phone, the thing that makes you look like a reject from a Star Trek convention. Around their waists they wore black nylon belts that held flashlights, cell phones, and multi-tools. Everything except what you needed most, which was a sidearm. Another strike against SecureTrex. Or maybe that was a plus. Not every clown should carry a gun.

They conferred briefly, then one guy unclipped his flashlight and headed up the steps to the front door while the other pulled the short straw and hoofed it to the far end of the block, probably so he could cover the back. Cover it with what, I wasn't sure. Maybe he would flash a light in the evildoer's eyes or do arm curls around his neck.

The first guy pointed his light on the ground as he went, even though it was broad daylight. He flashed it at the wrought-iron railing, the door handle, he even leaned over and lit up the window. Satisfied, he opened up the screen door and turned the handle of the main door. It didn't budge. He looked at it for a second and then he knocked. Standard procedure, I guess, but in my experience, bad guys don't answer knocks.

Shortstraw appeared from around the corner and shook his head when Flashlight glanced his way. They must've gotten instructions from the mother ship then, because they both abandoned the front porch and started looking around. It didn't take long for them to spot me, watching from half a block away.

I thought they were going to get in the SUV and drive over, but they were in too good a shape for that. They jogged instead, looking fit, young, and healthy. They stopped in front of me. Neither one was out of breath and wearing short sleeves in forty-degree weather didn't seem to faze them in the least.

"Excuse me, sir," Flashlight said. "We had a report of a break-in at one of these residences. Did you happen to see anything? Say, in the last twenty minutes?"

"A break-in?" I said. "No, sorry. I just got here."

"You didn't report the break-in, then?"

"No, I'm afraid not. Like I said, I just got here."

"What's your business here, sir?" Shortstraw said, eyes narrowing. His hair was cut even shorter than the other's, the half-inch bristles sticking up from his scalp. He made the word "sir" sound like an insult. Ex-military, maybe, with a touch of scorn for civilians.

"I'm waiting for a friend," I said.

They chewed that over, exchanging glances. This was a singularly unlikely spot to meet someone. You meet people at restaurants, coffee shops, bars. Not Pershing Avenue sitting on the hood of your car in December. Shortstraw got a look on his face.

"Can I see your ID?" He held his hand out. It was calloused on the pads and the palm, no doubt from the crosshatched grips of barbells.

"No," I said. "You can't."

He purpled around the eyes. Maybe he'd been a sergeant, used to giving orders. Or maybe he had a type-A personality and people did what he said. Or maybe he was just a rent-a-cop asshole and liked to push people around. I could tell he wanted to take a swing at me, then dimly remembering that following through on that desire would be assault, he tried the stare-down instead.

I gave it right back, staying relaxed and unconcerned. The trick was to stay still. If I'd moved, it would've broken the spell, turned it into something physical. And this showdown was about willpower, not knuckles. I'd like to think I can handle myself, but no way was I going to take a guy twenty years younger than me with wrists thick as drainpipes. You hit lunks like that from behind with a brick or you shoot them; you don't see which one of you can take a punch. I had to make sure it didn't come to that. So he scowled at me and I glared back, letting him know I wasn't going to snap in half, even if he stamped his feet and yelled mean things at me.

When I was a rookie, the guy who got stuck with me was a round, pasty-faced second-generation Russian named Sokalov. He laughed a lot, drank too much, and smelled like onions. He wasn't much to look at, but he was hell in a fight. The first time we got into it, I mean *really* into it, with a couple of punks down on Georgia Avenue, he stared down a half-dozen of them. I was sweating it, my hand near my holster, ready to draw and empty my pistol if any of them decided to earn their street cred by taking out a couple of cops.

Sokalov had looked at them, still and serene in the face of all their bluster and insults. It seemed a close call to me. But they'd all seen something, sensed something, that convinced them to drop it. The magic moment passed, that razor's edge where, at some other time, in some other place, six kids and two cops were killed in a street-side shooting in southeast DC. Instead, in this universe, we got dirty looks and the finger, but everyone walked away.

When Sokalov turned around, I was too self-conscious to ask him what had happened or how I could work the same spell next time I was in a jam. He knew, though, and said to me as he walked past, "Steel breaks bone." We got back in our squad car and cruised on out of there.

I still didn't know what the hell he was talking about. But I carried that phrase around in my head and, after a while, it made sense. It's what I thought of now as I eyed the iron-pumping freak in front of me. *Steel breaks bone*, I said to myself, and looked back at him as he tried to cut me down with his eyes. I saw a hesitation there.

"C'mon, Scott," Flashlight said, grabbing Shortstraw's arm. At that moment, a light brown Malibu rounded the corner and came to a cautious stop behind SecureTrex's SUV. I slid my eyes away from the two in front of me and toward the car. The door opened and Julie Atwater, still in her faded black-gone-to-gray pantsuit, got out of the driver's side, hesitating. She glanced from the SUV to her house to the three of us tough guys having our pissing contest halfway down the street.

"Hey, there she is," I said. "Just who I was waiting for."

The two SecureTrex clones, who had turned around when she'd pulled up, glanced at me, then jogged back in unison to Atwater. I stayed with my car, hands in my pockets, watching the gestured conference. I watched the fast-action pantomime as they described the call, their response, the fruitless result, and then—with fingers pointing—their encounter with me. Atwater squinted in my direction. Even at this distance, I could see her expression and it wasn't good. She turned and said something to the Dynamic Duo, who argued for a minute, then gave up and plodded back to the SUV. The black monstrosity started up with a roar and they drove down Pershing in my direction. As they passed, they gave me the kind of *You better watch out* look kids give each other when they peel out of a high school parking lot.

I turned to see Atwater stalking toward me, her fists curled at her sides as she walked. She must've been cold, wearing only the threadbare pantsuit, but I guess her anger was enough to keep her warm. She stopped five feet away, breathing fire. I sensed *steel breaks bone* wasn't going to work here.

"Singer, what the fuck do you think you're doing?" she said, with nary a hello.

"Waiting for you, Miss."

"I hope you have plenty in whatever nest egg you've saved up for your retirement, because I'm going to have an injunction on your ass inside the next hour. And that's just a start."

"For what?"

"Harassment is a good start. Falsely reporting a crime."

"Calling a former colleague isn't illegal. Mistakenly reporting a breaking and entering isn't either."

Her lips pressed together, forming a horizontal line across the bottom of a face that wouldn't have looked half bad if she'd smiled more often. A deep furrow creased the spot between her eyes. Her hair was longer than I remembered, falling past her shoulders. It was black with a streak or two of gray. Probably put there by guys like me. Strands fell in her eyes and she pushed them away with an impatient flick of her hand, a curiously girlish gesture. She had a ski-slope nose and large, dark brown eyes that snapped with anger.

"Calling six times?" she said. "Sitting outside my house, staking it out? You aren't a cop anymore, Singer. And you'd be out of your jurisdiction even if you were."

"Look, I get it. You're not a fan. If it makes you feel better, the feeling's mutual. But that's irrelevant right now. There's something going on that's bigger than our mutual dislike. I need half an hour. That's it."

"I don't want to give you a half hour, Singer," she said. "In fact, I don't want to give you the time I'm wasting right now. I don't want to talk to you and don't need to. This conversation is over."

I nodded slowly. "You're right, there's nothing I can do to you to get your cooperation. Officially. But we both know that I've got enough connections back at MPDC to make life rough for you, whether it's in the courtroom or not."

She didn't say anything, just continued to glare. I pushed it. "Give me some credit, Atwater. I might've been a pain in your ass back in the day, but I was never interested in wasting anybody's time, least of all my own. You know that. Thirty minutes and I'll be out of your hair."

Something I'd said got through. The anger was still there in the gritted teeth and squeezed fists, but, as I watched, the great surge of rage that had carried her over here leaked out and dribbled away. Her shoulders sagged. "What do you want?"

"Same thing as I did on the phone," I said. "Tell me about Michael Wheeler."

"Jesus," she said, closing her eyes for a second. "That case is done and gone. Wheeler is gone. Ten, twelve years ago. What could you possibly need to know at this point?"

"Let's just say something's interfering with my retirement and Wheeler's part of it. And that means talking to you."

"What're you going to do? Try a citizen's arrest this time?"

"Actually, I'd prefer if he tripped and fell onto the Beltway at rush hour," I said. "But I'll settle for finding out where he is. You can help."

She looked at me, weighing her options. Could she really be rid of me in a half hour? How much of a pain would I be if she didn't agree? Looking unhappy, she jerked her head back toward her house. "You've got thirty minutes. You ask me questions, maybe I'll answer, then we're done. You try to push me around again, I fight back. I'm not going to be on the hook forever. Deal?"

I nodded. "Deal."

CHAPTER TEN

I followed Atwater back to her town house, stopping for a second while she grabbed an attaché case out of the passenger's side of her tea-colored car. She walked ahead of me with a controlled stomp, completely silent. It would've been kind of cute, if it didn't look as though she was trying to put her heel through the ground. I'd thought she walked that way because she was angry with me. Now I realized it was how she walked all the time.

I held the screen door open while she unlocked the triple set of Yales on the front door. She banged it open and went inside, tossing her keys in a bowl of pennies sitting on a table by the door. She stomped down the entry hall, flicking some lights on. The walls were painted that shade of not-quite-white that you can buy by the tanker truck, a color a friend of mine had dubbed "nicotine." A lonely pair of sconces were the only decoration. The place smelled stale, inert, as though the windows had never been opened.

I trailed her into the living room. A couch with worn arms and two upholstered chairs faced each other in a companionable circle, though I had trouble believing there were two people in the world who wanted to talk companionably with Julie Atwater at any time. A small end table held an ashtray with a few butts in it.

She dropped her attaché case on the floor, then shrugged off her blazer and threw it over the far arm of the couch. Something made me look at her again. The simple, familiar move, in her home, transformed her into someone more normal and relaxed than I'd ever seen her in the courtroom. Her back was still ramrod straight and her expression wasn't even close to inviting, but the edges had been softened. She also had a nice figure that the tawdry jacket had concealed. I scooted one of the chairs to a better angle and eased into it, while she took the middle cushion of the couch. She got back up, fished a pack of cigarettes and a lighter out of her jacket, sat back down. The tip of the cigarette glowed ruby red while she lit it. She took a drag, then we stared at each other for a second until she made an exasperated *"well, what?"* motion with her hands, the smoke waving from her cigarette like a flag.

"This is your show, Singer," she said. "Twenty-eight minutes."

"Tell me about Michael Wheeler."

"You're going to have to be more specific than that."

"Where is he?"

Her eyebrows shot up. "Is? I have no clue. People can cover a lot of ground in twelve years."

"You never heard from him? He doesn't send you postcards, thanking you for getting him off a murder rap?"

She snorted. "I'm a criminal defense lawyer, Singer. People like Wheeler don't give a shit. Most of them think they should get off because they want to. No better reason than that. They don't think they're innocent. They just don't think they should go to jail. So, no, they don't thank me for saving them from doing twenty-to-life and they sure don't remember it twelve years later."

"So, you've got no idea where he is? You haven't heard from him?"

She took a drag, exhaled. "No."

"What about the days right after the trial? Where did he go? What did he do?"

She shook her head. "I don't know."

"You've had no contact with him since the day he walked out of the courtroom?"

"That's what I said."

"Gimme a break, counselor," I said. "Your first real client as a criminal defense attorney. A huge deal in the press. Maybe a landmark case against the MPDC, a bad cop goes on trial for murder one, and it gets screwed up on the way. And you're telling me you don't know anything about him?"

"That's right."

"You don't know where he lived, or ate, or what his forwarding address was?"

"Singer, you probably know as much as or more than I do. Up until the time I represented him, I hadn't even heard of Wheeler except in the papers. After I was brought on the case, he was in custody during the trial. I visited him a couple of times in lockup to get our strategy straight. After that, the only other time I saw him was when the bailiff marched him over to my table. And that's it."

"And after the trial," I said, still digging. "Nothing? He walked out of the courtroom and out of your life ten minutes after the verdict?"

"More like five, but yes, pretty much. We gave the obligatory statement to the press—it was big news, naturally—and then we shook hands and he took off."

"No phone calls, no visits, nothing?"

She smiled. "No matter how many different ways you ask, Singer, the answer's the same: I never saw Michael Wheeler after the trial."

I tried a new angle. "Don Landis."

The smile dropped off her face like a stone off a cliff. "What about him?"

"No congratulatory handshake? No commiserations? No gloating?"

"Don had just lost a high-profile, must-win case to a first-time criminal defense attorney. Because his own side had dropped the ball.

Do I need to remind you? He wasn't going to pat me on the back. And I wasn't going to shove his nose in it. Don was a good lawyer and it could've easily been me, then or later. In fact, it should've been me, except—" She stopped herself.

"Except what?"

Her mouth was so pinched that it seemed as if there were sutures pulling her mouth inward. "The screwup. I had a decent defense strategy, but I knew I wasn't going to get anything better than a reduced sentence. It didn't matter that your evidence against Wheeler was circumstantial; everyone was howling for a conviction. I told Wheeler to expect the worst, no matter how well I did. But thanks to your bungling, when the case got dumped, it all went away. The evidence, the bargaining, the trial. Everything."

"You don't sound very happy about it."

She refocused on me, but took a second to answer. "It was bittersweet. I put a lot of work into that case. As you said, my first real client. An important, noteworthy case. Lots of press. I wanted to win it on my own merits. Instead, I got handed a turkey. One that worked for me, but a turkey anyway."

I let the silence spool out. Then, "How did you feel about that?"

"What the hell do you care?"

"I've never gotten this close to a criminal defense attorney before. I'm curious."

She laughed, a short bark that fell flat. "What do you think? It should've launched a career. But it was a lame duck, a gimme. Everyone assumed if I was lucky, I couldn't be good. I got passed over by all but the dumbest or most desperate schmucks you can imagine. No one recognized the work I did on Wheeler's case *before* you guys laid an egg. And, since I was getting lousy clients, my win rate spiraled downward, netting even worse clients than before. So, what do you think it did to me, Singer?"

Despite my innate dislike of Atwater—and criminal defense attorneys in general—I'd never stopped to think how Wheeler's acquittal might've affected her. To me, a win is a win. If a bad guy happens to step off a curb and get hit by a truck instead of going to jail, well . . . it's harsh, maybe, but to me, justice is served. That's a cosmic balance I can live with. But what if your life and livelihood were predicated not just on the *results* of your work but the *appearance* of it? And your first chance to put that effort on display seemed fraudulent, fluky, pure shit luck? It could ruin you.

I cast about for a silver lining. "It was still a win. And it was twelve years ago. New clients come along. People forget."

She smiled sarcastically. "Yeah, except I didn't. When you get five years of shit clients, you start thinking it's you. That maybe you don't have what it takes and never did. I've gotten past that, but it took most of a decade for me to start believing in myself again."

I gave her a second, then said, "When I first called you and mentioned Wheeler, you didn't sound angry or disgusted. You sounded scared. Why was that?"

Her face twisted. "Don't you get it yet, Singer? I wasn't scared, I was pissed off. That case represents everything that's gone wrong with my career from day one. And you're the guy who started it all. Then you call and want to chat about it. What the hell is it to you, anyway?"

I watched her face. "He's back."

Atwater became very still. Her face, previously flushed with her anger, turned waxy. "What? What did you say?"

"Wheeler's here, counselor. He looked up Brenda Lane's daughter and left her a not-so-subtle reminder of her mother's death. You remember Brenda, don't you? The woman he murdered, no matter what the court said?" I leaned forward and stared at her. "He's after Brenda's daughter and I have to find him. I need to know where he is. I need to know anything you do."

She swallowed. Her hands squeezed each other so hard that, just like they say in the books, the knuckles turned white.

"Get out, Singer," she said. "Your thirty minutes are up."

◆　◆　◆

I left Julie Atwater sitting on her couch, tight of lip and rigid of body. No amount of cajoling or implied threats would get her to talk and she kept repeating that I should leave until, after the sixth time and with her voice starting to crack, I figured she meant it. I jotted my number down on a scrap of paper I found near the penny bowl by the door. It would probably end up in the trash by the end of the day, but I'd had less likely leads pan out before.

It sure would be nice if she called, since our encounter had raised a hell of a lot more questions than it had answered. That she didn't know where Wheeler might be was natural. It had been the longest of shots to begin with, the kind of jackpot question you have to ask in case you get lucky. It was her behavior that had me stymied. Like on the phone, her reaction first to Wheeler's name, then to the news that he was in DC, wasn't sarcasm, or irritation, or dismissal, or any number of other reactions I would've expected from a woman who, at the heart of it, hated my guts. It was fear. And that didn't make sense for a twelve-year-old case where the defendant had walked out free as a bird because of her.

So the long shot was one reason to leave my number. The other was, if Wheeler was around and had already threatened her or she thought he would, she might wise up and give me a call when she realized she couldn't handle it herself. It wouldn't hurt to be thought of as her temporary guardian angel . . . as long as it led to Wheeler.

But I went over the conversation again in my head as I tucked my hands in my jacket pockets and headed back to my car. Something wasn't sitting right. Atwater might've turned white when I told her Wheeler was back in town, but the first chink in her armor had appeared when I mentioned Don Landis, the prosecutor on Wheeler's case. Not that I had a fond recollection of the man, either. I had worked with Don on the investigation and would've preferred to forget all about him. But the ghosts of the case weren't that easily laid to rest. So when I got to my car, instead of putting it in gear and driving off, I turned on the heat and sat, thinking about a case I shouldn't have lost.

CHAPTER ELEVEN

The case against Wheeler took almost a year to put together and get to trial. This is considered light speed in the world of criminal trial law, but his defense seemed so paper thin, the man himself so smug with guilt, that I had trouble believing we hadn't already tried, sentenced, and buried him in the first month. I remember waking up some of those days, thinking about the work ahead of me, planning it out, and being astonished—toothbrush or razor frozen in hand—when I realized Wheeler's case was still at the top of my list.

Despite my bias, I was still a professional. I went about my business and conducted as thorough an investigation as I could. Interviews, diagrams, background checks, ballistics results, spatter reports, more interviews. Phone calls, long hours, late nights. We paid special attention to the case, did what we could, though we were stretched thin. Those were the heydays when DC led the nation in homicides.

Assigned to the case from the legal side was Don Landis, a silver-haired attorney in his mid-fifties with a decent reputation. Unlike the rest of the country, the District is a federal jurisdiction, so the United States attorney's office does the prosecuting instead of a district attorney. It sounds like a big deal, but the situation is identical to that of the rest of the law-abiding world, including the sometimes complicated relationship between cops and prosecutors. Some of them are crazy about getting involved early on, showing up at the scene to make sure everything is done right, micromanaging the site until the cops on the ground go crazy. Others don't move until the investigator's report starts to yellow and curl up at the corners.

There were worse cards you could pull from the deck. Landis fell solidly in the middle. I'd worked with him on other investigations and found him to be thorough, if uninspired. He did the minimum amount of work to see a case through, but at least he did it. The apathy meant he wasn't climbing any political ladders or looking for headlines despite a ton of trial experience under his belt. He was a clock-puncher, a nine-to-fiver. I expected a competent job from him and not much else. Consequently, I was astonished when I got a call at the break of dawn from him the day after Brenda Lane was killed.

"Singer," I answered from the bed. Even shut, my eyes were burning. I'd trawled the scene most of the night and hadn't gotten back until after three.

"Marty," came the phlegmy, pack-a-day voice on the other end. "Tell me about Mike Wheeler."

"Don?" I said, surprised, eyes opening.

"The one and only."

"You drew the short straw, huh?"

"You could say that," he said without humor. "At least it'll be more entertaining than the gangbangers and drug hits we usually get."

"Press been after you?"

"I got a couple calls in the middle of the night from friends at the *Post*. They only needed a couple lines for the morning blotter, but if I don't have a statement by this afternoon they'll be out for blood."

"Mighty nice of them."

"So what do you got?"

I described the scene and Wheeler's statements. I did my best to stick with the facts but, as far as I was concerned, Wheeler was guilty as hell. I was so convinced that I found myself speaking of him in the past tense. And I expected Landis to feel the same way. I was talking to the prosecutor, for crying out loud. He should've taken my cue that this was about as open and shut as you could get. We were beyond the what and the why; we should've been talking about the how and how long.

Instead, Landis asked, "Wheeler had some prior contact with this woman?"

"Yeah, scuttlebutt has it that she'd called the station a half-dozen times to complain about him hanging around. Borderline harassment. And the switchboard told me we've got a recording of her calling last night a minute before he shot her."

"Can you get me that tape?"

"Once I listen to it myself, yeah. We'll get it to you."

"This lady—"

"Brenda," I said. "Her name was Brenda Lane."

"Sure," he said. "Did she ever file charges on Wheeler? About the harassment?"

"Not that I heard asking around last night," I said. "We'll know more today."

"You don't know?" he asked, his voice peeved.

"I've been on the case for six hours, Don," I said. "And I've been asleep for three of them."

"If she didn't file charges, that's going to weaken the case."

"It's important, but that's not going to make or break this case. You talk to this guy once and you'll smell the stink coming off him."

"As in a confession?"

"No, not as in a confession," I said. "As in a string of goddamn lies. A two-year-old could see through the crime scene."

"Why don't you walk this two-year-old through it, then?" he said, his voice sarcastic.

I pinched my eyes with a finger and thumb until I saw stars. "There's no way the shooting could've happened the way he said it did. He calls it self-defense, but I walked through it and, physically, it doesn't work. The lab can give you the floor plan. You can see for yourself. As for the gun she was supposed to be pointing at him, unless she's got connections to a black-market arms dealer, it's a plant. And, for Christ's sake, the guy *thanked* me, like I was his sponsor at communion or something. He damn near came out and asked me to cover for him. I'm telling you, Don, he stinks."

His voice became brittle. "Marty, you might be able to play a hunch, but I need something more than how the guy smells. The union is coming out with a statement of support later today and the mayor's office is expected to comment after that. Half the city is going to want Wheeler swinging from the Fourteenth Street Bridge, the other half is planted directly behind him. If I'm going to prosecute this guy the right way, I can't afford to blow it on guesswork. It's my ass on the line when we go to court and I'm not going to let someone else fuck this up on my behalf."

It was obvious who he thought the someone else was. And I didn't appreciate it. "If this case goes down in flames, prosecutor, it's not going to be my team's fault."

Those were still the days of landlines and phones with bells in them, and the base made a nice ringing sound when I slammed the receiver down hard enough to crack the plastic casing. It's not like today where you have to punch a button to hang up and all you get is a "beep," no matter how angry you are. You have to throw the phone across the room to get any satisfaction.

Then again, if I'd known where the case was going, I would've slammed the phone down *and* thrown it across the room.

◆ ◆ ◆

Twelve years later, I found myself gritting my teeth as I remembered the memos Landis had sent to my office. The words "insufficient" and "inadequate" peppered most of the messages. The language was negative and harsh, criticizing my team and its work, while constantly urging us to double and triple our efforts. This on top of the three dozen or so other cases we'd been assigned. Only in books, TV, and the movies do cops get to work on a case at a time. And it seemed even more inequitable than usual for us. While other teams were going home at five, we were canceling vacations and sleeping in the office to handle the workload.

It didn't amount to squat. In court, Landis was unable to project the image of Wheeler as an obsessed stalker, refusing to make more than a passing mention of Brenda Lane's calls to the station complaining about his attentions. Atwater, despite her inexperience, used the same episodes to paint Wheeler as a devoted community peacekeeper, an example of his dedication to protect Brenda Lane and the neighborhood. She cited a rise in local crime to back up the need for vigilance—never mind that the "rise" consisted of statistics taken from the rest of DC and not the patty-cake problems the Palisades suffered from. Lawrence Ferrin, Wheeler's partner and friend, gave an impassioned description of Wheeler's service to the community and his fitness as a brother police officer. With sly looks in my direction, he described how brusque I'd been at the crime scene and my dismissive attitude.

The case progressed and Atwater ripped the lab team apart, describing their examination of the crime scene as a comedy of errors. She intimated that the body had been moved and created a colorful misinterpretation of the timing of things, deftly making Wheeler's alibi—impossible from what I'd seen two hours after the event—perfectly acceptable. The head of the forensics team defended his department's actions on the stand, but when Atwater pointed out several black eyes suffered by his unit in three previous cases, all having to do with crime scene taint, his credibility went down in flames.

The coup de grace was a chain-of-evidence fuckup of monumental proportions. The tape of Brenda Lane's call the night she was murdered—her panicky, gasping reaction to Mike Wheeler breaking into her house minutes before she was shot to death—up and lost itself.

Lost. Vanished. As in, we couldn't find it.

I'd listened to it dozens of times. But when the original was sent by courier to Landis's office, it never got there. It grew legs and walked off. No one had made copies, even though that was standard procedure, so the only evidence of Brenda Lane's damning call was the fuzzy memory of the harried switchboard operator on duty that night.

The dirty little secret that no cop or prosecutor wants to admit is that . . . it happens. Things go missing that shouldn't. But you don't lose something of this magnitude. The tape wasn't just a piece of physical evidence, one block among many in the wall we were building around Wheeler. It was that all-important emotional denunciation that juries lap up, the stand-up-and-point moment that knocks the defense's house of cards down like a hurricane hit it. Would anyone have truly believed Wheeler was there to check on a burglary after hearing Brenda's voice, the recognition in that one word, "*You?*"? Does a woman aiming a pistol at a potential attacker stay on the phone and scream "*Don't, don't, don't!*" instead of firing? Those twelve angry men would've been in and out with a guilty verdict so fast the door wouldn't have had time to swing shut.

Instead, Landis called us in a rage a few days before trial, wanting to know where the tape had gone. A massive, unsuccessful hunt for the thing followed, succeeded quickly by a lot of finger-pointing. No one seemed to know who picked up the tape or signed for it, or whether it even got to the goddamn prosecutor's office. My team ripped into each other until I told them to knock it off and concentrate on the case. Communication with Landis's office reached an all-time low in both volume and civility.

I was furious—not to mention dejected—at the setback, but still thought we had enough to pin Wheeler to the wall. As for getting the jury emotionally involved, we'd lost our ace when the tape went missing, but I thought we might have a chance when Wheeler took the stand. The man was so naturally arrogant that he was his own worst enemy.

But Atwater had coached Wheeler well. He was the model defendant: humble, courteous, contrite, nearly breaking into tears when he fielded a soft pitch from Atwater about how the shooting might mark the end of his law enforcement career. Landis did his best to rattle him and a few times I thought I saw the true Michael Wheeler rise to the surface. But each time that happened, either Wheeler recovered himself, Atwater objected, or Landis failed to follow through. Atwater took the point in that game and the defendant's testimony—so often the straw that breaks the jury's back—did nothing but pave the way for the eventual verdict.

Not guilty.

I'd been involved in enough trials to see it coming, but refused to believe it until I heard the actual words come from the jury rep's mouth. The crowded gallery broke into a raucous mix of cheers and groans; like the police, the city, and the public, the audience was split in their support. Landis stared straight ahead, his gaze caught somewhere between the floor and the judge's dais. He didn't even blink when the verdict was read. Atwater had almost the same look, with just the merest blush at her success. I remember thinking at the time that she seemed underwhelmed by the victory.

Then I caught sight of Wheeler. He was standing, surrounded by supporters. Lawrence Ferrin and Tim Delaney from the night of the shooting were there along with a bunch of other cops that I hoped I never had to work with. There were backslaps and jokes all around.

I stared at Wheeler, not quite believing what had happened. He was shaking someone's hand, when Ferrin—grinning so wide the skin of skull seemed ready to split—nudged him in the ribs and he turned my way. His face was so self-satisfied, so full of triumph, I almost vaulted the railing to get at him. Wheeler was guilty as hell and we'd let him slip away. It was, perhaps, the worst moment of my professional life. I kept my cool, but while he was still turned toward me I cocked an imaginary gun, aimed, and shot.

He just smiled, a jackal's grin, and shook his head.

The rest of the year petered out, sluggish and uninspired. To a man, my department knew we'd blown it. Half the fault might be the US attorney's, but you don't look at it that way. As a matter of survival, I forced everyone to focus on the current cases and let Wheeler go. There was no shortage of people out there killing other people and they deserved our attention. Over time, the team let the case slide from the front of their mind to the back and eventually out altogether.

Of course, I didn't follow my own advice. Months after I watched Wheeler swagger out of the courtroom and Kransky had left Homicide cursing my name, I would go home and look at my personal file of the case, wondering where we'd missed the golden nugget that would've put him away. I never found it. Or we'd had it and lost it. I blamed myself, my fellow cops, the legal system, the government. I blamed Atwater and the whole subhuman race of criminal defense lawyers, then I blamed Landis and every federal prosecutor who'd ever lived. More than once I sat in my living room with a fifth of whiskey on the floor to the right and the phone to the left, got stinking drunk, then called Landis to heap abuse on him. To my surprise, he stayed on the line and took it, at least the first three or four times. Even after that, he would simply listen for a minute, then hang up quietly. Dods—newly assigned to me—got wind of what I was doing and threatened to cut my phone lines, then my fingers, if I didn't stop.

If there was any silver lining, it's that I didn't have to see Wheeler afterward; he seemed to disappear after the trial. His cronies—Lawrence Ferrin and the others—gave me looks and threw some remarks in my direction when they saw me, but nothing ever came of it and they, too, seemed to melt away once the fireworks were over.

A year later, long enough that I didn't blame myself too much, Landis walked out of his brownstone in Old Town Alexandria, swallowed some pills, and lay facedown across the railroad tracks north of town. An exercise path runs alongside the tracks, separated by a narrow stretch of grass and a chain-link fence. His body, or what was left of it, was an early-morning find by two joggers I'm betting never took that particular trail again. The coroner found traces of alcohol and prescribed antidepressants in his blood. In the wake of the Lane trial and bolstered by testimony from his coworkers and his psychiatrist, an inquest deemed it a suicide, no contest.

When I heard, I sat at my desk for a minute, saddened, then went to lunch. I had only recently managed to forget about the debacle when Don killed himself, so I'll admit with some guilt that, when he was gone, he was one less reminder of our inability to put Michael Wheeler behind bars. Memories of the trial and our colossal failure surfaced like sunken debris that had been temporarily dislodged. I gazed dispassionately at my anger and frustration . . . then let them sink back into the murky bottom of my emotions from where they'd come.

IV.

She was older, of course, and taller, but there was still a lot of the girl in her that he remembered. The hair was the same and she was still slender. Her face had the same distracted air, like she was listening to someone or something no one else could hear.

There were differences. As a girl she'd been awkward and clumsy growing into her body, falling off her bike and cutting up her knees. As a woman, she was lithe and walked gracefully even when she was hunched over with her books. Shy twelve years ago, she seemed popular now: she smiled and chatted with students and teachers on her way to class.

From benches and doorways and street corners he'd watched for days, trying to remember her. He'd monitored himself, alert to any of the desire he'd had for her before, surprised when he felt a stirring of the old emotions. Not the rushing burn he'd had back then, but enough of a tickle to make him doubt what he was doing. He'd been dead inside for twelve years. Was he the same person? She had changed; maybe he had, too.

He'd arrived with a mission, strong and confident, ready to act. Now he felt the first stirring of doubt, a crack in the foundation of his plan. If he wasn't ready to do what needed to be done, he didn't deserve the chance. Second chance, he corrected himself.

Maybe he'd sensed his own doubt. The flower had been as much a test for him as a message to her. He'd felt a strange tumult of emotions when he'd left it for her, and later, when he saw her pick it up. Satisfaction at her *shock, cold rage at the thought of the years behind him because of her—but hardest of all—the unexpected wriggle of desire. He'd assumed he'd feel nothing but cold direction; now, his emotions were confusing and muddling his focus. He needed something to tell him how to proceed.*

It was time to push the boundaries.

CHAPTER TWELVE

I drove away from Atwater's house mad. Memories of the trial were hard to swallow, naturally, but the encounter itself was difficult to take, too. I wasn't used to having to dance around subjects or witnesses. When you're a thirty-year veteran of the MPDC, you usually get what you want. Not that I was a bully. I didn't slap people around like some Prohibition-era thug with a badge. But I had resources, from outright arrest to more subtle ways to pressure people into doing what I needed them to do. Like suggesting they might get a parking ticket on the hood of their car every day for the rest of their natural life. That kind of thing. Those days were gone. Atwater knew that I could make her life inconvenient, but when push came to shove, she could tell me to get the hell out of her house and that was the end of it. It was another adjustment I was going to have to make.

I blew out a breath and concentrated on driving. I felt like I'd had a load of bricks dumped on my shoulders. I hadn't done anything like face down the boys from SecureTrex or work on a reluctant subject like Atwater in months. It should've been a piece of cake. Now all I wanted to do was pull over to the side of the road and take a nap. I gritted my teeth, put my hands at ten and two, and blinked rapidly until I pulled in front of my house.

I dragged myself inside, shut and locked the door, and collapsed onto the couch. From my back, I tossed my keys on the table and meant to do the same with my phone, but only got as far as pulling it out of my pocket before I fell asleep with it in my hand.

Which was a stroke of good luck, since it was the phone that finally woke me. I'd had it on vibrate and apparently it had been buzzing and jiggling enough to send it tumbling out of my hand to the oak floor where it landed with a loud *clack*. The noise of its impact and the persistent vibration fished me out of the coma I was in.

I sat up, stupid with sleep. It took me a minute to register where I was, when I was. It had been early afternoon when I'd stumbled through the front door and fallen onto the couch. Now it was pitch black outside, Pierre was doing a hotcakes dance in front of me, looking for food, and my phone was making a sound like an angry cicada stuck on its back.

I scrubbed my face with my hands, then picked up the phone. I punched the button to stop the alarm, then checked the time. 9:25. The day before, I'd set the phone to go off on the nines, a.m. and p.m., to remind me to check in with Amanda. She was almost a half-hour late calling in. A walnut-sized lump of anxiety took shape in my chest, but I clamped down on it and hit the speed dial number for her. I began rationalizing. We'd only been doing the call-in for a day or two; it wouldn't be that strange if she'd forgotten or blown it off, though the second thought made me burn. If she wasn't going to play by my rules, she could find someone else to worry about her.

The call was on its sixth ring and headed for voice mail. I cursed, ended the call, then hit speed dial again. It chirped four times. Five. Six. I was about to hang up when I heard it pick up. A loud bang made me wince, then Amanda's voice came on.

"Hello? Marty?"

"Amanda," I shouted.

"Sorry, I dropped the phone," she said, out of breath. "Oh, shit. It's past nine, isn't it?"

"Yeah," I said. "You were supposed to call in, remember?"

"I'm so sorry. I totally forgot. I gave an exam two days ago and I promised my students I'd get their scores back—"

"Wait," I said. "Where are you?"

"I'm in the Krueger building," she said. "My office."

"Your office? On campus?"

"Yes."

"Damn it," I said. "I thought I told you to stay away from there."

"I know, but the only scanning machine in the department is here—"

"Did you call campus security, like I told you?"

"Not yet," she said, hesitating. "I was going to earlier—"

"Amanda, you need to leave. Now." I had a snap in my voice, the product of converting the sudden fear I felt into a tight, controlled command. "Don't clean up, don't turn any lights off. Just walk out."

"Marty, this is dumb—"

"No, it's not. I want you to grab your bag, turn around, and walk right out." I pinned the phone to my ear with one shoulder and put my shoes on. "What floor are you on?"

"The ninth."

"Are there elevators?"

"Yes."

I stood up and grabbed my jacket. "Go to the elevators, punch the down button, but head straight for the stairs. Don't get on the elevator."

"All right," she said. Her voice was small.

"Don't be scared, be smart," I said. "You have a can of pepper spray, Mace, anything?"

"Pepper spray."

"Pull it out and have it ready. In your hand. I don't care if it looks stupid. When you get outside, head straight for the biggest, most populated space you can think of, then call me. Student union, library, whatever. Don't stop to talk to anybody."

"Got it."

"Good girl," I said. I snagged my keys and headed out the door. "I'm on my way."

"Marty, you don't have to—"

"Yes, I do. I've been taking this way too lightly," I said, as much to myself as to her. I thought of the look of fear in Julie Atwater's face. "It's time to get serious about this. Now, no more talking, but keep me on the line."

"Got it."

A moment passed as I hopped down from the porch to my car. I could hear her clip-clopping down whatever polished academic hall she was in and I resisted the urge to tell her to tiptoe. I jumped behind the wheel, but as I turned the key in the ignition, I heard her gasp.

"What is it?" I said.

"Someone's coming up the stairs."

"You already punch the elevator down button?"

"Yeah," she said, whispering.

"Take your shoes off and head back to the elevators."

"My shoes?"

I wheeled away from the curb holding the phone to my head with one hand, glancing over my shoulder for traffic. "They're too loud. I can hear them over the phone."

A half minute passed where all I heard was her breathing, then, "I'm by the elevators."

"Get in one. Punch the lobby or first floor or whatever, but don't get out there. When it gets between the third or fourth floor, pull the stop button."

"Stop button?"

"The emergency button, the hold, whatever they call it. An alarm might go off, but that's what we want." She made a high humming noise, not quite a whimper. "What's wrong?"

"Elevator's not coming."

"Is he still on the stairs?"

"Marty, I don't know," she said. "I can't hear him anymore."

"Keep punching that button."

I wheeled the car back onto Route 50, heading to DC at twice the recommended speed. Luckily, at nine thirty on a weekday night, traffic wasn't what it could've been. I punched my hazard lights on, hoping that any one of the five or six police agencies that were entitled to pull me over would give me a pass, thinking it was an emergency. Which it was.

"How we doing?" I asked.

"I can hear him coming down the hall," she said, her voice a mouse's squeak.

"Elevator?"

"Almost here."

"Hang in there, kid," I said. "The elevator is as good as a vault once you're in there."

I heard a faint *ding* and a clatter. "I'm in."

"Close those doors and get moving."

Her breathing was fast and fluttering, catching in her throat as she tried to talk. "I think I'm all right. You shouldn't—"

And then the phone went dead.

CHAPTER THIRTEEN

My heart was thudding in my chest. I called Amanda's number two more times, fumbling with the phone one-handed as I raced toward Teddy Roosevelt Island and the District line. Both calls failed. I cursed, then lifted the phone again. At one time or another, I'd worked with every university and federal police force in the city, so I punched in the GW campus security number from memory. I hoped. I fiddled with the numbers, glancing down at the phone, up at the road, down at the phone, up at the road, trying not to kill myself or anyone else. They picked up on the second ring.

"GW campus police."

"This is Detective Marty Singer with MPDC," I said, stretching things. "I've got reason to believe one of your faculty might be in danger of assault."

"On campus?"

"Krueger, ninth floor."

"Hold on." There were some bleeps, then the voice came back. "Who is the faculty member, Detective?"

"Amanda Lane," I said. "She's got an office there. Women's Studies, if that makes a difference."

"Hold, please." The voice disappeared again. I flew across the Route 50/66 bridge. The headlights of the oncoming traffic were paired stars, whipping past me while the Potomac flowed underneath all of us, black and serene. I slowed down as the stoplights and cross streets of the city loomed ahead. The operator came back on. "I'll try to get a unit in place, Detective, but there's a rally on campus tonight that's got us tapped out. Patrols are tripled up."

"Christ," I said, squeezing the phone. "This girl's life might be in danger. You don't have one warm body you can get over there?"

"Trying, Detective," he said. "I'll peel someone away from the rally. We're looking at five minutes, maybe seven or eight. You on the way?"

"Yeah."

"ETA?"

"The same," I said. "Unless I run into your rally. Where's Krueger, exactly?"

"Twenty-second and M. Big, tall building, can't miss it."

"A big, tall building? In DC?" I said. "You're kidding."

"It says Krueger on the outside."

"Jesus . . . okay, I'll find it," I said. "I'm plainclothes, so ask your boys not to shoot me."

"Can do. Might want to put on a clip badge or something, Detective. Just to be sure."

"Thanks for the tip," I said and hung up.

George Washington's campus is snugged into a lower corner of northwest DC, its streets and buildings woven into those shared by nearby Georgetown and Dupont Circle. It's so integrated, in fact, that the only real clue a visitor would have that they were near a large university was the character of the street life and the GW logo embedded into the sides of the buildings.

While families were already asleep in the suburbs of the city, throngs of students wearing flip-flop and jeans were out in force here. I went as fast as I could through, past, and around them, trying not to plow into the ones that crossed the street with white headphones jammed in their ears, oblivious, or others too intent scoping out the opposite sex to care about my front bumper. I whipped the car over to the curb near a group of kids on Twenty-Second Street, three girls and two guys laughing at something one of them had said. The smiles drooped a bit when they saw me—even without the uniform and cruiser, everything about me screamed "cop"—but I was used to it.

"Hey, guys," I said, leaning over to talk out the passenger's side window. "Krueger building around here?"

The guys stared back, defiant and surly, and one girl was still laughing too much to answer, but the last two girls pointed to a gray stone building poking its head up over its companions a block away. Block construction and narrow windows made it look like a prison. I waved a thanks to them and stomped on the gas, blowing through a red light with the help of some honking and creative hand gestures.

I don't remember stopping the car, only jumping out and running up the shallow, scalloped steps to a long row of double glass doors protecting a brightly lit lobby. I yanked on the first door. Locked. I looked down the row. There were four sets altogether and I went down the line, getting more desperate with each door that didn't budge, until I nearly pulled myself off my feet when the last pair flew open. I ran through and headed for the back of the lobby.

Like the glass doors, there were four sets of elevators, fronted by brassy gold panels that matched the nameplate on the front of the building. The second from the left was holding steady on the third floor. I crossed my fingers that Amanda was holed up in there. By herself.

The other three were at the lobby level. I thought about it for a second. My adrenaline had given me a boost, but there was no way I was going to be able to run up nine flights of stairs and be ready to do anything except collapse like a pile of wet laundry. I jabbed at the up button on the third elevator. It opened with a soft chime and I got in. I reached under my shirt and pulled out my holdout gun from when I was on the force, a SIG Sauer P220 Compact. I squeezed the grip of the gun to fix the feel of it in my hand and waited an eternity for the "9" to light up above the doors. Finally, the elevator eased to a stop and

I flattened myself against the side wall as the doors slid back. I counted to five, then swung in to the hallway, gun out.

There was nothing in front of me except a dimly lit hall with a shiny composite floor and wall-mounted light fixtures shaped like upside-down punch bowls. I cocked my head and listened, but might as well have stuck my fingers in my ears. Warm air blew softly down the hall with a low roar that, coupled with a buzz from the lights and a hum from the elevator shaft, swallowed all other sounds, no matter how hard I concentrated.

But that could work both ways. I padded down the hall, noiseless in sneakers. The hall branched to the left several times, forming the bottom end of a T. At each branch I listened intently, then bobbed my head into the hallway for a quick check. I reached the end of the hall.

Nothing.

Nobody.

No Charles Manson or Ted Bundy or Vlad the Impaler. Definitely no Michael Wheeler.

I considered for a second. I didn't know which office I was looking for and could spend half the night checking doors and poking my head into rooms while Amanda might or might not be stuck in an elevator. And if Wheeler was holed up somewhere on this floor, it would be child's play to sneak up and pop me while I was going up and down hallways, rattling doorknobs. It wasn't a one-man job and I could afford to wait for backup. My first priority was to make sure Amanda was safe. Quick but cautious, I headed back to the elevators. Halfway there, my cell buzzed in my pocket. I answered.

"Singer."

"Detective Singer, this is the dispatcher with the George Washington University police. We spoke earlier. Are you in the Krueger building?"

"Yeah," I said, keeping my head up and watching the doors to at least a dozen classrooms as I continued the walk back to the elevator. "I'm on the ninth floor now."

"Is Ms. Lane in danger?"

"I don't know." I explained how I'd lost the call. "We'll need to get someone to override the elevator and bring it down."

"No problem. There's a unit arriving now. I'll let them know you're on the way," he said and hung up.

I reached the elevators and punched the down button, keeping myself half-turned toward the hall. When the doors chimed open, I did a quick check, then got in and headed for the lobby. On the way there, I slipped my gun back in its holster and pulled my shirt over it. A short ride later, I stepped out into the lobby. The elevator I hoped Amanda was in was still holding steady at the third floor. I tried her number a few more times, with no luck. Aside from banging on the doors and scaring her to death, there wasn't anything I could do to get her out, so I did a more thorough look-see of the first floor. I found nothing besides cold marble and locked bathrooms, so I headed outside to wait for the cavalry.

A GW police cruiser, lights flashing, showed up a minute later. To their credit, while it seemed like an hour since I'd called from the road, in reality it couldn't have been more than ten or fifteen minutes. Lousy response time for an MPDC unit, but if they were triple-booked like the switchboard said, not too shabby. Two cops got out of the cruiser, a man and a woman. They looked wary and ready. I let them get a good look at me and my hands and waited for them to approach me.

"Detective Singer? I'm Officer Hatcher," the female cop said. She was about five eight and wide as a truck's front bumper. She had a full-moon face that squeezed her eyes almost to a squint. Her hands hovered near her belt, ready to go for baton, spray, or gun as necessary.

"I'm Singer," I said. "I've already been inside. There's no sign of anyone, but I've got a hunch that Ms. Lane is holed up between floors in one of the elevators."

The two exchanged a look. *Uh oh*, I thought. I knew that look. I'd used it myself.

"Can I see your badge, Detective?" the male cop asked. He was black, thin but athletic, slightly balding, late thirties. His nameplate said "E. Robinson."

I shook my head. "No badge, sorry. I came straight from home when Ms. Lane called me."

"ID?"

"Sure," I said. "But would you mind if we get the poor girl out of the elevator first? Or maybe see if she's not alone in there?"

That last part seemed to spark a fire. Robinson went in and headed for the elevators. Hatcher arranged it so she could watch her partner while also staying square to me from fifteen feet away, with her hand resting on the butt of her gun. It was good technique and I said so. She wasn't impressed with my observation.

The cruiser's flashing lights were attracting attention and people stopped to gawk. Something about my stance and Hatcher's body language looked like a takedown in progress, so bystanders were now gathering on the sidewalk, unsure which part of the criminal equation I was on. A gaggle of kids whispered and laughed to each other. A studious-looking man with a beard and in need of a haircut raised his head from a book, glanced around, then kept walking. A thin, aging skinhead—dressed in shredded jeans and sporting too many tattoos—watched with an impassive gaze, hitching a backpack up on his shoulder every few seconds, waiting for some action. I ignored them, focusing on the lobby.

Robinson fiddled with his keys, then popped open the door of a control panel that I'd mistaken for another brass decoration. He switched out one set of keys for another, inserted them into some kind of mechanism in the panel, and then held it there while he turned and watched the elevator. The numbers began to count down.

I frowned. Robinson was taking things too casually. I hadn't been joking about Amanda not being alone in the elevator. I shifted my weight so I was facing the inside of the building and mentally walked through the steps of drawing my gun. Hatcher flicked her eyes to watch me, but didn't say anything.

The elevator bonged and the doors opened. I tensed, ready for anything.

Robinson said something and a few seconds later, Amanda appeared out of the back of the elevator. Alone, safe, and looking very unhappy.

I started forward and Hatcher said, "Hey!," but I ignored her and went inside. I walked over to Amanda and the cop. She looked up at me, eyes moist and shiny, but no tears.

"You okay, kid?" I said.

"Marty," she said. Then she had me in a bear hug, squeezing tight and shuddering without making a sound. It was like holding on to a sapling shaking in the wind. I let her go for a minute, patting her on the back, then gently pushed her away. The skin around her eyes and nose was a bright pink.

"You all right, Amanda? Did you see anybody, anything?"

She shook her head. "Nothing. I got in the elevator like you said. I thought I heard footsteps in the hallway, but I got the doors shut before they came too close."

"You *think* you heard?" Robinson asked. "You're not sure?"

She glanced at him. "No, not absolutely."

His lips twitched. "So we don't know if anyone is there or was there? Or might still be there?"

I looked at Amanda. "How likely is it that someone would be in the building this late?"

She rubbed the back of her hand across her nose like a child. "Any of the faculty could be. But with the rally going on and midterms coming up, most people are at home finishing up. It was too crazy at my friend's house for me to work, so I came in."

The two cops traded glances. Hatcher spoke, not looking real happy at the situation. Or maybe just unhappy with me. "Great. Anything else we can do? Get a cat out of a tree, maybe?"

"Look, this wasn't a bullshit call," I said, angry. "It's not going to kill you to check things out when there's a report. What the hell else is a patrol for?"

"We left an assault because of your call, *Detective*," the woman cop said. "We got puked on by a couple of drunk twenty-year-olds, broke up a fight, cuffed two of them, took them to a station for processing, then busted ass to get over here, to find out you don't have a badge, a suspect, or a crime. What you've got is a girl you conned into locking herself into an elevator—"

"Hatcher," Robinson said. She closed her mouth like she was a switch that had been turned off. He turned to me and held out a hand. "ID."

I pulled my wallet out and gave him my license. He glanced at it, then passed it to Hatcher. "Check it out, will you?" She stomped out with it in her hand and he turned to Amanda. "How do you know this man?"

Amanda glanced at me, then back at Robinson. "He was the detective in charge of my mother's murder. I've asked him to help me."

His eyebrows went up. I stepped in and explained the situation with Wheeler and the potential danger Amanda was in. He seemed mildly interested, as if I was reading him something from the back page of the newspaper. Hatcher returned from doing a background check on me, looking simultaneously sour and triumphant.

"He's retired MPDC," she said. "Homicide division. No priors. No PI license, either."

Robinson turned to me. "You want to tell me a story?"

"I needed you guys to move fast. It's not like I wasn't a cop."

"So you call our switchboard, impersonating an MPDC officer, to get us to trim a minute off our response time? Nice."

"I didn't call you guys for kicks, Robinson," I said. "Just because you didn't see anything doesn't mean there wasn't something going down. What happens next time if it's real?"

"You can call and we'll come. But don't tell us it's the MPDC to try and make us jump, all right? I don't care if you're the head of the FBI, we don't need you telling us how to do our job."

I made a face, then nodded. He had a point.

"Wait a second," Hatcher said, her complexion pink going to red. "This asshole claims he's a cop, wastes our time, and we're going to let him skate?"

"What do you want to do, call MPDC and tell them to come lock him up?" Robinson said. "Not worth it. Just drop it."

Hatcher gritted her teeth. I could see her drafting the complaint letter in her head already. Robinson could see it, too, and he shook his head.

"If you're not going to arrest me," I said, "is that it?"

"Well, since you were good enough to call the matter into the main office, we have to go up and check the entire floor, room by room. Appreciate that."

I grunted. I might be sorry for claiming to be a cop, but I wasn't going to cry them a river while they did their job. "You ready to get out of here, Amanda?"

"Yes . . . wait, no," she said. "I left my books and my pack up there."

"I'll go with you," I said. I turned to Robinson. "You mind?"

He shrugged. "Come on up. It's already a damn party."

He punched the elevator button and the four of us waited for it in an awkward, silent clump, our reflections peering back at us grotesquely from the gleaming elevator door. Hatcher and Robinson were in front of us and turned slightly away from each other. No love lost there. Amanda was hugging herself and had her head bowed, staring at her sneakers. I stood there feeling fine. It takes more than a false alarm and a couple of pissed-off campus cops to make me uncomfortable.

We rode the elevator to the ninth floor. Robinson turned to Amanda.

"What's your office, ma'am?"

"201-B."

"We'll take a look there first, then do the door-to-door thing," he said, shooting me a look. The two cops set off down the hall, shining flashlights down each branching corridor.

Amanda and I got off the elevator and trailed behind the other two. Displeasure was coming off her in waves. I glanced over, but she wouldn't look at me. "Want to talk?"

She stopped, putting her thoughts together. Her face was pinched, anger and fear washing over it. "I feel exactly how I didn't want to. Like a victim. Like prey. I was scared shitless, trapped in that elevator. It was like something out of a horror movie, waiting for it to start moving, then watching the doors open. I was huddled in the back corner when it got to the lobby and I swear I saw Michael standing there."

We both stood there for a moment, digesting what she'd said. The low, industrial hum did little to fill the void.

"What else?" I asked. "Are you angry that I made you feel this way?" She studied the floor. "Yes."

"Even though it could've been for real?"

"I know it's not your fault," she said. "You're doing exactly what I asked you to do. I just wasn't prepared to act or react this way. I told you before I refuse to be a victim. I'm not going to be bullied into fear."

"I get it, Amanda, but your attitude has consequences," I said. "There's no such thing as underreacting to a situation like tonight. If he'd been here, the bit we did might not have been enough. There's not always going to be an elevator around. I might not be fifteen minutes away. If we do any less next time—if there's a next time—then he wins."

"I know."

We stood there for another half minute. Sometimes you can't talk situations away. Sometimes you have to be quiet.

"That's why you came here to grade those papers, isn't it?" I said. "You could've done them anywhere. A coffee shop, the student union, the library. But you came back to the office, knowing it was deserted, knowing your name's on the door."

"Yes," she said, the word dragged out of her.

"Amanda, you can't do that. Or, more to the point, I can't do it. You want me to protect you, to get to the bottom of this, all right let's get it done. But I can't fight you and Wheeler at the same time. You have to be smarter than that."

She nodded. I was about to say it all over again, to make sure we were clear, then realized repeating myself would only be to make myself feel better, to feel righteous about making my point. There was no need. She got it. She'd done something stupid and she knew it. I reached out and squeezed her shoulder. "Let's get your junk and get out of here."

We headed down the hall, our footsteps sounding loud. I had the desire to creep heel-to-toe again. Hatcher and Robinson were out of sight. We got to the third T intersection and Amanda turned, stopping at the second office door on the right. Her name was penned in beside two others on a piece of paper taped to the wall.

"Don't you have your own office?" I asked.

She shook her head. "All the TAs have to time-share offices. We're like indentured servants."

I poked my head in. Robinson was standing by the desk, shining his flashlight on the surface. He glanced up as we came in. "Is this your stuff?"

Amanda gasped. I pushed past her.

A small desk lamp was still on, highlighting an eight-inch-tall stack of papers. A red felt pen, uncapped and resting where Amanda had dropped it, lay on a test paper. Her laptop lay open, an inane screen saver of swimming fish casting an erratic secondary light across the back of the closet-sized office.

And scattered over everything, like a crisp December snow, lay handfuls of white petals.

CHAPTER FOURTEEN

We both stared at the desk, and what was on it, for a minute, then Amanda moved forward, as if to pick up some of the petals.

"Wait," I said, my voice sharp. "Don't touch anything. Let me make some calls first, see if I can't swing a favor or two and get someone to look into this."

Robinson looked up, confused. "What the hell are you talking about?"

I'd already pulled out my cell phone and speed-dialed Kransky's number. I motioned Amanda to tell Robinson what was going on, then walked out to the hallway to get some privacy.

Kransky answered on the third ring. I summed up the situation, keeping my voice low and glancing up and down the hall. I knew rationally that Wheeler wasn't around anymore, but I couldn't shake the feeling he was in the next room over and was counting to ten before he jumped out.

"Not my department but, still, I should be able to get someone over there with a kit in half an hour," Kransky said. "You know how it goes: if there's no blood, there's no rush. Plus I'm going to have to let GW in on it, naturally. What'd you say the two cops' names were?"

"Robinson and Hatcher. You'd make Hatcher's day if you put me in cuffs when you show up."

"For what?"

"Impersonating a police officer."

"That a joke?"

"Kind of," I said. "She hates my guts for pulling her away from a frat party."

He huffed, a lame grunt that tried to sound amused for my sake. I said good-bye and hung up, then leaned back into the office. Robinson passed me coming out, telling me he was going to clue Hatcher in on what was going on. I motioned Amanda into the hall to get her away from the evidence.

"What now?" she asked.

"That was my old partner," I said. "He's still on the force and can swing a unit over here."

"What for?"

"If we're incredibly lucky, Wheeler left his prints around when he threw those stupid flowers on your desk. Or he snagged a thread, or left some mud on the floor, or shed some DNA on something that we can pin him down with. If we get a positive ID, then we've got leverage to ask MPDC for a full investigation. And if for some reason it's not Wheeler, then we've got a hell of a lot more information than we had before."

She was quiet, then said, "So, what you said back at the elevator means something completely different now."

"Yeah?"

"It wasn't a false alarm, it wasn't me being scared for no reason. It really happened. You said there's no such thing as underreacting to a situation like this, that we couldn't afford to do any less." She said the words like she was discovering something for the first time. "And if we hadn't, if I hadn't gone into the elevator like you said, he would've been right here. Coming for me."

"Don't dwell on it. He didn't and he won't. This is a reminder that we've got to be smarter than he is, that's all. And, as scary as it is, this might be a break. If he screwed up and left something Kransky can use, we might be on the downhill side of the problem."

"What if he didn't?" she asked. "I can't stop teaching and I can't run and lock myself in an elevator every time someone walks down the hall. And where am I going to stay?"

What I said next surprised both of us. "Stay with me."

"What?"

I frowned, trying to figure myself out even as I answered her. "Stay at my place. I know it sounds weird, but it's the only safe house we can be sure of."

"But Michael came here, to the office, not where I was staying."

"He only has to follow you once to find out where you're living. If you're careful when you go to class and don't pull a stunt like you did tonight, you'll be ten times safer at my place than at a friend's house."

She didn't answer and I felt the heat crawl up my neck. When's the last time I'd blushed? "Look, I might not be able to run down here or to your friend's house or the middle of campus if something comes up again. And it will happen again if all he has to do is follow you from your class to a friend's house."

She nodded, or I imagined she did.

"The safest thing would be to tuck you away in some no-name hotel in Crystal City, but that's talking a lot of cash. It could be a while before something comes to light."

"Or never."

"Maybe. But we have to deal with what we know, what we've got in the short term. And that means keeping you safe."

She was quiet again. I felt uncomfortable. In thirty years as a cop, I'd never extended myself like this, never brought a victim or someone affected by a crime this close. It was stupid, something you learned in your rookie year to avoid at all costs. And now here I was helping the first damsel in distress to come knocking. Or was I trying to play makeup? Twelve years ago, I hadn't allowed—or forced—myself to find out what had happened to Amanda after her mother had been murdered. I'd let the frustration and disappointment of the case fade away and let the system take care of the rest. Including this girl.

Oh, and I was a fifty-three-year-old single guy asking a twenty-four-year-old woman to stay at his house. Whatever the reason, despite the best of intentions, I now felt like the worst kind of middle-aged creep. "Look, forget it. If it makes you feel uncomfortable, I understand—"

"Yes."

"Sorry?"

"I think it's a great idea," she said. She had a tentative, thread-thin smile so fragile it looked like it would float away at any second. "I don't have many places to go anymore. They've . . . they've all been taken away."

"You're sure?"

"I am. Thank you, Marty."

The knot of anxiety and embarrassment I'd felt melted away. Something tugged at the corners of my mouth and I said, "You're welcome."

The forensic crew showed up not long after that, beating the half hour Kransky had set for them. The team was a cop named Owens and an evidence collection expert named Benkov. I filled them in on the basics, told them what we'd touched and hadn't, then let them get to work.

Robinson was tired and pissed off while trying to put a good face on it at the same time. I'd worn that same look enough times myself. Hatcher looked like she'd swallowed a pickle. I introduced them all around, then turned to Robinson. "Look, if you didn't think this was real before, this is damn good evidence that someone's at least harassing Amanda, and probably getting ready to do something a whole lot worse. You need to take this seriously. Can you set up some kind of protection for her?"

He ran a hand over his scalp. "I can't guarantee anything, Singer. Our department isn't exactly teeming with bodies."

"I get that. But you're all going to be looking for jobs if something happens to Ms. Lane on your watch."

He held up a hand to placate me. "I'll see what I can work out. Where can I reach you?"

Amanda and I gave him our cell numbers. Then she said, "I'm going to be staying with Mr. Singer until this blows over."

Robinson's eyebrows flicked upward, which was all the surprise he showed. Hatcher had a leer on her face that made me want to grab her nose and yank, but neither said anything.

"Got everything you need from us?" I asked, talking to everybody in a uniform. They all either nodded or ignored me. I turned to Amanda. "Let's get the hell out of here."

We took the elevator—hopefully for the last time—down to the lobby. I was still jumpy and kept Amanda close while I scowled at the corners. Another small crowd had gathered on the sidewalk in front of Krueger. Not surprising, considering the MPDC and GW cruisers, reds and blues flashing, parked outside the building. Then there was my car, which, I saw as I got closer, was up on the curb like a stunt car in a *Starsky and Hutch* episode. Old habits die hard.

"Dude, what's going on in there?" a teenage kid with matted dreadlocks asked me.

"Finals," I said, and kept walking Amanda to my car. We got in, I backed the car up, and we drove away.

We made a quick stop by the friend's house where Amanda was staying to pick up her stuff, then she gave me her schedule as we headed back to my place. Since she didn't have a car of her own, I told her I'd drive her to campus most days, so it was going to be Singer's Taxi Service for the foreseeable future. We scrapped over that one, since she wanted to do things like take the Metro line into school or ask friends for rides, but I pushed back: they all had the same inherent risk as grading papers at nine o'clock at night in a campus office with her name on the door.

"Wheeler was a cop," I said, trying to convince her. "A bad one, but still a cop. He knows how to tail people without being seen, he knows techniques you aren't aware of. He might have a partner or is paying someone to tip him off when you leave campus. Let's do it my way for a week or two."

She caved. Which was lucky for me, since I was running out of steam mentally, emotionally, and physically. My body, running on adrenaline, was shutting down. We were still a couple miles away and I was having to chew the inside of my cheek raw to stay awake. Checking the rearview mirror and imagining Wheeler tailing me home with a shotgun in hand helped. But when we got to my place, I had just enough energy to shut the car off, stagger up the steps, and unlock the door before I landed on the couch I'd vacated a few hours before.

"Thanks for holding the door," Amanda said, as she struggled up the steps with her bags.

"Sorry," I said, but made no move to get up from the couch. I felt like I'd been glued down. "Put them anywhere. I'll show you around in a second. The guest room is—"

She never heard the rest. With a squeal, she dropped her bags to the floor and scooped up Pierre, who had charged down the stairs to kill me with the death of a thousand cuts for not feeding him all day. The last thing he expected was a forced cuddle from a twenty-something with the grip of a python. I laughed weakly at the look on his face.

"Oh my God, he's so cute," she gushed. "What's his name?"

"Pierre."

She laughed. "Pierre?"

"Short for Robespierre," I said. She raised an eyebrow and I shrugged. "I'm a history buff. And if you saw what he did to mice, you'd know the name fits."

In less than a minute, she had him purring like a two-stroke engine. I told her where the cat food was, which is when I lost him forever. She doled out cat treats for fifteen minutes, making him sit up and paw at her hand for them while I watched. The interval gave me back a bit of energy and I hauled myself out of the couch with a groan.

"Let me show you around," I called. Amanda left him and I gave her the nickel tour of the place, including the tiny room she could call home. I winced at how stale the room seemed. It had been a while since I'd had anyone over long enough to be considered a guest.

But Amanda didn't seem to notice. She dumped her bags on the bed and turned to me. Her eyes were wide. "Marty, thank you for this. And for everything. I'll try not to be a pain."

"Don't mention it."

We stood there for a second, awkwardly, then she stretched up and kissed me on the cheek. "Good night, Marty."

"Good night, Amanda," I said, retreating. I closed the door behind me.

It was the second time that night I found myself blushing.

CHAPTER FIFTEEN

The next morning was odd.

I'd slept as badly as you might expect, knowing that today would bring the first round of chemo. Or maybe it was because I knew Wheeler had been within arm's length last night. Or, maybe it was realizing I had someone staying at my house that wasn't a one-night stand or a distant family member flying in from out of town. Whatever the reason, it wasn't much past five when I gave up, groaned, and rolled out from under the blankets. Normally, this would dislodge Pierre from the foot of the bed and send him running for the food bowl. Or, more often, he'd be perched on my chest, boxing my nose or chin until I took a swing at him. This morning, neither was the case.

"Pierre?" I called.

Nothing.

I got to my feet and threw on some sweats. I called for him again in the hallway. Nothing. Which is when I remembered last night and Amanda and the food. I walked down the hall. The guest room door was open a crack; maybe she'd gone to the bathroom or something in the middle of the night. I eased it open a hair, feeling like a dirty old man, but I couldn't help myself. Was my cat sleeping with someone else?

Sure enough, caught in the act, Pierre was curled up like a dishrag at Amanda's feet. The poor girl was twisted like a sideshow contortionist, having succumbed to Pierre's voodoo magic ability to make a human relinquish ninety-five percent of a bed in his favor. He opened one sleepy eye to look at me, but refused to budge despite my peeved finger waving and silently mouthed threats.

I gave up after a minute and backed down the hallway, but left the door open cat-wide in case Pierre decided to let me back into his life. I crept downstairs, trying to avoid the worst squeaks and creaks in the steps, already seeing in my mind's eye the coffee being scooped into the filter. My mind's nose could already smell it. Just the thought of coffee gave me a lift . . . until I remembered that I wasn't supposed to eat or drink anything except water in preparation for the chemo.

It's hard to describe how much my spirits sank after that. Instead of sipping a cup of coffee at five thirty in the morning, staring out my kitchen window like I'd done for thirty-odd years to wake up before a shift, I was standing there with a glass of tepid water in my hand, glaring at the refrigerator. My mind alternated between being completely blank and dwelling on the sordid facts I'd picked up about chemo and cancer survival rates. When my mood hadn't improved by five forty-five, I tossed the rest of the water in the sink and started cleaning the fridge. I know when some physical activity is called for. Amanda found me an hour later putting the drawers of the crisper back, after having removed them—and everything else—for a cleansing so complete that it approached sterilization.

"Hey," I said from the floor when I heard her shuffle into the kitchen.

"Hey," she said back, her eyes at half-mast. She wore an oversized GWU sweatshirt and plaid flannel bottoms. "What are you doing?"

"Ah . . . couldn't sleep," I said. "I didn't wake you up, did I?"

She shook her head, still sleepy. Pierre, the traitor, was threading his way through her ankles. "Do you have any coffee?"

I winced. "Sorry. I should've put it on," I said. My knees popped as I got to my feet, pulling on the refrigerator door for leverage. "Gimme one sec."

"Don't you drink coffee?"

"Yeah, a ton of it. But I have to go to the doctor's later today and they told me no can do. All I get is water until this afternoon."

"Oh, jeez," she said. "That's lousy. You don't have to make it just for me."

"No, no problem," I said, trying hard not to grit my teeth. "Coming right up."

She fed Pierre while I grabbed the can and set up the coffeemaker. The smell made my mouth water. I turned away and grabbed a mug out of the cupboard.

"It's nothing serious, is it?" Amanda asked as she cleaned off the cat food spoon at the sink. She put the spoon back in the drawer, then turned and leaned up against the counter.

"What?"

"The doctor's visit."

"No," I said. The fridge smelled of disinfectant and cold. I shut the door. "Only a checkup. When you hit fifty, they drag you in all the time."

"You're fifty?" she asked.

"Yeah. Well, fifty-three. Why?"

"You don't look it."

"Well, thanks," I said, feeling pleased. Cancer be damned.

"What time do you have to be there?"

"Eight thirty."

"I've got class from eight 'til eleven. Do you know when you'll be done?"

I thought about it. Demitri had said a couple of hours should do it. Maybe I should hedge my bets and assume it would be longer than that, but why not think positive? "I should be done with enough time to come pick you up. If not, I'll call and either get a cruiser to come get you or ask the GW beat to give you a lift."

"That's not going to attract attention or anything."

"Might not be an entirely bad thing. I mean, if Wheeler is out there thinking that it's only you against him, he might get bold and try something more dangerous. On the other hand, if he knows we're on to him and you're protected and we're on the lookout, then maybe we'll scare him off for good or force him into doing something stupid."

"Or run him to ground so that we'll never find him."

"Maybe," I said. "But I'd rather err on the side of caution. If I can't make it, and you get in a cruiser, I know you're safe. I'm not going to use you as bait only to draw him out. Well, not yet, anyway. That's plan B."

"Thanks a lot."

"No problem," I said, glad to see she'd gotten some of her spunk back. Not becoming a victim isn't only about going to work and acting like nothing's wrong. Sometimes it's keeping a sense of humor or being chippy with people when you don't agree or, conversely, keeping your cool when no one would blame you for blowing your top. In short, acting like a human being. But it's easier said than done.

The coffeemaker gurgled to a stop. Amanda poured herself a cup. "So, that's plan B. What's plan A?"

I chewed the inside of my lip, trying not to look at her cup. "I'm tackling it in two ways. The guy I called last night, Jim Kransky, is my old partner. He's still on the force and he's going to pull some strings, try to turn up the info on Wheeler that we can't get ourselves. If he finds something, I can follow it until it either peters out or I find Wheeler and make him stop."

"And part two?"

"I'm doing my own digging. I've talked to his defense attorney from the trial. I didn't expect much—it's been twelve years, not to mention she's got no love for cops—and I didn't get far with her, but you never know what you'll find."

She nodded, but did it staring down into her cup.

I watched her for a second, then said, "Sound passive?"

She gave me a wan smile. "Maybe. Last night made it very real. I'm not sure I can take sitting back and waiting for Michael to make another move."

"Yeah," I said. "It sucks. He's holding a lot of the cards right now and the best we can do is react when he decides to show us some of them. The key is to hit him hard when he does. And, meanwhile, keep scratching away with the expectation that we'll find something that leads us to him. And then we're the ones holding the cards. And won't *that* surprise Mr. Cheap White Carnations."

"Can't we go to the police?"

I hesitated. How to explain? "I know this sounds stupid, but we don't have enough to show them. If we take this to the MPDC, they'll file it under pranks and cranks, not as a death threat. They'll argue that anybody could've dumped those petals on your desk."

"What about your friend on the force?"

"Kransky? He's helping already, like I said, but it has to be behind the scenes, so to speak. Technically, he shouldn't be involved unless and until a crime gets committed."

"Jesus," she said. "Do I have to die before someone makes a move?"

"No. It might seem that way, but try to keep the faith. Wheeler doesn't know where you are and we're going to keep it that way. I'm looking for him nonstop and Kransky is hell on wheels when he gets ahold of something. We're not going to let him get you. It's that simple."

It was the lamest pep talk I'd ever given, but something I'd said must've sounded good, because she nodded.

"Marty, I want to contribute something. No, really," she said as I waved whatever she was going to say away. "You're doing more than anyone could reasonably expect. Maybe I could chip in for food or something."

I thought about it. There are times when you can be more generous by letting others share a burden rather than taking it all for yourself. "Tell you what. You buy the coffee as long as you stay. I might not be able to drink any right now, but I'm going to celebrate with a pot and a half when I get back. That'll be your job."

She gave me a look. "Marty. Please."

"I'm serious. Coffee's important. You buy it and make it. I'll drink it and beat up the bad guys. And you feed Pierre. He's ignoring me anyway. Fair?"

She wrinkled her nose, not happy, but playing along. "Fair."

I glanced at my watch. Six thirty. "I gotta get dressed. Can you be ready in an hour?"

"I can be ready in fifteen minutes."

Amanda was as good as her word, sitting on the couch reading over her notes for the day by the time I got downstairs, her damp hair hanging down over her papers. We'd been able to dance around each other without mishap as we each got ready for our day, despite the fact that my place only has one shower and, while standing in the hallway, you can reach out and touch every door on the second floor.

It was strange having someone else in the house. There were different sounds as she walked around the guest room getting dressed. Smells of flowers and strange spices wafted out of the bathroom after she'd showered and even the few things she'd left lying around—cosmetics, a damp towel, the extra coffee cup in the sink—reminded me of what a single, solitary human being I'd become. I couldn't tell if I liked it or not.

We jumped into the car and took off ten minutes early. I took a winding, complicated route away from my place, looking for a tail, but saw nothing. I started in on some small talk, but the attempt fell flat. There was the radio, but the chatter would put my nerves on edge. I tried relaxing, letting my mind wander, but my thoughts looped back to the upcoming chemo appointment every time. It was like being in a horrendous pinball machine. Cancer, chemo, death. Cancer, chemo, death. Not good. I stared at the bumper of the car in front of me in an effort to keep my mind blank.

Amanda, I assumed, was brooding over Wheeler and her own safety. Or maybe how, exactly, she was supposed to function as a teacher and a student when surely everyone on campus had found out by now that she was being stalked. News travels fast when your professor or colleague might get whacked in the middle of class. Her next few hours were going to be every bit as nerve-wracking as mine.

Her directions took us to the Fiddler building, another squat, unremarkable scholastic hall of learning. Knots of kids, looking bedraggled and genetically incapable of being up this early, moseyed along the sidewalks, trying to eke out a few more minutes of freedom before class. I circled the block until I saw a campus police cruiser parked nose-out in the delivery entrance. A young cop—white, close-cropped hair, wraparound shades—sat in the car with the window down and his arm on the door frame. He watched as I eased in next to him. I rolled my window down.

"Hey," I said. "I'm Singer. This is Amanda Lane. I talked to Robinson last night about a protection detail."

He raised a hand. "Looking at it. Matt Przewalski."

"Anyone else?"

"Nope. Well, there're two bike cops that'll be around on patrol, but they're not assigned to this. I can pull them in if I need help."

I didn't like it, but it's not like GW had their own Secret Service. We were lucky that they'd put someone on it at all.

"You want to go in the delivery entrance?" he asked. "There's a fire door we can use, too."

"No. I want deterrence as much as protection. If we get Wheeler to make you, maybe he'll back off long enough for us to track him down. And the last thing we need is for him to jump the two of you in an empty stairwell or coming through a back door nobody uses."

We talked more about Amanda's schedule and when I'd be around to pick her up. I wanted a safe, smart handoff. Przewalski—I made him spell it out so I could remember it—was young, but he seemed to get it and didn't have any of the attitude I'd gotten from Hatcher and, to a lesser extent, Robinson.

We finished and I turned to Amanda as Przewalski got out of his car and came around. "Looks like you're in good hands. I'll give you a buzz when I'm on my way. You stick to this guy until I show up, even if—"

"—I have to ride around with him for the rest of the afternoon in the cruiser," she said, finishing my sentence. "I got it, Marty."

"Right," I said. "You sure?"

She leaned over the console and gave me a quick hug. For Christ's sake, I blushed again. "I'm sure," she said, smiling. "Good luck at the doctor's."

Przewalski opened her door and the two of them walked to the front doors of Fiddler. A few students whispered to each other and pointed as the two entered the building. I waited to make sure they were inside, then backed the car up and drove around to the far end of the block. I shut the car off, hopped out, and backtracked as quickly as I could, picking a spot diagonally across the street to set up camp. I checked my watch. I had some time before I had to be on the road, assuming I'd break some speed limits to get to Demitri's office.

I scanned the sidewalks, the streets, and the building entrances, my eyes skimming over people and objects, letting my mind and my intuition do the work of looking for the break in the pattern, the thing that jumps out. I'd learned a while ago that trying too hard screws with your attention. You focus on a bright, shiny object and realize too late that it's a handbag when what you're actually looking for is a gun. I didn't let my eyes get lazy—though Lord knew I was feeling the effects of last night's circus—but I trusted heavily in my instinct with a nudge from my experience. When something seemed to snag my attention, I gave it a five-second stare, then moved on.

Ten minutes into my one-man surveillance, the streets filled up as kids cut it close, rushing to make their eight o'clock class. I watched as the dreadlocks, the backpacks, the sandals, the piercings, the black eye shadow, and the tattoos passed by, some kids scooting now as they tried to slip behind a desk at the last second, others sauntering along unconcerned. All of the kids dressed like felons to my aged eye, but nothing screamed "Michael Wheeler" at me. No one stalked along with a handgun and a mission. No one flung white carnation petals all over the sidewalk. In fact, the place became strangely empty before a new surge of kids, probably just getting off the Foggy Bottom Metro, crowded the sidewalk again. I glanced at my watch. I had to go. I'd done what I could for Amanda and had to trust that I'd delivered her into good hands.

Now I had to go do the same for myself.

CHAPTER SIXTEEN

Nurse Leah whisked me back to an exam room ten minutes after I walked through the door.

"Hey," I said, surprised. "Not this again. I thought I was supposed to go to the lounge?"

Leah smiled. "I'm going to check your vitals, then I'll go over the chemo procedure. After that, you get the easy chair. Same routine, every time."

I groused some but at least they hadn't made me wear a paper bag again. Leah took my temperature, blood pressure, and so on, then handed me a laminated pamphlet. It was entitled "The Folfox Protocol," which sounded like a Robert Ludlum novel to me. Underneath was a list of medicines and chemical names like I'd never seen, most of them ending in "zan" and "vorin" and "zine." Leah pointed each one out as she launched into a spiel worthy of any flight attendant. This one was for nausea, that one was to protect the stomach, this one killed the cancer, another flushed the last one out before it could kill the patient.

She took some blood through the Mediport and disappeared with the little plastic tube. A minute later she was back to go over the same side effects Demitri had told me about, the weird lineup of fatigue, cold sensitivity, and numbness, none of which seemed related. I nodded politely, tired of listening. There was a knock on the door and another nurse opened it to hand Leah a sheet, which she scanned quickly, bobbing her head as if to a song. She looked up, smiling. "All clear. Let's get started."

She led me back to the easy chairs. Four were occupied. Leah put me between an elderly woman with an elaborate knitting project in her lap and a young black guy sound asleep with headphones on. Even through the headphones I could hear the tinny beat of whatever lullaby had knocked him out. Everyone who was conscious gave me a smile or a wave as I sat down. I was part of the club.

Leah introduced me to the woman, whose name was Ruby. The other lucky suckers were Jim, a phone line technician; Mandy, a cake decorator; and Leroy, who slept in a chair for a living. I got the sense it was fine to mention this was my first time, but maybe not so cool to ask how far along everyone was, for the obvious reason that the question would reveal where they stood with the disease. But I was spared making conversation when Jim and Mandy went back to their books.

Ruby, on the other hand, had waited her whole life to talk to me. I told her I'd been a cop and those were the last words I managed to get out in that hour, interrupted only by Leah coming in and switching some tubes around. I learned about Ruby's favorite police TV show, her favorite police novel, the best police film ever made, and so on until I was ready to rip the tubes out of my chest and sprint for the door. In one of the few lulls in the monologue, I asked about her knitting to change the subject. That was the second sentence I uttered and definitely the last one I remembered as the previous night's hijinks caught up with me. My last conscious view was of Leah coming in, shooting me a sympathetic look—for the chemo or for having to listen to Ruby, I'm not sure which—and changing my lines one last time. After that, Marty Singer was on the fast track to la-la land, helped on his way by Ruby's nonstop vocal drone.

◆　◆　◆

Aside from two concussions I'd received in the line of duty, I awoke feeling more stupid and dizzy than I ever had in my life. This was comparable on the wooziness scale, but those other times I'd also experienced massive pain on waking, which is what happens when you've been hit with a pipe (the first) and a fist (the second). This time, at least, there was no pain, but it was as if someone had taken my brain out, scrubbed it, then put it back upside down by mistake.

I focused on the room around me. Ruby and her knitting were gone, thankfully. Jim and Mandy had also finished, and apparently Leroy had woken up long enough to walk out. He'd been replaced by a woman in her forties or fifties, also wearing headphones and with her eyes closed, but drumming her fingers on the arm of her chair. My brain commanded my arm to lift and I glanced at my watch. It was after eleven. I groaned out loud. I'd promised Amanda I'd be picking her up after class about now.

Leah moved into view. "How're you holding up?" she asked. "You've been out for a while."

"I feel . . . I feel weird," I said.

"Weird like sick?" she said, looking around. For a bedpan, I assumed.

"No. More like you did a lobotomy on me."

"We tried," she said. "But we couldn't find anything to take out."

I wanted to laugh, but nothing came out. Instead, I said, "How much longer is this going to take?"

She grabbed a small plastic cup off a cart and handed it to me. "Here. It's apple juice. What's the rush, sport?"

"I have to pick somebody up," I said. It sounded stupid even to me, seeing as how I was having trouble keeping my eyes from crossing.

She looked at me quizzically. "You're kidding, right? What part of 'have a friend to take you home' didn't you get?"

I shook my head. What was I supposed to say? *I didn't think it would be this bad?* "Can't help it. I gotta."

She shook her head. "Sorry, but you're not going anywhere. I'm serious. Maybe later, when you know your limits with the treatment, but you're in no shape to hit the road. Is there any way your friend can get a ride from someone else? Or can we call a cab?"

I shook my head again, not to disagree, but because I suddenly felt numb all over. Useless. Helpless. It was as though someone had ripped away the proverbial curtain, showing me that what I'd been thinking and what was real were at complete odds with each other. I'd been treating cancer like it was the flu, an inconvenience that I'd have to put up with temporarily. Except cancer wasn't just a sore throat and a fever, and chemo wasn't just a shot in the arm. Cancer wasn't a bump in the road—it *was* the road, and I'd better make plans to treat it that way. My life, as I knew it, had changed for good.

Leah put her hand on mine. Her fingers were cool, dry, and soft. She smelled like soap and fabric softener and flowers and a bunch of other things that were solid and good.

"It's real now?" she asked.

I swallowed. "It's real."

"That doesn't mean it's over, okay?" she said. "It's going to be the number one thing in your life, but it's not going to be the *only* thing, got it?"

"I think I figured that out," I said. "Took me a while."

"Do you have anybody at home we can call?"

My face froze into a mask and I could feel my throat tighten up. "I have a cat. Pierre. And he can't drive."

She smiled, then squeezed my hand. "What's your friend's name, the one you have to pick up? Let me give them a call, see if they can make it without you. Maybe they can even swing by and help you home."

I shook my head, but I was too tired to explain that I was the one who was supposed to be helping people, not the other way around. I fumbled for my cell, thinking of calling Amanda to let her know I wouldn't be coming, but before I could concentrate on punching the number, somebody toyed with the focus on the camera and the room went fuzzy. I sank back into a big black pit where all the noises came through a ten-foot layer of cotton, everything smelled of flowers and apple juice, and no one talked about cancer, or drugs, or death.

◆ ◆ ◆

"So what should I do when I get him home?"

"There's not much to do. Help him get comfortable and stay positive. He'll be tired and woozy. Don't try to get him to eat or drink if he doesn't want to. He'll tell you when he's ready. We're sending him home with some antinausea stuff if he's not. That was a hell of a reaction he had."

"Is it always going to be this bad?"

"No. This is the tough part, where we have to wait for the drugs to work through his system. His reaction here and at home helps us grade the strength of the chemo regimen for next time. I know Dr. Demitri planned an aggressive dosage to try and get the best results, but it doesn't make sense if it ends up making Marty feel like this every time."

"God, I hope not. He looks terrible."

I opened my eyes, though they felt like they had to be unzipped first. I was still in the easy chair. A blanket had been draped over my lap. Amanda and Leah were standing nearby, heads close together.

"I can't look that bad," I croaked, trying to interject some humor into the situation, but the only words that came out were "can't" and "bad." The two looked over. Amanda had a worried expression on her face that twitched into concern and anger when she saw that I was awake.

"Marty," she said, coming closer. She had her enormous backpack with her. Just looking at the thing made me tired. She dropped it to the ground and leaned down next to me. "What the heck were you thinking? I can't believe you agreed to help me knowing you were starting chemo, for God's sake. Why didn't you tell me?"

"I'm feeling much better, thanks," I said. Leah poured me a plastic cup of water, which I knocked back and held out for more. I looked at her. "I thought you said the worst would be like having bad Mexican."

She bit her lip. "We can't always predict the reactions people have. I'm afraid you tipped the scale in the wrong direction."

No kidding, I thought. Then I looked back at Amanda. A mistake. She was glaring at me. "Marty, this is crazy. All of it. We need to get you home, then I'll find some other way to handle Michael."

I swallowed, then shook my head. "No." She opened her mouth to say something, but I held up a hand. "Home first, then talk. Believe me, I'm not up for doing anything heroic and stupid right now."

Amanda frowned, a crease forming over the bridge of her nose, but said nothing.

I pushed the blanket off and, with their help, I was able to stand, pull on my coat, and totter out to the front desk, where I made a follow-up appointment with the receptionist. I kept nodding, agreeing to whatever date and time she was saying so I could get the hell out of there. Leah walked us out the front door, her hand under my elbow. She got us to the door, where she watched, her arms folded across her chest, as Amanda helped me into my own car.

I stared straight ahead, trying not to think, and failing. Amanda had almost been attacked the day after I'd taken the job, I was flat on my back from a chemo treatment, and she'd had to be the one to come get me. Why didn't I hire her instead? I wasn't ready to start an investigation or stop a potential killer. I didn't feel like an ex-cop, I didn't feel like a bodyguard. I felt like an elderly relative, ready to go back to the nursing home.

My bones felt heavy, as though they were sagging through my flesh. Slush spattered the windshield and the world outside was gray. I put the seat back and stared out the window, wondering if I had enough life left to preserve and, if I did, why bother?

V.

She was gone.

The lock had been easy—ten seconds' work—but he was still cautious. Kids at school had more electronic equipment than entire police departments did a decade ago. If she had a security camera with a motion sensor, his break-in was already playing in real time on a website somewhere while he stood in the doorway. If so, it wouldn't be long before a patrol car would be on its way.

With his back turned to the room, he pulled a ski mask on over his face, then did a circuit, looking for outlets and cords in particular. Few webcams operated on batteries, so he pulled every plug he found. An alarm clock began its urgent, neon 12:00 . . . 12:00 . . . 12:00, and there would be lights that wouldn't come on when their switches were thrown, but he didn't care if he left that kind of evidence behind. She would know, in her gut, it was him. That was the point, after all.

He prowled the small apartment, asking himself what he'd learned with the flowers. This wasn't a courtship. There were no sunsets to ride into. This was about exorcising demons, about obliterating the past. He needed to admit he was enjoying teasing himself and her; some part of him couldn't resist the delicious twist of the petals, that there was a sentimental reminder that only the two of them shared. It was dangerous. Self-indulgent. He'd have to be more disciplined. Emotions like that had almost tripped him up the first time.

And could ruin things for him now. He'd watched in shock as Marty Singer, of all the people in the world, had skidded to a stop on the sidewalk outside the classroom building and ran around like a super cop, just like he had twelve years ago. And even though nothing Singer had done had touched him then, the man was dangerous. There'd be no more chances to scatter flowers.

He searched thoroughly like he'd been taught, looking for clues as to where she'd gone. As he upended boxes and pulled out drawers, the scent of her caught in his nostrils. Thoughts of Singer vanished, replaced with visions of Amanda as a little girl. Riding her bike. Lying on her bed. Playing in the yard. The memories elicited an involuntary croon from somewhere deep in his chest, a small animal noise that started to uncoil and grow. A prickling sensation started along his hairline and ran up and down his arms. He gulped in air, trying to clamp down on the feeling and the sound, choking both. This wasn't the time to give in. He stood there for a long moment, breathing heavily, gaining control. When he felt like he'd recaptured his focus, he opened his eyes and assessed.

Dishes were piled in the tiny, utilitarian sink. Garbage swelled in the trash can, pushing the lid off. Clothes and papers were strewn around the fake hardwood floor. It would be tempting to believe this was just how a recent college grad lived or that maybe she was only gone for the day. If you didn't notice the small things. No checkbook or cell phone charger. Dresser drawers closed, but half empty. A jewelry box with impressions in the red velvet liner, but no tenants. She'd left in a rush and meant to be gone for a while.

Only one thing of note was left: a small glass figurine of a unicorn, lying on its side on the top of a dresser. It was the kind of meaningless keepsake a little girl wins at a carnival and keeps on a shelf with pink ribbons and candles. He stared when he saw it, letting the barest memory float to the surface of his mind and take shape. He'd seen it that night, the night everything had changed. The night, though he hadn't known it yet, that his life had gone to shit.

He placed the figurine in the center of the apartment, as though choosing a place of reverence. Resting his foot on it with exaggerated care, he ground it into the floor until it was nothing but grains of multicolored glass. He liked the crunching sound it made and he twisted his boot several times to hear it again.

He took off his mask and walked out, leaving the door unlocked and open behind him.

CHAPTER SEVENTEEN

We pulled up to the curb in front of my house. I managed to get out of the car and stand up, all on my own. As long as I held on to the door. Amanda came around from the other side and threw one of my arms over her slim shoulders. She was surprisingly strong. We made the thirty feet to the front door in under a minute. A voice inside my head was screaming that we should be checking the back door, looking for signs of a break-in, and generally showing more caution than we were as we limped along. But that voice was drowned out by the one that needed me to lie down . . . now.

We got inside and I collapsed on the couch, a neat parallel to how I'd crashed onto it the day before. Amanda bustled around the first floor, turning lights on, feeding Pierre, and generally not looking in my direction or talking to me. I did a silent physical inventory and was relieved to find that I wasn't nauseous or in pain, simply wiped out beyond belief. I watched Amanda go about her self-appointed tasks, then flagged her down on her third flyby through the living room.

"Hey," I said.

She stopped. "Yeah?"

I waved to a chair. "Can you sit down? Please? I'm going to apologize now and I'm too tired to yell to you in the kitchen."

She sat, managing to huff without making a sound. Her mouth was set in a firm, unrelenting line and her hands were carefully arranged on the arms of the chair. I stared at her for a second, trying to judge the best way to start, came up with nothing. So I dove right in.

"So. I've got cancer. I'm sorry. I should've told you. But I hadn't gone to chemo yet, as you probably guessed. I thought I had everything under control. Why not? It's been a long time since I got hit with something that I couldn't handle, so I fought it in my usual stupid way, like nothing was wrong. As if a little bit of luck and a couple visits to the doctor were all I needed. Apparently, that was a mistake. I've got to face the fact that things might not work the way they did before, that I can't make an assumption like I'll drop you off in the morning and pick you up later after a little dose of chemo."

Amanda was quiet and had moved only to breathe, so I continued.

"But, the nurse said something back there, before you showed up. Cancer is going to be the main thing in my life from here on out, but it's not going to be—it can't be—the *only* thing. I'm going to have a life after cancer. And that life is going to include things like helping protect you and putting away human stains like Michael Wheeler for good."

I pinched the bridge of my nose and closed my eyes for a second. "But I shouldn't ask you to put your life in my hands, to risk your neck just because I want to prove I can take cancer on headfirst and beat it. This isn't about me thumbing my nose at my disease. It's about keeping you alive and giving you your life back. This is a serious question. I guess what I'm saying is, do we find someone else to take this one, to watch your back? Or do you want me to stay on the case?"

I choked up and stumbled over the last few words, surprising myself. The possibility of having to step aside—good reasons or not—scared me. A black depression welled up in my heart at the thought of returning to the empty, meaningless days when retirement had yawned open in front of me.

I didn't have time to dwell on it, though. Amanda launched herself across the room and, with a sob, wrapped her arms around my neck in a bear hug. Not easy, considering I was slouched sideways on the sofa.

I closed my arms around her and hugged her back, feeling how small and seemingly fragile she was.

"I'll take that as a yes," I said, and squeezed.

◆　◆　◆

My confession seemed to patch things up, which was a good thing, as the rest of the afternoon was a wash. Between bouts of fatigue and waves of sleepiness, I reclined on the couch and stared off into space. I'd like to say I was busy solving the mystery of where in the hell Michael Wheeler was hiding, but in reality, my mind was completely blank, as empty as an upside-down bucket. Amanda puttered, asking me how I was doing every so often as she got familiar with the house and where I kept things. I felt guilty, watching her act as my impromptu sick nurse, but there wasn't much I could do about it. When there wasn't any more puttering left to do, she came in and asked me if I wanted the TV or some music on to keep my mind occupied.

"No TV," I said, cringing at the thought of being pinned to the couch, helpless, forced to watch the crap that passed for innovative programming. "That's my weather and sports box only. And, um, the music I like isn't for relaxing."

She looked at me, curious. "Really? I thought cops were jazz guys. Smoky bars and saxophones, that kind of thing."

I groaned. "Jesus, no. I can't stand that stuff. All that honking and tooting drives me nuts. It's so random. It never seems to end."

"So what do you listen to? Like, doo-wop stuff?"

She'd said it with a straight face, so either she was a great actress or she wasn't actually trying to insult me. "No, Amanda, I don't listen to doo-wop. I grew up in the seventies, not the fifties."

"Like what?"

"I . . . look, I doubt we're on the same page, musically speaking."

"Try me."

I sighed. "The Dead Boys? Television? The Voidoids?"

Her face stayed blank. It was like I was explaining the inner workings of a jet engine. I tried again. "The Stooges? Chelsea? The New York Dolls?"

She shook her head.

I tried to find something to bridge the gap. "The Clash? Iggy Pop?"

Nothing. Then I thought of it. "The Ramones? You gotta know the Ramones."

She lit up like a lightbulb. "I gotta be sedated," she crooned.

"No," I said. "But close enough."

"So you're into . . . punk?"

"You got it, sister," I said. I sat up, trying to get comfortable. "Hard to believe, huh?"

"I don't know. I can't see you with a Mohawk and a pierced nose."

I waved that away. "That came later. We wore jeans and T-shirts."

"So, you still listen to that stuff? Where's the collection?"

I pointed at the dining room with my chin. "In there. Inside the big wood thing hides a wheel. That's a machine that was invented to play round, plastic disks we call 'records.'"

She smiled sweetly as she got up to investigate. "I know what they are, Marty. I've been to the Smithsonian."

A faint *thunk* told me she'd opened the cabinet containing my stash of LPs, something I hadn't done in a long time. Two years? Three? I realized with something like amazement that I'd become a boring old man. I'd thought it had been cancer that had sapped me of joy and energy, but maybe it had started earlier than that.

From the dining room, I heard the whisking noise of albums being pulled out and slipped back into place. Amanda giggled a few times, probably at the atrocious covers, then I heard the faint click and buzz as the stereo was turned on and some scuffing noises as she put a record on the turntable. I got the shivers when I heard those first few seconds of rhythmic static—a mechanical thrill you can't get from a CD or a computer file—then the opening bars of the Business playing "England 5, Germany 1" jumped out of the speakers, looking for blood.

She listened to it for a few seconds, then cranked it. Jesus, it was loud. For a second—just a second—I almost yelled for her to turn it down. But then she leapt into the living room, dancing a lunatic jig to the beat, her hair flying around like a storm. I started to laugh and it felt good. Amanda kept up the dance for the full 2:54, throwing in some air guitar for good measure. She only stopped as Steve Kent's last chord faded from the speakers. She grinned at me, totally out of breath, her hair wrapped around her head like a squirrel's nest. I was still laughing, but the sudden silence let us hear what had probably been going on for a while: someone knocking at the door with a hard, businesslike rap.

"Oh, shit," Amanda said, and ran to turn the record player off.

I heaved myself off the couch, anxiety twisting in my gut. I thought about getting my gun, but dismissed the idea. Killers don't knock when they want to increase their body count. Though that brought up another unpleasant thought: if it had been Wheeler, we would've never heard him come in the back or through a window with the Business's greatest hit cranked to ten on the dial. So much for lighthearted memories of the punk generation.

I opened the door. Standing a foot away with her hand raised to knock again was Julie Atwater. I couldn't have been more surprised than if Michael Wheeler himself had been standing there with a box of chocolates and a signed confession. Her mouth was set in a flat, livid line. The cold December wind blew her hair across her face and she pulled it away with an angry gesture.

"Counselor," I said.

"Singer." She stood there, glaring at me.

I raised my eyebrows. "Can I help you?"

"You were lying," she said.

"Sorry?"

Matthew Iden

She crossed her arms over her chest. "What is your game, Singer? What are you trying to get out of me?"

"Get out of you?" I repeated, confused.

"Michael Wheeler," she said. "Tossing his name at me. Like I'd crack in half. You're after something and I want to know what it is."

"I'm trying to find the guy—"

She plowed ahead. "I hope you know a hell of a lawyer, Singer, because you're going to need one. I'm not intimidated by cops, ex-cops, or other assholes who think they can get what they want by throwing their weight around. I gave you a chance to ask your stupid questions."

Before I could say anything in my defense—whatever that was going to be, since I didn't know what I was being accused of—I felt Amanda push past me through the doorway and take a step outside, right into Julie Atwater's grille. Atwater might've been on fire about something, but Amanda was a half-foot taller and didn't have the most accommodating look on her face, either.

"Lady, I don't know what the hell's wrong with you, but this guy doesn't need this right now. If you've got something important to say, I suggest you call it in, because I'm not going to let you stand here and rip strips off him."

Atwater looked at Amanda like she'd fallen out of the sky. "Who are you?"

Amanda put her hands on her hips. "I don't give my name to bitches who stand on other people's porches and scream at them in the middle of the night."

"What did you call me?"

I put a hand on Amanda's shoulder to try and restrain her before we had a full-scale brawl in the front yard. "Hold on. Jesus Christ, would you both calm down for a second? Let's pull this inside or we're all going to freeze to death."

"I don't think so," Atwater said. "Whatever it is you're trying to squeeze out of me isn't going to come out whether you try to scare me or sweet-talk me."

"Atwater, I got to tell you, I have no idea what you're talking about," I said. "Really. You look like you're ready to blow a gasket over something, but if it's my little stunt with your security firm, I thought we were over that. I'll apologize if that'll make you feel better."

Atwater put a hand to her chest and gave me a look of amazement. "Really? Apologize? And then what? Try your story about Michael Wheeler wandering the streets again?"

I exchanged a look with Amanda. "He *is* wandering the streets again."

She shook her head. "Singer, just stop. You're no good at this. If you want to scare me or extort me into something you're going to have to try harder."

I started to argue, but at that moment the world started to tilt and I grabbed onto the door frame. Amanda took my elbow.

"Is this supposed to impress me?" Atwater said. "Get a little peaked bullying other lawyers you know?"

"He was at his oncologist getting chemo," Amanda said, propping me up. "Good enough for you?"

"Hey, now—" I said, but Atwater interrupted me.

"Chemo?" She looked stunned.

I winced. So much for my privacy and dignity. "I had an appointment early this morning and I've been flat on my back since. No time to intimidate public defenders, I'm afraid. Or anyone else, for that matter."

Atwater opened her mouth, shut it again. She glanced at Amanda. "Who are you, anyway?"

"Amanda Lane," she said with an edge, still angry. "Who the hell are you?"

Atwater stared back at her. The encounter wasn't going according to plan for her, obviously. I tried to diffuse the situation.

"Amanda, this is Julie Atwater, Michael Wheeler's defense attorney at your mother's murder trial," I said. "Counselor, this is Brenda's daughter."

Atwater still didn't say anything. Her face was inscrutable. We stood there for a moment, an awkward triangle of three, then the wind gusted again and what little adrenaline and energy I had was swept away in the face of an angry winter. "Look, I know you're still mad, confused, whatever, but why don't you come inside and talk. Because we've got to talk. And I'm not going to do it standing here with the door wide open."

She didn't move.

"Please," I said.

Something broke through. Maybe she saw how hard I was holding on to the door frame or the fact that we were telling the truth became self-evident. Whatever it was, her face—a mask of anger and accusation a moment before—relaxed. A fraction.

"I think I owe you an apology," she said.

"Forget that," I said. "We need to talk about Michael Wheeler."

It was late, but everyone was up for coffee. The three of us shared a chill that had nothing to do with the cold draft finding its way through the cracks of my house. I grabbed the cups while Atwater settled into an easy chair across from the couch where I'd flopped most of the day. She pulled her hair behind her ears, revealing gold hoops that, coupled with the black jeans and a cream cable-knit sweater she wore, made her look stylish and ten years younger than when I'd seen her in court wearing drab business suits. I handed out the coffee, then sat down and looked at her.

"Can we get a few things straight?" I asked. "It sounds like you think I'm trying to scare you into doing something illegal. Or maybe just to harass you. I'm not. I'm after one thing and one thing only: to stop Michael Wheeler."

"It wasn't a put-on," Atwater said, lacing her fingers around her mug.

It hadn't been a question, but I treated it like one. "No. I'm sorry if my approach was, um, duplicitous, but you didn't have any reason to give me the information I needed."

"Hanging up on you probably didn't help," she said.

I smiled. "It didn't. And if you throw gas on a fire, well, you know how it goes. I got my back up and didn't make it any easier on you. I apologize for that. But the truth is that Michael Wheeler is back in DC, Counselor."

She got a peeved look on her face. "Would you stop calling me that? Julie is fine."

"Okay . . . Julie," I said, trying it out. "In any case, you're one of maybe four people who might have a scrap of information about him. So I had to talk to you."

"How do you know it's him?" she asked.

I gave her the whole story, with Amanda chipping in here and there. Throughout it all, Atwater kept her eyes focused on the floor, her fingers stroking the side of her coffee cup. Her eyebrows were knotted in a frown, causing a little ridge to develop at the bridge of her nose.

"That's what we know," I said when we were done. "Maybe it helps make sense of what I was doing at your place. Now, are you ready for some questions?"

"Like, why did I come over here ready to rip you apart?"

I nodded.

She put her coffee cup down on the table between us, then put her hands to her face for a minute. I thought she might cry, but she took a deep breath and smoothed her hair back several times, a ritual-like gesture. I thought we'd passed the moment and she was going to hold it together, but she crumbled forward instead, burying her face back in her hands and this time she really did start to cry. Quietly, with her shoulders jogging up and down and no sound coming out. I looked on, useless. I'm good for nothing when people cry. But before I could open my mouth and say something stupid, Amanda walked around the coffee table, knelt down, and put a hand on Julie's shoulder. She traced small circles on her back until the heaves subsided. I made myself useful and brought some tissues from the kitchen, which I put on the table. She grabbed one and blew her nose, then stared into some middle distance.

"God," she said in a whisper. "I hate him. For everything. For every goddamn thing that's gone wrong in my life for the last twelve years."

I said nothing.

"My career wasn't just a mess because people thought I'd been handed a lame-duck case. That was half of it." She wiped her eyes, balled up the tissue, picked up another. "The other half was simple. He scared me. It was so obvious he'd done it. He never came out and said it, but he'd . . . brag about it. Describe how it felt. It was all for my benefit. He'd watch me, waiting to see my reaction, telling me what it was like to watch her—to watch her die. He'd laugh if I showed the smallest emotion, the tiniest tic. He'd pat my hand and tell me not everyone was cut out for it. Cut out for killing."

I felt rather than saw a small convulsion in Amanda, a ripple that went through her back and shoulders. I looked over, but her face was stony, impassive.

Julie cleared her throat, getting a measure of control back. "He never threatened me. Not directly. But he seemed so sure that he was going to get off, so smug about it, like he had some kind of insurance. Like if he didn't make it, it could only be because of me. And if I screwed it up, I'd pay."

Something dawned on me. "You stopped taking homicide cases after his trial."

She took a breath. "Not all of them, just most. It doesn't really make sense, after all. Not every violent criminal is a murderer. There're plenty of people out there you should be afraid of who don't kill. If I'd wanted to be one hundred percent safe, I would've dropped criminal defense work. Done corporate law or something. I stopped short of that. Trial law is what I was born to do. But I won't take a murder case if I can help it. I just can't do it. Won't do it."

"No more Michael Wheelers," I said.

She nodded. "I feel safe. In control."

"But not the easiest ride."

"My career took a hit. I'm considered a second-rate attorney and earn a tenth of what I should. But I'm alive."

"Then I showed up," I said.

"When you told me he was back in town, it all came back. I could hear his voice, feel his hand on my arm. His hand was always hot, burning up. I could feel it through my sleeve. I can feel it now."

I gave her a second, then asked, "Why tell us this?"

She sighed. "I'm tired of being scared. Twelve years tired of it. And not just scared. Guilty. I helped that bastard walk out of the courtroom and get on with his life, while the rest of us were left holding the bag. You, me, Amanda. Sometimes it seems like he's the only one that got away intact."

We all were quiet for a minute, then I said, "There's a way to change that."

She looked at me for a long time, then nodded.

"You think there's anything in your files that can help?" I asked. "Something that would pin down where he is right now?"

"I don't know," she said. "I recorded our conversations and logged a lot of hours coaching him, trying to get our story straight. There might be something buried in all that paperwork."

Amanda, quiet for most of the conversation, spoke up now. "Did he . . . did he say why he did it?"

Julie glanced at her. "I'm sorry, he didn't. For all his bravado, he was still careful. Whenever he talked about it, you know, trying to get a reaction from me, he always described things in the third person, distantly, as if he were an observer. It's not like I'd take the stand against my own client, but he still chose every word with care."

"Don't worry," I said. "When I get my hands on him, he'll tell us anything we want."

Amanda smiled at me, but it was empty. There's precious little consolation in bringing a killer to justice. If I had my hands around Wheeler's neck right now, it still wouldn't bring her mother back. I squeezed her shoulder, then turned to Julie.

"I don't want to scare you," I said, "but getting involved in this means you're going to make Wheeler's short list."

Her face was pale, but she nodded. "I understand."

"And, while I trust SecureTrex to guard you against things like squirrels and paperboys, Wheeler would chew those lug nuts up alive. Do you have another place you can hole up? A friend or relative?"

She shook her head, then blew her nose. "I can find something. A hotel, a short-term apartment, something."

"Be smart, okay? Wheeler was a cop once. He's got some basic deductive instincts on his side, so if you register under Jenny Atwater, he's going to find you."

"I'm not that stupid, Singer," she said, annoyed. "If I were, I'd use your name."

Amanda snorted and I almost smiled. "Funny," I said. "What about getting to work? Travel is the weak point here."

"There are private gates at my office," she said. "Full metal garage doors, keycard access only."

It sounded good. "All right. Last thing would be to not get tailed there or on your way to a hotel." I spent a few minutes giving her some basic anti-tailing advice, the accumulated tricks I'd picked up over thirty years of police work on both sides of the tail. I thought she'd be dismissive, but her eyes were locked with mine as she listened to the whole thing. She asked some smart questions after I was finished, and my estimation of Julie Atwater clicked up a few notches.

The evening was closing in on midnight by the time we were done talking and I could feel myself fading. Both women must've seen it, because in a matter of a minute, Julie was standing and putting her coat on with Amanda next to her. I started to get up, but Julie pushed me back onto the couch. She was surprisingly strong.

"Get some rest, Singer," she said, not unkindly. "There are two of us counting on you now."

CHAPTER EIGHTEEN

I wish I could say the next few days were interesting or that I had an epiphany about Michael Wheeler's location or that I hit the lottery and had my rectum lined with gold. But what actually happened is that I underwent chemo exactly as ordered for three solid days. And nothing else happens on a chemo day except chemo. I fretted about the wasted time—we were giving Wheeler all kinds of opportunities—but I had to be alive to help Amanda. And to stay alive, I had to have chemo. Further complicating things was that Amanda had to keep teaching if she wanted to keep her position at GW. At least, that's what she said. It seemed stupid to me that you'd risk your neck for the sake of a job, but of course that's not what it was about. It was about showing her spine. I admired her for it while it simultaneously drove me nuts. We had a tremendous argument.

"Look, would you at least let Kransky or me drive you to class?" I said.

"You weren't in any shape to drive after your first treatment," she pointed out.

"Granted," I said. "But Kransky should be able to take you if I have a repeat performance. Would that be all right?"

"Yes," she said, reluctantly.

"And the GW cop will be outside your classroom if you need him?"

"I don't like it," she said, but when she saw my face darken, she followed up with, "but that'll have to be okay, I guess."

"Great," I said, though I didn't mean it. I had no idea if Kransky would be willing to chauffeur Amanda around twice a day or not and I didn't feel good about putting her life in the hands of a college rent-a-cop the rest of the time. But she wasn't under lock and key. All I could do was tell her the risks, do my best, and let her decide how she should live her life. I got on the horn with Kransky and explained the situation to him, including the fact that Julie Atwater was on our team now.

"Christ, what did you do that for?" he said, his voice rich with disgust. "Might as well take an ad out and draw Wheeler a map to your place."

"There's no connection. If you could've seen her face when I told her about Wheeler, you'd believe me when I say she wants to put him away as badly as you do."

"Not possible," he said.

"Okay, you want Wheeler more than anybody," I said. "But could you bury the hatchet long enough for us to get to him? She's the last connection we have to the guy and for all I know what we need is stuck somewhere in her files."

He grumbled some more, but agreed to be civil as long as I acted as the go-between. He was more receptive to driving Amanda to school and back, which was a relief, and said he'd get out to my place within the hour. I hung up and told Amanda she had her ride into the city.

"What's Kransky like?" she asked.

"He was my partner for a couple of years around the time of your mom's case. He took it hard when Wheeler walked."

"Why is that?"

"I don't know. Maybe because Wheeler was a cop. Or could be because of his daughter. She's about your age and I could see him wondering what it was going to be like for you, growing up without parents. Or maybe it was the straw that broke the camel's back. Not all cops are cut out for Homicide."

"Is it the violence?"

I considered. "That, and the fact you see a lot of the guys walk. They get seven years for ending somebody's life, which then gets knocked back to three for good behavior. The futility of it can ruin you if you let it."

She nodded. She knew what I was talking about.

◆ ◆ ◆

Kransky eased up to the curb in a Corolla that looked like it had pulled duty in a war zone. It was an older model, the one that Toyota tried to make look sporty, all angles and sharp corners. At a guess, it had once been white; now it was a dingy gray that reminded me of a dirty sink. Where there was paint, that is. A quarter of the car was covered in patches and bodywork that gave it a leprous, diseased look. He got out of the car and slammed the door without locking it, then hurried up the steps, hands in his pockets against the cold, without a coat or jacket as usual. I held the door for him as he ducked inside.

"What is that?" I said.

He stopped. "What?"

"That," I said, pointing at the car.

He glanced over his shoulder. "Impound. Some junkie's piece of crap."

"Is it going to make it? You can borrow my car if you need it."

"It'll be fine. I had it checked out last week," he said. "It just looks bad. It runs great."

I was about to say it was hard enough to keep Amanda alive without endangering her life on the road, but she clomped down the steps at that moment. Kransky turned to look up at her. I turned, too, but was still halfway facing the door, so I had a good view of his expression.

Kransky always had one of the best poker faces I ever saw. It had been indispensable when we questioned suspects or reluctant witnesses. I'm not exactly cut out to play the good cop, but when they got a look at

Kransky's stark, unforgiving stare, I had no choice but to play the patsy in any two-on-one interrogation. It took me years to learn that it was when his face lost all expression that he was showing the most emotion.

As Amanda came down the steps, his face took on the flatness of a marble countertop. His skin was pale, the cheekbones and the lines in his face standing out in sharp relief. His mouth was a slash and his eyes were like small chips of glass. Amanda looked at him with a hesitant smile, then stuck a hand out as she got to the bottom step. "Hi, I'm Amanda Lane."

His hand shot out automatically and he pumped it up and down one, two, three times, before he said simply, "Jim Kransky." Then he stood there, mute. Amanda turned to me, eyebrows raised. I stepped in.

"Um, you know where you're going, Jim? GW campus. Amanda will show you the building. A university cop will meet you outside."

He blinked. "Got it."

I turned to Amanda. "I'll catch a cab back from the doctor's. Call Kransky if anything goes wrong, looks wrong."

She nodded. "Are you going to be all right?"

"I'm going to ask them to take it easier on me this time. And I won't be driving, which should save some lives on the Beltway."

She smiled, then her eyes went wide and she said, "Forgot my backpack," as she ran upstairs.

I waited a second, then grabbed Kransky's arm. "You all right?"

"Yeah, why?"

"You looked like you were going to pass out when you saw her."

He didn't answer for a moment and I was going to repeat myself when he said, "You don't get many chances to do things over, do you? You look down at a body in an apartment or you see a kid in an alley torn to pieces from a bad batch of crack and you think, there's another one. Again. We never save anyone. We're punishers, not saviors."

I didn't say anything.

"And helping this kid won't bring Brenda back. But it still feels like a second chance if we do it right." He took a sudden, deep breath as if coming up for air, and shook his head. "I'm okay. How do you want me to do this?"

I described how, after the first time I'd dropped her off, I'd doubled back so I could watch the building and the foot traffic for signs of Wheeler. "You got a few minutes to do that, too?"

"A couple. I can't stake the place out until lunch or anything," he said. "I'm hoping to hear back from a guy in Records today, too. I put him on running down anything related to Wheeler that I can't find myself."

"Great. Call me when you hear anything."

Amanda came back down the steps toting her enormous backpack and then she and Kransky headed out. I watched them from the front porch, feeling strange. Kransky and I'd had our differences, but there weren't many people in the world I'd trust more than him to protect Amanda. The problem was, I was one of those people. I should be the one in the car driving her in. My hands balled into fists and I squeezed until I couldn't feel the fingers anymore.

Chemo followed the same procedure as the day before, though Leah assured me that they'd backed my dosage off so I wouldn't fall into a heap of wet noodles at the end of it. The lounge, as I'd come to think of it, was barren except for a guy with earbuds stuffed in the appropriate places, mouthing the words to his favorite song. Ruby and her knitting and unrelenting monologues weren't there to distract me, so I spent the four hours hooked up to the IV drip sitting and thinking.

It didn't get me very far. I had to face it—I didn't have much more to go on than when Amanda first approached me. Julie might discover something in her files, or she might not. Kransky might dig something up that we could use, or he might not. And if neither option panned out, we would be forced into being purely reactive, waiting for Wheeler to make a move. Since I believed he was a killer and mentally unbalanced, it was fair to assume that this move would be both violent and possibly lethal. Not the kind of circumstances I would've picked while waiting to throw a counterpunch. Assuming I got the chance.

I sighed and squirmed around in the chair, restless. What had I done in a former life to be glued to a chair for four hours at the exact moment Wheeler was out there somewhere making plans to kidnap and maybe kill someone I'd sworn to protect? I groaned in frustration and the guy with the earphones opened his eyes. I raised a hand in apology, embarrassed, and settled back. I forced myself to relax. I tried doing multiplication tables, naming all the presidents in order, listing all the state capitals, anything to pass the time. I was just dozing off when my cell phone buzzed, making me jump. I pulled it out.

"Kransky. What's up?"

"You got a sec?" he asked.

"For you, Kransky, I have an uninterrupted hour. In a recliner, no less." There was a humorless silence. I sighed. "What do you got?"

"The results are back from the girl's office."

"Yeah? Get anything?"

"Nothing. No prints, no tracks, no fibers. The petals could've come off any carnation from any grocery store in a two-hundred-mile radius."

"So they are carnations?"

"Yeah, why?"

"I was thinking that Wheeler is a cheap bastard on top of everything else," I said. "He could at least use rose petals."

"Well, he's a careful cheap bastard," Kransky said. "Nothing in any of the trash cans on any of the floors and they'd been cleaned hours before all the excitement started."

"Dumpster out back?" I asked, hopeful.

"Nothing. I had two guys go through it. Rotten bananas and office supplies."

I closed my eyes to think. I had something I wanted to ask him, something important . . . then my eyes snapped open. I'd zoned out and I fumbled around, trying to get back on topic. "GW cops have any tape?"

"On the exits, you mean?"

"Yeah," I said.

"Nope. They've got cameras covering a few public access spots and some of the dorms, but nothing inside the campus buildings. Not much call for it."

"And let me guess, nobody remembers seeing a guy walking around with a bouquet of carnations, wearing rubber gloves and surgical booties?"

"We sent out an appeal through the GW media for witnesses to step up, but you know how effective that's going to be. And, even if we net something, it'll take a few days."

"So much for the scene," I said. "How about the background check on Wheeler?"

I heard the sound of papers being shuffled around, Kransky coughed, then I could make out a light thumping sound. I smiled, but sadly. I could picture it perfectly. He was tapping his pencil on the desk as he scanned the report. I'd seen it a thousand times before, back when we'd been partners. "Here's the thing. It really does look like he dropped off the face of the earth twelve years ago. But part of the problem is that it *was* twelve years ago and a lot of this stuff either wasn't automated at the time or wasn't entered in later."

"You ran his prints?"

"Nothing. All they had was when Wheeler joined the force, then his initial arrest in the Lane case."

"Any of the databases have anything?"

"All old stuff again, or out of date. No phone calls, no purchases, no job applications, nothing. Exactly like when I first searched for him."

"Damn," I said. I'd hoped Kransky might've raked something up but, realistically, I wasn't surprised. Something cops like to keep secret is that it isn't that hard to fall off the map if you know what you're doing and are willing to put up with some inconveniences. Wheeler fit both descriptions. Granted, he never struck me as the sharpest tack in the barrel and his experience would've been from the mid-nineties, but a lot of the rules were the same: use a fake name, never get fingerprinted—so no federal jobs, don't commit a crime—and don't use your own Social Security number. That was about it. And, if he'd stayed current on some of the more elaborate identity theft scams, he could've been living a brand-new life for the last decade.

Kransky sensed my frustration. "The well hasn't dried up yet. My buddy in Records hasn't called back yet. Since this is off the books, it's going to take some time, but he's still a good source."

I racked my brain trying to think of something he hadn't, an angle or a new avenue to go down, but came up empty. "All right. Disappointing, but it's still good work. You know, another thirty years and you might make captain."

"Jesus Christ, I hope not," he said and hung up.

VI.

He stalked down the sidewalk, planting the heel of each boot hard on the ground, like he wanted to crack the cement under his feet. Electric worms moved under his skin, poked out of his eyes. In stir, this rage had helped keep him alive. It was a force field that communicated with others on the most primal level. It said: don't fuck with me. The vibe had been just enough to keep him in one piece on the inside, but out in the real world, it had an even better effect. People walking toward him kept their eyes on their shoes or found a reason to cross the street.

But anger was a dangerous luxury. He turned into a small park where he sat on a chewed-up, graffiti-covered bench, forcing himself to get control. More than one group wanted to get their hands on him and lock him up for good. Stomping around in a blind fury was a great way to get picked up, plucked right off the street. He'd been on the move for days, living off whatever he could steal, trying to dodge the thugs he'd seen around the campus he knew were looking for him. So busy looking over his shoulder he'd had no time to search for Amanda. It didn't take a genius to guess she was with Singer, but finding them was going to have to take a backseat to staying free and alive. The thought that he could find her so easily, but couldn't actually do anything about it, made him furious. His hands curled into fists.

What he needed right now was discipline. Calm. He sat very still, emptying his mind and slowing his breathing. It wasn't easy. He couldn't stop the self-recrimination. The one break he'd been given he'd squandered, indulging himself with the stupid flowers again, unable to resist one more time when what he should've done was made his move right there. Then she'd disappeared, only to come back with Singer escorting her and handing her off to one of the clown cops, the campus police. Again, he should've struck, but he'd been spooked. Was he being set up? Were they baiting him with the rent-a-cops, daring him to go after her while a SWAT team was in the next room, ready to unload on him? He gave a moan and gritted his teeth, almost crazy with frustration. He sat like that for long minutes, waging an internal war with himself, until a girl at a nearby park bench caught his eye. Tired of trying to conquer his anger and his hunger, he gave up, letting his mind follow his emotions for once.

The girl was slender and tall, a sapling amongst a bunch of stumps. He hadn't noticed her when he'd first sat down, but he stared at her now, unable to look away, vibrating with impotent energy. She was leaving, tucking slab-thick chemistry and physics texts in a backpack. Slim hands smoothed her hair back and tied it into a ponytail. By the time she stood up to go, his leg was jogging up and down like a pump. He had to squeeze both hands bloodless to keep from reaching out as she walked by. He almost barked at the complete indifference she showed.

He got up and followed. It was stupid, but he was kidding himself if he thought he was in control anymore. He followed her for blocks, almost without blinking, focusing on her legs, her backpack, her hair. She saw him once at a red light, then again from a casual glance thrown over her shoulder. Her pace quickened.

She knew.

A tremor ran from his groin to the crown of his head, tightening the skin at the back of his skull. It's what he wanted, to have her know he was back there, coming for her.

That's when it all finally made sense to him. The flowers. The long, watchful nights outside the apartment. Trailing her through the streets. It was so obvious. It was the hunt as much as the result, the journey as much as the destination. He couldn't shortcut the approach any more than he could *simply do away with the ending. Both were integral. He almost wept with the relief the realization brought to him.*

The girl was almost running by the time she passed through the glass doors of her dorm, waving her electronic key fob at the security panel in panic. He saw her again out of the corner of his eye. She'd stopped in the lobby, fearful, gasping, waiting to see if the danger she'd sensed had been real or imagined, ready to be embarrassed at a moment of excessive and unnecessary caution.

But he had already forgotten her. He knew what he needed to do now. No more wooing or elaborate gestures; the drama was crying out for its end. He forgave himself his lapses and concentrated instead on the new feeling of purpose that ran through his soul. His pace was steady as he walked by the girl, his gaze straight ahead as he smiled beatifically to himself, as though he'd found the answer to the most difficult question in the world.

CHAPTER NINETEEN

I put the dumbbells on the floor with a groan and collapsed on a workout bench that was in worse shape than I was. Foam padding erupted out of splits in the cover and there was more rust than steel in the frame. The dumbbells were filthy as well as rusted and my hands were covered in stains from the couple of sets I'd done. I'd made it home from chemo in one piece, but I was scared and frustrated with how weak I was. If this is how I was going to feel all the time, all I'd be able to do to Wheeler would be wave a fist at him.

"Work out," Nurse Leah had said, when I'd complained.

"Huh?"

"Go to the gym. Walk around the block. Anything."

"I would've thought you'd want me to rest."

"Look, we're blasting your red blood cells with drugs," she said. "That's why you feel tired. It's not the chemo that makes you feel like crap, it's the fact that we're destroying your source of energy. If you exercise, you'll replace some of the good cells that we're killing. Not to mention it's a great way to take your mind off things."

So, after I got home, I scratched Pierre on the head and clomped down to the basement to dig out my old weights. I managed to move some boxes out of the way before I had to take a break. Then I got the dumbbells lined up in order of their poundage, which required another sit-down. All told, I was able to knock out one set each of curls, presses, and squats before black spots swam in front of my eyes and I decided to call it a day. It wasn't really a workout, but—hell—it was something. I crawled back upstairs and stood in front of my sink, gulping water straight from the tap. I didn't stop until I could hear the water swilling around in my belly, at which point I tottered out to the living room, still sweaty, and crashed on the couch once again.

I lay there, making the furniture unsavory, until guilt and restlessness overcame fatigue. With a sigh, I got to my feet, clambered upstairs, and returned with Wheeler's folder. Every cop knows and hates the adage: when you don't know what else to do, start over. I flopped onto the couch, opened the case file, and read the first page. Again.

Five hours later, the file wasn't done, but I was. Any sense of well-being and health I might've gotten from my abbreviated workout had drained away and now I felt dull and light-headed. And no closer to solving anything. I could've been reading the phone book for all the sense it was making. I got up and stretched, popping the vertebrae in my back, and let out a huge yawn. My chest was sore, and I realized I'd been fiddling with the skin around my Mediport while I'd been reading. I was going to have to cover it with duct tape or I'd be scratching the thing right out of my body.

I went to the kitchen to pour a cup, then headed back to the living room, when I heard the low burble of a truck engine outside. I pulled back a curtain to peek out. A powder-blue Toyota truck with tinted windows was parked out on the curb. As I watched, the truck's cab seesawed as someone got out of the driver's side and came around the front. I tensed, ready to grab my gun, until I saw it was Kransky. He gave the street the once-over, then glanced at my front door. I opened it to show him I was there. He raised his chin once, then opened the passenger's door and hustled Amanda inside. I shut the door behind them, but watched the street through the window while I talked.

"Any problems?"

"No," Amanda said. Her voice was short, clipping the ends of the words off like she was trimming them with a knife. I glanced away from the window and looked at her, then Kransky.

"Any problems?" I asked again.

Kransky shook his head. Amanda said, "I've got to get some work done. Marty, can I use your office?"

"Sure. Move the files"—I said to her back as she sprinted up the stairs—"out of your way."

Kransky watched her go. I turned to him and said, "What's going on?"

He pinched the bridge of his nose. "She doesn't want this thing to impact her life. She wants to teach class and grade papers and walk around campus like Wheeler is a guy who won't stop asking her out instead of a killer."

"And?"

"If I'm going to do this, I'm going to be careful. So I went up to her classroom when the schedule said she was supposed to be done and told some kids to clear off."

"She didn't like that?"

"I wasn't real diplomatic about it. She was mad the whole way home and I took an hour to drive back here. No sense in giving her an armed escort at GW, then leading Wheeler right back to your house."

I glanced up the steps. "I'll have a talk with her. She hasn't totally grasped the implications of keeping herself safe from him."

"That might help."

"What happened to the Corolla?" I asked, gesturing toward the street.

"I stopped by the Impound again, got the truck instead."

"They let you do that?"

"I can keep it up for a few days," he said. "It might mess Wheeler up if he's watching."

Matthew Iden

"Good move," I said. I lifted my cup. "You got time for some coffee?"

He shook his head. "No time. There's something else, though."

"What?"

"My friend over in Records called," he said.

"And?"

"Wheeler's file was expunged."

"Expunged? As in missing?"

"No, as in gone. Deleted. The whole thing. At least, that's what he assumed, since there isn't even enough of a trail to tell that there *was* a record."

I stared at him. "This isn't good."

"No shit. There're cops that did some terrible things and you can still find their files. They might be eyes-only, but at least you know they're there. This one was rubbed out."

"No mistake?"

"None."

"How would that happen? Who's got the authority to do that?"

"Aside from accidents," he said, "which I don't believe in, maybe a dozen people could do it. No way peons like you or me could've ordered something like that. I don't know, maybe captains on up."

"Any idea on who had it done?"

"No, that's the thing," he said. "The file is totally gone, so there's not even a record of the record, if you know what I mean. He's going to keep looking, and maybe he'll unearth something, but in a year or two it'll be like Wheeler never existed."

"If only," I said. "Anyway, why would somebody do that?"

"To hide something."

"Hide what? What are we talking about here?"

"Maybe the why and the what aren't as important as the who. Someone that's in the, say, top ten movers and shakers in the force cared enough to have Wheeler's record disappear for good."

Kransky took off after that, promising to be back the next morning to chauffeur Amanda. I watched him go, then flopped on the couch and watched some travel show on TV about a place in South America I'd never go to. Unable to summon the energy to change the channel, I watched as it was followed by an inane half-hour program promising to reveal the "secrets" of Las Vegas that were probably already common knowledge to millions of people and would soon be revealed to millions more after the commercial break. That gem was chased off the air by a two-hour special on Mardi Gras. The run-up to the show touted scenes of blurred, topless women and people dancing in the street but the cop in me just saw a city full of assholes violating ordinances left and right and creating a week's worth of headaches for anyone in uniform.

Halfway through the show, Amanda came downstairs and dropped into a chair. We watched the on-screen chaos for a while, then I looked over at her. "Frozen pizza sound good to you?"

She nodded, mesmerized by the scenes of floats and jazz musicians. I got up and went to the kitchen, where I fished out a pizza box using tongs from the drawer. The nurses at the clinic had told me that the chemo would make me cold sensitive and I'd learned the hard way they weren't lying. The day before I'd reached in for something and yelped when I felt like I'd grabbed ahold of the wrong end of a hot plate.

I was watching the thing burn in the oven through the glass window when Amanda came to the entrance to the kitchen and leaned against the doorway. "How are you feeling, Marty?"

"Better than yesterday," I said. I didn't want to tell her that the tangy cheese smell coming off the pizza was making my stomach do a handstand. Maybe oatmeal would've been a better choice. I cleared my throat. "Kransky said he got under your skin today."

"He told two of my students to fuck off," she said.

"Ah," I said.

"What?"

"That's what he meant by undiplomatic."

She folded her arms over her chest. "What's his problem?"

"Trying to do his job. Maybe too serious about it. Then again, this is serious stuff. We don't get any do-overs on this. Kransky knows that."

"It doesn't mean he has to be a jerk about it," she said. "I appreciate what he's doing, but would it hurt to act a little more human? When he wasn't scaring the shit out of my students, he acted like a robot. He said two words on the way in and nothing on the way back to your place."

"I'll talk to him," I said. "He's good folk. I wouldn't want anyone else besides myself looking out for you."

The timer dinged on the stove and I turned the oven off and opened the door. A wave of smells hit me and I had to do some serious mind-over-matter stuff when I pulled the pizza out. I put it on the stovetop and backed off, feeling queasy.

"Marty? Are you okay?" Amanda asked.

"I'm good," I said, my voice tight. "Help yourself. I'm going to give it a sec."

I walked back out to the living room, but the smell had expanded to fill the entire first floor, so I went out on the front porch and stood there, hands in my pockets, breathing deeply until I decided I was more likely to freeze to death than throw up. I ventured back inside, where Amanda was picking at a piece of the pizza on a paper plate in front of the TV.

I headed for the kitchen, waving Amanda back to her chair when she moved as if to get up to help. She'd thoughtfully wrapped all the slices in foil to cut down the smell, which helped. I ignored the pizza and reached on top of the fridge for a loaf of bread. I pulled out three pieces and choked them down. It was the single most bland and unsatisfying meal I've ever had, but it stayed down, which was the point, and it ensured I wasn't going to die of starvation.

I went back out to the living room and eased back into the contours of the couch, watching TV and trying to act like this was another normal domestic evening for Marty Singer.

CHAPTER TWENTY

Standing in my living room at eight the next morning, with his head bent to take a sip of coffee, Kransky gave me a look that could've pinned a dart to the wall. "You want me to fuck around with her life on the line."

"No," I said. "Think about it from her point of view. No parents. Foster homes and social workers half her life. A stalker that, for all intents and purposes, has been after her for twelve years. She's got baggage a daytime talk show host can only dream about. Her future is something she's making up as she goes along and right now it revolves around teaching. Being independent. Living within her own rules."

"Living being the key word here."

"Understood. But there are ways and there are ways. Think about her for a second the next time you've got to insert yourself into her life. Ask her a couple questions on the way in. You've got a job to do, but you don't have to be an asshole while you do it."

He turned his head, a sour look on his face, which for Kransky was like throwing his cup across the room and kicking the TV over.

"We okay on that?" I asked.

He nodded, obviously unhappy, but I could tell he was thinking about it. I heard some banging from upstairs and Amanda came down the steps, toting her backpack. Pierre slunk down with her, but stopped to watch everyone from halfway down the steps.

I gave her a thumbs-up. "All set?"

She smiled. "Good to go."

"Same routine as yesterday. This will be my last day of chemo for the first round, so I'll be able to take you in after this. We'll give Jim a break so he can get back to his job."

"Sounds good," she said, then smiled. "By the way, don't call a cab for your appointment."

"What? Why not?"

The smile grew wider. "I made alternative arrangements."

I frowned. "Like what?"

"You'll see," she said, reached up and patted me on the cheek, then tossed her hair—along with my concerns—over a shoulder. "Don't worry, Marty. It'll save you a couple bucks. Just keep a lookout by the curb."

She turned to Kransky and said, her voice as cheerful and bright as a new penny, "Ready to go, Detective?"

He handed me his empty cup and they walked out. As he reached back to shut the door, I heard him say, "You know, I've got a daughter your age."

They left. I sat and glared at the wall. I hate surprises and people who knew me better than Amanda would hesitate to spring one on me. For a chemo appointment, no less. I slumped in the easy chair and went through the possible ideas a twenty-something would think would be neat-o. A limo? A clown car?

I got up every few minutes to peek out the curtain to see what she'd arranged and on the third trip to the window I saw a familiar brown Chevy Malibu pull up. Julie Atwater got out wearing a lime-green poncho with the hood up and green Wellies. She came around the front of the car and walked up to the porch. I went out to meet her.

"Counselor," I said as she approached. "I hope you didn't make a trip over here for nothing. I have to take off in a minute for my chemo appointment."

She looked at me like I was an idiot. "I know. That's why I'm here."

"What?"

"I'm your ride, Singer. Amanda called me last night."

"You're kidding," I said.

"No, I'm not and"—she peered at her watch—"if we want to make it, we better get going. You know everybody in DC loses their mind when it rains."

◆ ◆ ◆

I was at a loss for small talk so, aside from me mumbling the address to the oncologist's and both of us making the small noises and hyperconscious hand movements of people trying to think of something to say, we rode the first few minutes in silence. Lucky for us, the light mist that had been falling all morning turned into a thrashing rain that sounded like a million rubber mallets hitting the car. We peered into the middle distance, trying to make out stoplights and bumpers. The windows steamed up and trapped the smell of her perfume in the car. Julie played with the climate control, trying to defog the windows.

We were stopped at a light on Wilson Boulevard when she said—casually, almost out of the side of her mouth—"So, what's it like?"

"What's what like?"

She cleared her throat. "Cancer."

I blinked. Nobody had actually *asked* me about my cancer. Not a single person. Everyone, including me, had just assumed it was the worst fucking thing that could happen to you and left it at that. No one had asked me to define it until now. I thought for a long minute, trying to fit words to the single most life-changing event in my world.

"Never mind," she said, taking my silence for anger. "It's a stupid question."

"No, it's not. I just don't have a quick answer," I said. "It's lousy. I thought I'd have another ten, fifteen years before I'd even have to think about retirement. Then I'd find a hobby, take a few trips, read the books I hadn't gotten to yet. I was so busy being in the middle of things I hadn't thought about the possibility of it all ending. Can you believe I've never been to the White House? Lived here thirty-five years."

She smiled. It was a small, barely noticeable upward tug of the lips. "Me neither. Or the Lincoln Memorial."

I glanced over. "The Lincoln Memorial? How could you have never visited that? You practically have to drive through it to get out of DC."

"I don't know," she said. "You skip things. Like you said, you always think there's a later."

"And then maybe there isn't," I said, then shut up as I realized how self-pitying that sounded. She didn't answer and the silence became awkward again. We stared straight ahead. Cars were jammed in the intersection for no apparent reason and when the light turned green, we inched forward only to see it cycle to red again before we'd made it a single car length. Like she'd said, when it rains in the greater DC area, everyone takes their brain out and locks it in their glove compartment.

I cleared my throat. "Have you dug up anything about Wheeler in your files?"

She shook her head. Her earrings swung with the movement. "No, unfortunately not. I'm starting in on the transcripts of my interviews with him, though. If I've got anything at all in the records, that's where it'll be."

"Why's that?"

"That's when they let the personal stuff slip. They get caught up telling me their life story and ramble on about things that have nothing to do with their trial. It's an ego trip. I have to sit through it all in case they say something that might be important later."

"Is that legal? To share with me?"

She glanced over at me. "Who gives a shit? I'm not going to tell anyone. Are you?"

"I guess not."

"What's your plan if I don't find anything and you don't find anything?"

"Our best bet is still Kransky," I said. "He's got access to all of the networks that you and I don't."

"And what if that doesn't pan out?"

I gazed out my window, watching car rental offices and parking lots slip past. "Then we go into reactive mode, which is what we're in anyway. We shield Amanda, but he gets to make the next move."

"Then?"

"Then we hit him so hard and so fast there's no time for him to think."

"Is that possible with two guys?" she asked.

No, I thought, *probably not*. Out loud I said, "We'll have to make it possible."

It took us another fifteen minutes to get to Old Town. We spent it complaining about the Redskins, which I found to my surprise was one of Julie's favorite topics. Several times she reached for her jacket pocket, where I saw the outline of her cigarettes, and pull her hand away. As we got nearer to the clinic, conversation tapered off and we were quiet except for my occasional directions, but it had more of a companionable silence to it and less of the awkwardness of the start of the drive. In a few minutes, we arrived at Demitri's office. She pulled up to the mossy sidewalk and I got out, then leaned my head back in.

"Thanks, Julie," I said. "You didn't have to do this."

"I don't mind. Well, not that much," she said, then smiled.

"I can get a cab back."

"That's stupid. What's it take, two, three hours?"

"About three."

"I brought the transcripts with me," she said, pointing toward the back. Her tatty briefcase lay on the seat. "I'll find a Starbucks and come back at eleven."

"You really don't have to."

"Shut up and do your chemo, Marty," she said, then looked surprised, as though shocked she'd used my name.

"Well, when you put it that way."

"Look, the only nice things I get to do are for guys who hit other people with pipes. Would you let me do this thing, at least?"

I smiled. "Okay."

"Good," she said, then held her hand out. I reached across and grabbed it but it seemed stupid to shake, so I held it. She didn't pull back and we stayed that way for a minute. Her hand was cool and dry and felt small in mine. I imagined I could feel her pulse through the contact we'd made. We looked at each other and I got an odd sensation in my chest. Then she squeezed my hand and I shut the door. I stood on the sidewalk and watched her car roll away in the rain.

Three and a half hours later, the rain was still going strong as we drove north on the George Washington Parkway, splitting gray puddles in half and throwing arcs of water into the other lane. We talked about neutral topics that kept us both safe, like the waiting times at airports and the price of houses. But I was swimming in the chemo funk and ended up paying more attention to the sound of her voice than the words. She had a low, late-night whiskey voice that I had thought contrived when she'd been behind the defender's table at Wheeler's trial, but now seemed perfectly natural. I sat and listened, grunting or throwing in single-syllable answers to keep her going. Traffic in the middle of the day was practically nonexistent and we made it back to my place in half the time it had taken to drive down.

She parked at the curb, then turned to me. "Are you going to be okay?"

"I'll be fine," I said. "A nap, a shower, and it'll be like it never happened."

"I'm going to keep working on the transcripts. At this pace, I'm hoping to get through them in another day."

"Call me as soon as you find anything," I said. "Any time, day or night."

"I will."

I got out of the car and shut the door. She smiled and pulled away, leaving me on the curb. I watched her go, getting a curious knotted-gut sensation that had nothing to do with cancer or chemo or Michael Wheeler. Something fundamental had just changed, a corner in my life had been turned. But the rain can do that to you. The clean smell of water on pavement, the haze that tints everything in view; it makes everything seem dramatic. But I stood on the sidewalk anyway, the drops hitting me in the face, until long after her car's taillights winked and were gone.

Hours later, after a nap and a shower had brought me back to life, I peeked out the window in time to see Kransky and Amanda pulling up to the curb. We went through our street-watching routine and then the two of them came inside, talking all the way from the car to my house. I let them in and opened my mouth to add something to the conversation when my cell phone rang. I fished it out and walked out to the kitchen.

"Singer," I answered.

"It's Julie."

Already? "I don't have chemo again for a while, Counselor."

"Shut up and listen. How much money do you have in your wallet?"

"Depends. For what?"

"Enough to pay for dinner at a nice restaurant?"

"If there's a good reason, sure," I said.

Her voice was breathless, excited. "Start counting, then. Because I think I know where Michael Wheeler is."

CHAPTER TWENTY-ONE

Julie refused to tell me anything over the phone, instead holding out for the big dinner. I agreed we could meet her at Fitzroy's, a steak place and Irish bar in a strip of shops called Pentagon Row. It was halfway for both of us. I hung up with her and went out to the living room to tell Kransky and Amanda.

"She knows where he is?" Kransky asked.

"That's what she says," I said. "Can you make it down there with us?"

He glanced at his watch. "If she gives us something useful by six. I have to do some work before they fire my ass."

I turned to Amanda. She looked some parts excited, some parts sick. "Progress," I said. "Finally."

She smiled. "And we get to go somewhere besides your house or school."

I told Kransky to give us some time to clean up. I shaved with elaborate care, then put on my best pair of jeans and an oversized, zippered turtleneck that covered my gun in its waistband holster. I should've probably worn a blazer and an underarm rig but, for once, I didn't want to look or feel like a cop when I left the house. I had a good vibe going for the first time in weeks, though I tried not to notice that my jeans hung on me like I was a clothes hanger and I was now using the last notch on my belt.

Amanda changed into black slacks and some kind of green, silky blouse thing that looked trendy and expensive. Sophisticated, knee-high boots put her close to six feet and a black leather jacket gave her the look of a runway model on the prowl. We trooped out to the Town Car Kransky was driving. Amanda went to sit in the back, but I waved her up front. I wanted to be able to watch the streets and roads around us for a tail as Kransky drove. It also let me face out so I could alternate between scanning the back and driver's side windows every ten or fifteen seconds. When we hit the highway, he stayed in the right lane so we could make a quick exit if we had to. I tracked each car going back fifty yards, noting its make and model, if it sped up or hung back, if the driver seemed too careful.

I kept up the vigil the whole way, looking for the odd car out. It wasn't easy. Like everywhere in the DC Metro area, people drove like complete nutcases, passing on the far right, poking along in the passing lane, swerving for no good reason. Some decided to camp out in our blind spot; I watched these until I was sure they were idiots and not legitimate threats. After a few minutes, Kransky got off the highway and took a series of back streets, even stopping and sitting with the lights off at one point. We stayed there for five minutes while I peered at the passing cars.

Kransky looked at me in the rearview mirror.

"Looks good," I said. "Even for a couple of paranoiacs." We'd pulled more evasive moves than an FBI training course. If Wheeler could follow us through all that, he deserved to get us. Kransky put the car in gear and we made a beeline for the parking garage at Pentagon Row. Our precautions had doubled the time it usually takes to get there. Kransky drove around the garage before he found a corner spot under a light, then parked so badly he took up two stalls, ensuring plenty of empty space around the car when he came back.

Pentagon Row is a strange place. An artificial corridor forces pedestrians past shops and windows before opening up onto its most distinctive feature, a vast courtyard filled with a scene right out of a Currier and Ives print: wooden benches, gas lamps with wrought-iron curlicues, and an ice-skating rink. Shops and several restaurants, including Fitzroy's, faced the rink so that patrons could feel the ersatz magic. We stopped short of the courtyard to scan the crowd.

After a second, Kransky said, "Well, shit."

I concurred. The prefabricated cheer of the ice-skating rink had done its thing. There were easily two hundred people in the area. Three or four dozen were skating endless loops on the ice to show tunes that tinkled out of pole-mounted speakers. The constant swirl of bodies and colors from the rink was distracting and made it hard for me to get a feel for the place. I let my eyes relax and, instead of people, concentrated on patterns and anomalies. Who was moving too fast, or not moving at all? Who stayed in one position and didn't participate in the normal nose-scratching, head-nodding habits that everyone everywhere uses when they interact with others? Nothing jumped out at me, but that didn't mean much.

Kransky glanced at me. "She beat us here?"

"Probably," I said. "You want to check the bar?"

"Give me a minute," he said, then headed for the entrance to Fitzroy's, a big oak door twined with Celtic knots and harps. A blast of noise—flatware on plates, conversation, laughter at the bar—spilled out into the courtyard as he went inside. I pulled back into another doorway and tugged at Amanda's sleeve.

"Are you that worried?" she asked as she followed me. "You two are acting like I'm the president. I mean, I appreciate it, but I don't want you to lose your minds looking out for me."

"Not worried," I said. "Cautious. If I were worried, we'd be in my basement with a shotgun pointed up the steps."

"But I thought you said we were safe? That he couldn't have followed us."

"He didn't."

"Then why the paranoia?"

"Because he could've followed Julie. Why look for the needle in the haystack when you could follow the haystack? If he's still thinking like a cop, he might be at the point where his best option is to latch onto someone close to the case and see where it takes him. We used to do it when we didn't have anything else to go on. When in doubt, ride it out. In this case, if he followed Julie, he'd hit the jackpot."

"So, you're cautious."

"We're cautious."

Kransky appeared at the door again and raised his chin, looking for us. I stepped out of the doorway. He saw me and gestured with his head. *Come on.* We crossed the courtyard, weaving our way in and out of couples and families out for the evening. As we walked, I kept my eye on the crowd around us while scoping out the darker corners of the courtyard.

She was right. It was extreme. We probably could've driven straight to the restaurant, parked on the street, and waltzed right in. Gone for a spin on the ice rink. But I'd known for a while that I wasn't on my A-game. As bodyguards go, I was definitely subpar. The only way to compensate for that was by going overboard. Skirting paranoia. Exaggerating every precaution. Doubling every effort. And even that might not be enough.

We reached the door and Kransky held it open for us, watching our backs as we went inside. The noise we'd heard before was doubled now, the raucous sound of a popular restaurant at prime time. I stumbled a bit as I stepped inside. The smells of a steakhouse going full throttle bore down on me, odors of spilled beer and grilled steaks and melted butter hitting me in the gut like a fist. I blinked and took a breath. Which was a mistake.

Kransky grabbed my elbow and yelled, "You okay?"

I nodded, waved him away. He raised his eyebrows, shrugged, then leaned in again. "Booth. In the back."

He led the way through the maze of tables, dodging waiters in white shirts and long black aprons. We steered clear of the crowd near the central bar, a glass, brass, and oak monstrosity the size of a bowling lane. Julie was in an odd nook where they'd stuffed a booth to maximize the seating, but which put us away from the blare of the bar and the ruckus coming from the kitchen. Her head, bowed as she dug through the papers in her attaché case, lifted as we came near. Excitement sparked in her eyes, though they dulled when she saw Kransky.

"Evening, Counselor," I said, hesitated, then slid in next to her, figuring that Kransky didn't want to sit near her and Amanda would want to face Julie while she talked. The booth was small and I took up more than my share. I tried to keep my distance, but even so my thigh was pushed up against hers from hip to knee. I looked across the table as the others sat down. Amanda's face was cautiously hopeful, Kransky's a flat mask. I squirmed in place, as disconcerted by my gun digging into my side as I was by the warmth of Julie's leg against mine.

"Detective," Julie said, inclining her head in Kransky's direction.

"Counselor."

Amanda looked from one to the other. "You know each other?"

"It's a small world down in the halls of justice," Kransky said.

"Detective Kransky and I have met," Julie said to Amanda. "Though usually on opposite sides of the bench. Sort of like now."

He smiled without humor. "I'm on duty in a half hour, Atwater, so you won't have to put up with me for long."

I turned in my seat to face her, but couldn't get much more than halfway, so I had to throw an arm along the back of the booth just to talk to her. "Now that the introductions are over, what did you find that's worth a steak dinner?"

Julie leaned forward. "I've had no luck the last few days, since I wasn't even sure what I was looking for. And I wasn't holding out much hope that whatever I found was useful, since even if I found an address or a phone number or something, it was going to be so old it would be useless."

I nodded.

"So, I checked the usual places and tracked down what I could find. The only thing that was relevant was Wheeler's apartment address at the time he was arrested, but it was in a building that was torn down in 2002. Likewise, phone numbers he gave were reassigned or out of service."

"A dead end."

"On that stuff. Then I wondered about my interviews with him leading up to the trial. It was my first major case, so I was paranoid about keeping notes and transcripts of everything, making sure I was not only aboveboard, but meticulous."

"What do you mean transcripts?" Kransky asked. "Did you tape the interviews?"

"Yes," Julie said simply. "He didn't know it, but after he turned creepy I wanted some kind of record. Inadmissible in court, but maybe enough to start an investigation if I needed it."

"What did you find?" Amanda asked.

"It was early on in my defense prep, when I was asking him about character witnesses, people who could put in a word for him. I also wanted to know who might crawl out of the woodwork and offer to testify for the prosecution. When I pressed him hard, he mumbled something about a sister."

"What?" I said, glancing at Kransky, who had straightened up in his seat. "Wheeler didn't have a sister."

"Well, there's someone he feels close enough to for him to call her that." She dug through the case next to her, then pulled out a thin sheaf of papers, which she handed to me. "Here."

My pulse jumped a notch or two, hitting me like a physical thing. I took the papers and turned them sideways so the other two could read. The type was old and faded from too much photocopying, but still legible and laid out like a play for two actors. I skimmed it, lost, until Julie pointed out the important part.

> ATWATER: Mr. Wheeler, I need you to give me the names of anyone that could help us in your defense or harm us by helping the prosecution. Are you sure there isn't someone you're overlooking? Someone you haven't told me about?
>
> WHEELER: [mumbling]
>
> ATWATER: What was that?
>
> WHEELER: Layla.
>
> ATWATER: Layla? Layla who, Mr. Wheeler?
>
> WHEELER: Layla Green. My sister, lives south of here. I don't want her mixed up in this. Not that she'd help me out, but she's close enough to DC that the media might sniff her out. Make her life hell.
>
> ATWATER: That's good. What else can you tell me? Would she help us?
>
> WHEELER: Probably. But I don't want you to use her unless you absolutely have to.

I lifted my head from the paper and turned to Kransky. "You remember anything about a sister?"

He was already shaking his head. "Nothing. Never found any family."

"Any way we could've missed something like that?"

"No way," he said. "Granted, this"—he flicked at the transcript with a finger—"was twelve years ago. We didn't have shit for resources. What passed for a thorough background check in '96 would be an hour's work on the Internet today. But, still, a sister? No way in hell we would've missed that."

"What's he talking about, then?"

"Maybe it's figurative?" Amanda said. "You know, my brother, my sister. Somebody close to him, but not necessarily related."

"Wheeler?" I said, making a face. "Stranger things have happened, I guess, but I don't see it."

"Could be he was just lying," Kransky said. "It'd fit his personality to say something stupid like this, even to his attorney."

"Julie, did you check the name at the time?" I asked. "Did he give you an address?"

She shook her head. "You can tell he didn't want me to contact her. He said he'd give me the information only if we needed it later. And we didn't, so I never got it. I did a quick search online when I found this transcript today, but came up empty."

I turned to Kransky, but he was already sliding out of the booth, reaching for his cell phone. He spoke while he dialed. "I have to go anyway. I'll call the name in, see what the system can find. Maybe we did miss it the first time around. If I get a hit, I'll get back to you."

"How are we getting home?" I asked.

"Maybe your new buddy can help you out," he said, nodding at Julie. With that, he left, his phone glued to his ear, weaving through chairs, tables, and patrons as he headed for the door.

"Well, he hasn't changed much," Julie said after a minute.

"Still a complete jerk, you mean?" I asked.

"Yes."

Amanda watched as Kransky left. "What happened to my vigilant bodyguard? The one that told my students to screw off so he could protect me?"

I sighed. "He figures we covered our bases coming in, that we're safe enough now, and is leaving the rest to me as punishment."

"For bringing me in," Julie said.

"Yes."

"That's childish," Amanda said.

"Yes," I said. "Although it also shows how much faith he has in me to protect you."

Amanda shook her head. I steered the conversation back to the news about Wheeler and his sister. It was exciting to finally get our hands on a clue even halfway meaningful, but I was careful to rope in any excessive enthusiasm.

"Could it be this easy?" Amanda asked. "We get one name and just look it up in some police phone book?"

"No," I said. "It's not hard to stay off the grid if you want to and it sounds like this Layla Green wants to. But we've got a ton of tools at our disposal that we didn't then."

"There's the simple fact that Wheeler might not be with her, either," Julie said, trying to inject some extra caution into our debate. It was smart. The feeling around the table was approaching giddy. "She could be a law-abiding citizen who happens to be related to the guy and nothing more."

Amanda picked at the edge of her place mat. "So what now?"

"Status quo," I said. "Keep you safe, wait for Kransky to run down any information he can, then move on it."

"Move on it how, exactly?" Julie said. As she turned her head to talk to me, I could smell the lavender scent of her perfume. "You're not a cop anymore. There's no kicking down doors or shooting people."

"I never kicked doors down," I said, lying. "And almost never shot anybody. Assuming we find an address for this mysterious sister, I'm talking about casing the place, seeing if there's any evidence of Wheeler at all. There are plenty of ways to get information. Legally," I added quickly, seeing Julie open her mouth.

"What if he's there, with her?" Amanda asked, looking worried. "Do you . . . make a citizen's arrest or something?"

"No," I said. "With Kransky on our side, we start surveillance. Knowing where he is means we'll be two steps ahead of him. We can keep him away from you. Kransky gets a true investigation going, then we pin a raft of charges on him that will put him under for somewhere between a hundred and a thousand years."

"Marty, Michael is . . . unbalanced. Dangerous. What if he pulls a gun on you, tries to kill you? Or me, for that matter?"

I smiled, like Kransky had earlier, without humor. "Then I'll just have to defend myself."

CHAPTER
TWENTY-TWO

Julie had earned her steak dinner, so we flagged our waiter down and ordered, then chatted about inconsequential things, jawing about nothing more dramatic than traffic, politics, and sports.

Then the food came.

When we'd first walked into Fitzroy's, I'd been able to control my nausea with a supreme effort of will. Then, once we'd sat down and I was distracted by the conversation, it was easier to ignore the little man in my gut that wanted me to empty its contents on the floor. But when Julie's porterhouse was passed under my nose and set down on the table, sweat broke out on my forehead and my pulse started to hammer hard enough to make my vision bounce.

Julie glanced over. "What's wrong?"

I gritted my teeth. "Nothing."

I was prepared to tamp my stomach down with nothing but ice water and willpower, when I remembered the antinausea pill the nurses had given me. I fished it out of a pocket and swallowed it almost before I got it out of the wrapper, silently urging it to get to work. In a moment, relief washed over me and I gave the other two a shaky thumbs-up. We got through the rest of the meal without me making a scene, though both of the women were careful not to enjoy their food too much or too audibly. The waiter came by and cleared away the plates while the ladies made appreciative yummy noises.

As he moved away, I sensed motion at the edge of my vision that didn't fit in with the pattern of the rest of the diners. A guy—bookish twenty-something, thick-rimmed glasses, blond hair sitting flat on his skull, complexion the color of skim milk—was walking toward us from the bar. His eyes were locked on Amanda from thirty feet away and an alarm clanged in my brain. The fact that this kid couldn't possibly be Michael Wheeler didn't matter. What did was the fact that Amanda appeared to be his goal and I needed to be between the two of them before he reached it. Four strides from our table, he was surprised to find me appear directly in front of him, like I'd sprouted there. My left hand rested on his chest, the fingers spread almost collarbone to collarbone. My right hung down and slightly back, near my hip, a few inches away from the butt of my gun.

"Hi," I said. "How are you doing this fine evening?"

The kid, startled, took a half step back, then his face screwed up, anger playing across his features. Before I could tell him to stay cool, Amanda had hopped up next to me and taken his arm.

"Jay," she said. "What are you doing here?"

"Hey . . . Amanda," he said, glancing between her and me, confused. I relaxed and took my hand off his chest. "What's with GI Joe?"

"Oh, sorry. This is Marty. He's a friend. I had a, uh, problem with a guy once and Marty helped me out," she said, then turned to look at me. "Jay is another grad from GW."

I held out a hand. "Marty Singer. Sorry about that."

"No problem," he said, his handshake as slack as a moist towelette. He looked at Amanda. "I came out for a drink with Sandy and Al, but now they're obsessing on deconstruction and Derrida and some other crap. I got bored and started looking around when I saw you in the corner and thought halle-fucking-lujah. You want to come over and save me?"

Amanda hesitated, then turned to me with a look that spoke volumes. She wanted to be with her friends, she wanted me to have a good time with Julie, and she probably wanted to get the hell away from me for a while. I sighed and closed my eyes for a second. The safe, anonymous, surgical strike for a quick meal and some good times had gotten complicated.

I opened my eyes. "You know the other two?"

"They're grads in the English department," she said, then smiled. "But I won't hold that against them."

"Fine," I said. "But come around to this side of the bar where I can see you."

Jay got a look on his face, as if to say *what the hell is this?* But Amanda nodded, tugged at his arm, and went around the bar. Two girls in matching black jeans but different tops gave her hugs and the four of them moved to my side of the bar as requested, then dove deep into a discussion. I walked back to our booth and took the spot Amanda had vacated so I could sit across from Julie.

"What was that about?" Julie asked. I told her about giving Amanda the chance for a dip back into normal life. But I glanced back at the bar and away. Then back again.

Julie raised her eyebrows. "Problem?"

I sighed. "The chances of Wheeler finding Amanda at my house, tailing us over here without me noticing, then waiting an hour before launching a surprise attack in the back of an Irish pub are about the same as us getting hit by lightning. Twice."

Her mocha-brown eyes flicked back and forth, searching mine. "But you're worried."

"You don't play the odds if you want to keep someone safe. You go with absolutes, even if it means hiding under a blanket with the lights off and the doors locked."

"Why is tonight different?"

I shrugged. "She needed to get out. I needed to get out. She has to have a taste of freedom if I don't want her climbing the walls and maybe doing something stupid. And Lord knows I could use a good time. But now I have to roll the dice and be ready to react. With the result that I almost bodychecked her friend Jay there and can't stop watching them at the bar. When I think I'd rather be watching you."

A blush appeared across Julie's nose and the tops of her cheeks, ending at her ears, which turned into two little scarlet candles. Her eyes dropped to the table, where the fake wood veneer was of sudden and immense interest to her. My smile faded. I'd expected a snappy comeback or a sarcastic put-down, either of which I could've handled. But she said nothing. Heat crept up my neck, climbed the sides of my face, prickled the skin around my hairline.

"I'm an ass," I said. "That was a stupid thing to say."

"No," she said. "No, it wasn't."

"It is. It's idiotic. We're supposed to be working to find a lunatic stalker who might want to kill Amanda. You and I are miles apart, romantically speaking. And—oh, I almost forgot—I'm fighting cancer. Talk about turnoffs."

"Singer, if I was going to be turned off, it would be the ex-cop thing."

"Really?"

She gave me a sour look. "Have you forgotten some of the things you said to me in the hall outside the Kaplan trial? Or on the way into court when I had to depose that scumbag in the Mark Aldridge case?"

I glanced away, looking for answers on the back of the malt vinegar bottle. "What did I, um, say, exactly?"

"Do you want it verbatim?"

"Not really. Maybe we can consider it all water under the bridge."

Her face broke into a predatory smirk that reminded me of a lioness I'd seen on a documentary, just before it sank its teeth into the butt of an antelope. "I don't think so."

And it took off from there. We circled each other verbally, wary but interested, dangling emotional pieces of ourselves at the end of a figurative ten-foot pole. She talked about being a defense attorney, the prejudice against women that still existed in the courtroom, living in fear of her own clients. I told jokes, or tried to, and I saw Julie Atwater laugh for maybe the first time. When she thought something was truly funny, she let out a heavy, snorting laugh that made me grin just hearing it. The furrow between her eyes that I'd thought was a permanent feature melted away.

"No deep secrets to divulge?" she asked after a while.

"You know all of them already. Or could guess. Divorced, no kids, ex-cop, cancer."

"What about helping Amanda out?" she said. "That's something special. Different."

"Who wouldn't?"

"Lots of people. You did your job twelve years ago and it didn't pan out. That's life. You're doing her a monumental favor."

I turned my head to take in the bar and the grad school nerds. The four of them were perched on stools in a rough circle, laughing at a joke, engrossed in the conversation. They spoke quickly and passionately, gesturing to make a point one moment, then becoming completely still as one of them led the discussion in a new direction the next. A furious back-and-forth debate erupted between Amanda and Jay, which the other two girls watched closely, smiling. Amanda's face was animated, happy. I realized I wanted it to stay that way. Why? Was it feelings of guilt from a job poorly done more than a decade ago? I'd probably done worse things to more people over the years and I wasn't hustling to make amends with them. Was it paternal? Misplaced feelings for a kid I'd never had? Maybe. But the real reason was closer at hand. It didn't take much imagination to wonder what I'd be doing right now, how I would feel, if she hadn't had the guts to walk up to me outside that café in Clarendon and ask for help.

I shook my head. "She's the one doing me a favor."

CHAPTER TWENTY-THREE

My mother was shaking me, a hand on my shoulder, trying to get me up in time to make the bus. I'd stayed up too late the night before, watching an Ed Wood movie, and now it was almost impossible to break through the membrane of sleep and surface completely.

"Marty," she kept saying. "Marty, wake up. Jesus, would you please wake up?"

My eyes snapped open. My mother would never have said that.

I sucked in a deep breath and sat up. I was in the backseat and Amanda was leaning between the seats, a hand on my shoulder. I looked around. The car was off and we were stopped on Chilton Street, a block away from my place. It was dark out and a strong wind was making streetlamps and porch lights sway, creating the illusion that the whole world was tilting from side to side.

I rubbed my eyes until I saw stars. "What's going on?"

Julie glanced at me in the rearview mirror. "You fell asleep and we didn't want to wake you, so we took the long way home. We drove past your place before we parked, trying to be cautious."

"Good work," I said, grimacing. "I'm glad somebody's on the ball."

"As we cruised past your house, we both saw it."

"Saw what?"

Amanda spoke. "A flash. Real muted. From the second floor."

I sat up straighter, no longer quite as tired. "Like the light being turned off and on real quick?"

They glanced at each other. "No," Julie said. "Smaller than that. You've got a couple windows in the front and only one was lit up by this . . . whatever it was. I think a light being turned on would've lit up both windows, even if it was only a second."

"So Julie kept on driving while I watched," Amanda said, "but it didn't happen again."

"Then we pulled over here and woke you up," Julie finished. "What do you want to do?"

"Amanda, do you have your cell?" I asked. I rattled off Kransky's phone number. "Save that and call him in twenty minutes if you haven't heard from me."

"You're not going over there," Julie said.

"I just want to check it out," I said. "We'll call in the Arlington PD if I see anything dangerous."

"You're not serious," Julie said, turning around in the seat to look at me. "Singer, you were passed out in the backseat the whole way home. You're not in any shape to go taking on some whack job with a gun. You're exhausted from the chemo and probably don't have half the reaction time you think you do."

"That's why I'm only going to check it out," I said. "I don't plan on making an arrest or anything. But if we call the cops right now, they're going to come with sirens blaring, no matter what I ask for. And, if this is Wheeler, we might have a chance to string him up if we go in quiet. I'll scope it out, then call Kransky."

Julie's mouth pinched shut, which took away from her cuteness.

"I promise," I said. Then, to Amanda, "Remember. Twenty minutes, then call Kransky."

"Got it," she said. "Be careful."

I grunted and got out of the car, throwing my jacket on the backseat as I did so; it was cold as hell but the jacket would get in the way. That left just a stylish turtleneck between me and the chill. The door clicked shut quietly. I looked around, getting my bearings. Julie had circled the block, so I was on the opposite side of the block from my house. I could cut through a few backyards and sneak up on my place from the back. I trotted up a neighbor's brick sidewalk and into their backyard.

The wind was fierce and I had to squint to keep leaves and dust from blinding me. I rounded the corner of a split-level brick-and-siding home. Was it the Tuttles'? Or the Cohens'? I couldn't even guess. I hardly knew my neighbors on either side of my house, let alone the people on the far side of the block. The disadvantages of being a bachelor cop most of your life. I did remember that they had a big chocolate Lab named Barkley that ran around the neighborhood chasing cats and knocking over garbage cans. I kept an eye out for him. One thing I didn't need right now was him taking a chunk out of my leg or barking his head off. I would also rather not have to explain to his owners what I was doing on their back patio at ten o'clock at night.

I padded along without encountering Barkley and crouched near the back fence. I looked back at the house. Flickering blues and whites of a large-screen TV lit up one living room, while the lights in the kitchen and dining room blazed away. From the house next door, the only illumination was the glow of a second-floor lamp leaking through a closed blind.

I slipped through their back gate and into the no-man's-land where the backs of all the properties met. My own yard was bordered by a simple split-rail fence, so I had a clear view of the back of my house. I squatted and watched for a minute. I didn't have much time before my twenty minutes were up and Kransky got called in, but still, I had to exercise some patience. I counted to two hundred. No one came out and danced a jig on my back deck, so I squirmed between the rails of the fence and ran to the back door, trying not to punt any sticks or tools I might've left lying around.

The deck was new, so I didn't have to worry about making noise crossing it, but my screen door was the old-fashioned kind with a spring that squeaked and popped when it was opened too far and would bang shut with the sound of a shotgun going off if you didn't stop it. I took a full minute to open the door, pulling it back a fraction of an inch at a time. When I had a foot of clearance, I propped it open with a shoulder and tried the knob. Locked. I fished my keys out and eased it open wide enough to slip through, praying that—if there *was* someone in my house—that Pierre had holed up somewhere safe and stayed there. If not, and he heard me, he'd come running and probably start an unholy yowling that might get us both killed. Another minute and I was in the kitchen, closing the screen door behind me an inch at a time. I shut the back door in case the wind blew something over. Or tipped off whoever was in my house from the change in air pressure.

I eased my gun out as my eyes adjusted. The kitchen was empty and the basement door was closed. No light showed beneath the door. So they hadn't broken in to do any surreptitious weight lifting. Check. The fractured glow from my neighbor's back porch light gave the small table, chairs, and appliances a sinister look, though nothing seemed to have been disturbed. Drawers were intact, the chairs were pushed in, cupboard doors closed. The faintest smell of pizza still lingered in the air. I moved in a stooped crouch to the doorway between the kitchen and dining room. My more elaborate dining room table and chairs had the same serene, spooky look as those in the kitchen. The stereo and record collection were safe and as disorganized as when Amanda had last rooted through them.

My thighs ached from the way I'd been squatting and I desperately wanted to stand up and stretch. Instead, I held my crouched, slumping walk and moved to the transition area between my dining and living rooms. I made myself stop and listen.

Nothing.

I started to straighten up and move to the bottom of the stairs when some instinct made me freeze. I suddenly paid attention to what I was feeling, instead of the nothing I was seeing.

You know your own house. There's a smell and a feel to things that you recognize as integral to your home. Anything else is alien. You know when you've had guests and visitors, you know the way it sounds when rain hits the roof, or how the pipes rattle when you take a shower.

And you know how it feels when there's someone else in the room.

Standing in the pitch dark, with his back to me, was a man. He was watching the street through one of my door's side windows, being careful not to tug the miniature curtains too far, only enough to see out. Every ten or fifteen seconds, he would glance up the stairs.

My heart jumped up in my throat. I'd been a second away from strolling past him like he was a piece of furniture. I got my breathing under control, watching him the whole time. Weak light filtering in from a streetlamp traced his outline, but he was dressed in black or navy blue from head to toe and was close to invisible. He was white, shorter than me, slim. Salt-and-pepper hair. Gloves. Nothing in his hands, but that didn't mean he wasn't carrying. He wore a peacoat or something else cotton that didn't shine or make a noise like synthetics do when they rub together.

It wasn't Wheeler. A dozen years had passed and people can change their appearance in less time than that, but Wheeler had been over six feet tall, with a round body and moon-pie face that not even a celebrity diet could've changed. This guy was lean, with an eagle's beak for a nose.

I had to fight not to jerk my head at a deep, rolling rumble coming from upstairs. The guy by the door glanced up the steps, then went back to staring out the window. The sound was repeated five more times. It dawned on me that it was the filing cabinet being opened and closed, once for each drawer. A succession of dull thumps followed: files and folders being dumped on my desk.

I thought about the situation. My legs and calves were on fire and it wouldn't be long before they gave out on me. I knew how many bad guys were in the house and I had the jump on them. It was time to act. I brought my gun up to train it on the guy by the door when quick footsteps sounded overhead and whoever had emptied my filing cabinet came hurrying down the steps. In the dim light, I couldn't make out many details. He was short and wiry and his face looked pushed in around the nose and cheeks, like he'd been a bad amateur boxer. He was dressed in black like his partner. A stack of folders was tucked under one arm and he held a Maglite in the other hand. The guy by the door looked up.

"Find anything?" he said.

"Yeah," the guy on the steps said. The flashlight was on and the light waggled across the walls and stairs as he came down.

"Turn that fucking thing off," the first guy said. "Why don't you throw all the lights on, let him know we're here?"

"I already figured it out, boys," I said, training my gun on them.

They were fast, I'll give them that. The first guy yanked the door open and was halfway out before I'd stopped talking. The short dude on the steps sidearmed the Maglite in my direction, then sprinted back upstairs still holding the files. The flashlight tumbled end over end, covering the room in wild arcs of light. I sidestepped the flashlight and squeezed off a round at the guy by the door. I missed and drilled a hole in my front door, sending splinters of wood everywhere.

I jumped across the living room and poked my head out the front door in time to see the first guy sprinting across my front lawn and down the street. Cars and trees blocked my view and my shot, so I turned to go after the guy behind me. I flicked the hall light on—there was no element of surprise left—and moved up the stairs, gun ready. When I was halfway up the steps, I heard a crash and the sound of breaking glass. I took the stairs three at a time and ran down the hall to the office. I kicked the door open, swinging my SIG in short movements to cover the room.

A cold, cruel breeze blew through my office from the broken window, scattering papers across the room. The short guy had thrown my office chair through the window, then jumped off the roof of my front porch. I spun and raced back through the hall and down the steps, bursting out the front door and off the porch. To my right, at the far end of the street, backup lights flared from a parked car, maybe an SUV or pickup with a cab. They illuminated the short guy, who was halfway between me and the car, hoofing it as fast as he could go. I fought the urge to put my sights on his leg or arm, to wing him, but this wasn't the time to play the Lone Ranger. Taking low-percentage shots in urban neighborhoods is a great way to end up killing the wrong person.

I jogged down the street after them. The short guy had a lead on me, but was slowed by a limp—probably from the fall off my porch roof. Tucked under one arm like a football were the files he'd lifted from my office. Combined with the limp, the awkwardness of the papers and binders kept him from breaking into a full sprint. In a matter of seconds, I'd be close enough to take a better shot or at least get a license plate number. Piece of cake.

But I'd gone about fifty feet when my feet started to drag. It was as though I had an extra person along for the ride. My steps slowed to a shuffle. Digging deep, I called on that extra kick I needed to catch up, but . . . it wasn't there. Halfway down the block I was lurching like a zombie while the short guy was almost to the SUV. By the time I took five more steps—all I could manage—he'd yanked the passenger's door open and jumped inside. I stumbled to a halt and watched the back of the SUV as it peeled away. The license plate was strategically covered with mud and I was still too far away to take a shot. The bad guys took off down the street and I leaned over, my hands on my knees, gasping for breath and cursing.

I was sifting through the disaster the two guys had made of my files when Kransky came up, looking rumpled and tired. He stood in the doorway for a minute, watching me.

"Any news?" I asked, picking some papers off the floor and putting them in a folder.

"No," he said, sitting down in the one remaining chair in the office. The other was still on my front lawn. "It's on the wire, so Metro patrols are looking for it, but there's not much to go on. A black, four-door SUV driven by two white guys is going to scoop up half the cars on the road."

"I know. Still worth a try." I closed my eyes for a second, trying to banish the exhaustion I was feeling, then slammed the files I was holding onto the desk. "I wish to fuck I knew who those guys were."

He watched me for a second. "Neither one was Wheeler?"

I shook my head. "No way. Wrong shape, wrong look. And two of them?"

"Partner."

"That would work if he'd been the other guy. But I know Wheeler. I interviewed him a ton of times, saw him every day for weeks at the trial. Neither one of those guys was him, even twelve years later."

"Hired hands?"

"Maybe," I said, doubtful. "Seems strange for a guy like Wheeler to sub out his dirty work. He's no kingpin."

"What did they take?"

I gestured to my desk. "Files."

Kransky leaned forward. "Let me guess, something to do with Brenda Lane and Michael Wheeler?"

"And a couple of others, maybe to throw me off, or maybe just mistakes."

There was a noise in the hall. Amanda and Julie poked their heads in the door. I waved them in.

"Marty, what's going on?" Amanda asked.

"I don't know," I said. Something more reassuring was in order, I guess, but I didn't have the energy or the creativity to come up with anything else. "It wasn't Wheeler, that's all I know. Whoever it was, they like to look through old case files. Including Wheeler's."

We were all quiet, looking at what had once been a neat and tidy office. Every drawer of the desk had been emptied and spilled onto the floor. Files had been removed from the cabinet and the papers that had escaped were being blown by the wind coming through the broken window.

"What are you going to do now?" Julie asked.

I glanced at Amanda. "First, we've got to get you out of here. I don't know who those clowns were, but my place is now officially compromised. Which sucks, I know, but we can't take any chances."

She gave me a pained look. "I just got here."

"I know. I'm sorry. But, until we know where those guys fit in, we can't act like everything's fine. Whoever it was that busted in here tonight knew about me and about Wheeler, which means they probably know about you."

"What are you going to do?" Kransky asked.

I waved at the mess that had been my office. "Clean this up, get some sleep, and then I think it's time to chase the one good lead we've got."

"The sister," Kransky said.

"Assuming you got an address for me."

"Waynesboro," he said. "I got it right as you called about your shooting match."

"What if Michael is there?" Amanda asked.

"Unlikely," Kransky said. "He's making a six-hour round trip to throw flowers on your desk?"

I held up my hands to stop the guesswork. "Either way, now that I'm done with chemo for a few weeks, I can run down there and get some answers."

"You might be done with chemo, but how do you feel?" Amanda asked.

"Like shit in a cup. But I'm angry, so it's a wash," I said. "Besides, I don't have the luxury of feeling lousy. Whoever broke in here tonight upped the ante in a big way."

Julie had been leaning against the door frame to my office, arms folded. Now she spoke up. "You shouldn't go alone. You weren't in good enough shape to even run down the street after those guys."

I colored. I didn't need to be reminded that I'd nearly passed out jogging a half block. Before I could defend myself, though, Kransky said, "I'll go."

"No," Julie said, with some force. "You should stay here. I'll go."

Kransky turned slowly in his chair to look at her.

She raised her hand. "Before you lose it on me, listen for a second. We just got done saying Wheeler probably isn't down there, which means he's where? Here. In DC. Amanda can't stay at Singer's and I'd put her up, but I'm a target, too. I'm living out of a hotel room. If he finds out where I'm at, or if tonight's two goons do, we're sitting ducks."

Kransky said nothing.

"So Amanda stays with you. You watch her. Singer and I go south and find out what we can. We come back in a day or two at most and take it from there."

I started to protest, more because I was still stinging from Julie's remark about being out of shape than any problem I had with her plan. Then I shut my mouth, because it wasn't such a bad idea.

"Can you take the time off?" I asked him.

"Yeah," he said. "It'd be better if we didn't have to chase around GW, though. With you gone, I've got no backup."

"Amanda?" I asked.

She said, "My classes are done for the week and I can cancel office hours. What about Pierre?"

I turned to Jim.

"You've got to be kidding," he said.

"I'll take care of him," Amanda said quickly. "You won't even know he's there."

"That's it, then," I said, ignoring the look on Jim's face. "You two hole up. The counselor and I are heading south. And Layla Green is going to tell us everything she knows about her brother."

VII.

"He had nothing?"

"We've only skimmed the files," the man said. He took a deep breath and got ready to take a verbal beating. It wasn't the news he'd been told to get. "But, no. Nothing off the top."

But instead of swearing, the old man simply grunted. A minute passed with only rasping, labored breathing coming over the line.

"Chief?"

"We're in good shape, Taylor," the old man said. "Or at least we're not in bad. Singer doesn't have a clue. It would've been nice if he'd had a map, I suppose, and painted a big red X telling us right where we wanted to go, but this news . . . it makes me realize we're all in the same boat."

"What about . . . ?"

"The girl's with Singer, right?"

"Her stuff was there."

"So, she hasn't been found. Which means all three of us are operating in the dark. But those two more than us. And maybe we can use that."

"What do we need Singer for, then? Take him out, grab the girl, make the rest happen the way we want it to."

"Maybe," the old man said slowly, considering. "But I like having Marty as a control. I know how he thinks. How he works. It's what let me lead him around by the nose twelve years ago. Plus he'll keep my . . . he'll keep the target occupied, distracted."

"Removing the problem worked last time," Taylor offered.

"Because nobody gave a damn," the old man said, his voice calm. "That's not the case with Singer. The man's got friends. His body turns up somewhere and we'll have a load of hurt. No, keep an eye on the girl. Put Jackson back on patrol. We just might get lucky."

CHAPTER
TWENTY-FOUR

The next morning, I packed a day bag for the trip south to Waynesboro. It should've been three hours away—and in most parts of the country, I could get there and back in a day—but in our neck of the woods, traffic could turn the trip into a full-day extravaganza.

Julie and I met at the parking garage for the Vienna Metro Station, as innocuous a spot as we could think of to stow her car while I drove us to Waynesboro. She was waiting for me in the multiday parking area, looking preppy in jeans, black boots, and a fleece. I popped the trunk so she could chuck her overnight roller bag into the car. She slammed the trunk shut, then flopped down in the passenger's seat.

"Hey," I said.

"Hey." She had wide, dark aviator sunglasses on that gave her a sophisticated look. Her hair was held back by a simple band. "Ready for some answers?"

"If we get lucky," I said, then tried to backpedal when I saw her smile. "You know, with what we're trying to find out."

She reached over and patted my hand. "Why don't you just drive, Singer?"

Any drive south and west of DC starts with Route 66 west, which, around DC, isn't the romantic highway of song and film; it's more like the world's largest continuous strip mall. Green trees arched into sight over the highway wall from time to time, but more often we were treated to unending stretches of shopping centers that could've been airlifted from anywhere in the US. There were so many pizza joints, nail salons, and big box stores that I wondered who went there. If everyone worked at these places, who was left to go shopping?

In time, the malls released their hold on the land and gave way to farms and the kind of grassy, green hills you typically only find on postcards. When we saw horses grazing and running through fields on either side of the highway, I knew we'd left the parts of Virginia that are really just suburban extensions of DC. The Blue Ridge swelled on the right, the hills layered in the distance like two-dimensional cutouts, with one set of slopes giving way to a larger, smokier, more beautiful set right behind them. Weathered plaques along the side of the road marked the sites where Civil War battles had been forgotten, Confederate flags flew in yards where they hadn't. Julie spent most of the drive on her cell phone, doing lawyer-type things and arguing with people while I concentrated on driving. When signs for Waynesboro started showing, however, she ended her last call, snapped the phone shut, and looked over at me.

"What's the plan?" she asked.

I scrounged around a pocket near the armrest and handed her a map. "Kransky wrote down where she lived. We can try and find it on the map or we could go to the visitors' center and ask—"

I stopped because she'd tossed the map on the backseat and had pulled her phone out again. "What's the address?" she asked.

"460 Catalpa Street."

"Hold on," she said and peered at the two-inch screen of her phone, biting her lip as she concentrated. She typed into the phone with two thumbs faster than I could with ten fingers. "Got it. When you hit Market Street, turn right at the light, go three blocks. Take a left, then go about two miles."

"You sure we don't want to go to the visitors' center?"

She shot me a look. "I'm sure, Singer. It's GPS, for Pete's sake."

We followed Waynesboro's broad, sleepy streets to the historic town center with its red-brick Federal-style homes and right out the other side. Main Street fell behind as the road snaked its way to the outskirts of town where homes became modest and modern. Brick and wood gave way to vinyl and plastic, front porches and gliders to cement steps and folding chairs. The lawns were larger, but more apt to have pink flamingos and gazing balls in them. We pulled onto Catalpa and counted house numbers until we neared the one that Kransky had given me. I eased up onto the gravel shoulder when I was fifty yards away and we took a long look.

The house was like the others in the neighborhood, a two- or three-bedroom rancher with a cracked asphalt driveway and in desperate need of landscaping. An ugly, half-height cyclone fence surrounded the property. Fake shutters screwed into the siding made a passing attempt at colonial respectability that was obliterated by a herd of plastic deer arranged in a semicircle around a birdbath. The lawn had been cut recently, though weeds and grass grew in the no-man's-land between the fence and the street. A beat-up blue Chrysler minivan rusted away in the driveway with a license plate too far away to make out clearly. A robin took a crap on the front porch. There was no one in the yard and no movement from inside that I could see. I shut the car off and unlatched my seat belt.

We sat for ten minutes.

Julie wriggled in her seat, trying to get comfortable. After five more minutes, she asked, "What are we doing, exactly?"

"We're waiting."

"For how long?"

"For a while," I said. "Wheeler could be sitting behind the door with a shotgun. It would kind of ruin my day if I got smoked strolling down the driveway."

"We'd have our man, at least."

"*You* would have your man," I said. "I would have a whole new set of medical bills."

She sighed and folded her arms across her chest and we both stared across the road some more. The highlight was when a Mazda RX-7 with custom rims and a pimped-out spoiler sailed by, going too fast, barely keeping it on the road. The drone of its muffler hung on long after it disappeared from view. It got chilly sitting there, so I started the car to turn the heat on for a minute, then shut it off. The hot air accentuated the light perfume Julie was wearing. I cleared my throat and cracked the window.

A minute passed and she sighed again. "Did you bring anything to drink?"

"A couple of sodas," I said. "Cooler's behind your seat."

I expected her to get out and open the back door, but instead she climbed onto the console between the seats and rummaged around the backseat from there, trying to open the cooler lid from the wrong direction. Her hip was pressed up hard against my shoulder as she leaned into me, while her butt was next to my face, waggling back and forth as she struggled to get the cooler open. I tried to keep my attention on the house across the street.

"What the hell is wrong with this thing?" she asked, her voice muffled but peeved.

"Let me get it," I said and put my seat back so I could reach the cooler. She yanked back on the lid at the same time. With the support of my shoulder gone, her momentum tumbled her backward onto the steering wheel, where her butt landed on the horn, honking it. She said "Shit!," jerked away from the horn like she'd been burnt, and slid from the steering wheel directly onto my lap.

I froze. She froze. Her face was three inches away from mine. Her sunglasses had slipped so that they now dangled from her ears and under her chin. Wild strands of hair had come loose from the band and they hung down over her eyes and across her face. I had a hand on her back and another on her knee. I guess I'd put them there when she'd dropped into my lap. We sat there for a long moment. I raised the hand that was on her knee and gently removed her sunglasses. Folded them and put them on the console. Raised my hand again and brushed the strands of hair away from her eyes. Her lips were full and parted and I could see her nostrils flare minutely as she breathed.

"I've never made out in a car," she said. "I've led a sheltered life."

"Would you like to break out of your shell?"

"Yes," she said, breathing the word and leaning in.

◆ ◆ ◆

So much for our stakeout.

It had been thirty years since I'd tried getting it on in a car and it wasn't any easier now than it was then. And that had been in a backseat. We squirmed around like two sardines in a can, honking the horn once more in our passion, until Julie found the lever that reclines the entire seat. We fell back with a grunt. She straddled me and worked at the buttons and zippers of her clothes while our mouths were glued together like we would stop breathing if we ever separated. I got myself in disarray before she did and helped her with the fleece, shirt, and bra. The jeans were the hardest part and I thought one of us was going to pull a muscle trying to shuck her pants off until she slapped my hands away, rolled onto the passenger's seat, slithered out of them, and crawled back on top of me. Somewhere in the back of my mind I was nervous, self-conscious, wondering what the cancer would do to me or what it had already done. I'd become weaker, fatigued, less of myself than I was used to in every other way. Why would this be any different?

But her hunger and mine overrode it all. My worries faded as she set the pace, straddling me, biting her lip, clutching at my shoulders. I let her go, enjoying it, conserving myself, until it wasn't my choice to make anymore and I became a part of it. Months of anxiety spent worrying about death and illness and fear were wiped away as we clutched and pushed and exploded with each other. I slipped into a heavy waking dream, content and blank and exhausted.

I moved as she stirred under my hands. She lifted her head from my chest and looked at me with a neutral expression on her face—wary—until I smiled. She smiled back, then took a deep breath. I glanced at the clock. Our episode had lasted for all of ten minutes. I'd slept for about two more, though it had felt like an hour.

"Do you think Wheeler was watching?" she asked, stretching and arching her back.

I let my eyes follow her body, watching with interest what the stretching did. She had put the fleece back on, but was bare from the waist down. It was a wonderful style, one that I thought women everywhere should adopt. "I don't know. I'm more worried about some country cop catching us like we're two seventeen-year-olds after prom."

"That was more action than Catalpa Street has seen for a long time," she said, then grinned.

I laughed. "Forget Catalpa Street. That was more action than I've seen in a long time."

"Not counting people breaking into your house."

"I can do without that kind of action."

She gently eased herself off me and clambered to the passenger's seat, giving the outside world a few choice glimpses in the process. In a minute she was put back together like nothing had ever happened, though that's not how I preferred to think of it.

I cleared my throat. "I like looking for sodas in the cooler. I think we should do it again."

She raised her eyebrows. "Right now?"

"Jesus, no. Not right now. Soon."

She smiled. "Good."

"So, not weird?"

She leaned back over the seat and said, "Not weird." Then kissed me.

When we came up for air, I coughed and said, "I don't care if Wheeler is sitting behind the door with a bazooka, there's no way I can sit in the car for another half hour."

I started the car and we eased past the house. Nothing jumped out at me, but I noticed that the yard kept going behind the house for an acre or three, which was disappointing, since I'd wanted to circle around and maybe get a look at the back. I did a quick U-turn and parked right outside the house. Julie and I got out.

Next to the road was a mailbox with the address and the name "Green" in cheap, stick-on letters that were peeling away like sunburned skin. Below it sat a bright yellow box holding two old copies of the town newspaper, still in their plastic bags. I opened the gate and walked up the cracked concrete path to the front door, taking my time and watching the windows.

You never get used to waltzing up to what you have to assume is a place of danger, the home of the guy who pulled the trigger or held the knife or swung the pipe. A knot of anxiety starts to unravel somewhere behind your belly button and spreads throughout your body. You do your best to ignore it and experience takes care of the feeling once things heat up, but the first few minutes before something goes down are the worst. Of course, Wheeler might not even be here. I had to treat the situation as if there was an armed lunatic hiding behind the door, but act as though I'd shown up to chat about the weather. Layla Green might be a sweet Southern belle and invite me in for iced tea, or Catalpa Street might see more bullets flying in the next five minutes than it had since the Civil War.

I peeked in the window. The blinds were down, but I could make out the living room through a bent louver.

"See anything?" Julie asked.

"Old, beat-up couch. Paper plates on the coffee table. Some crap on the floor. Big plasma TV."

"At least she has her priorities straight," Julie said, looking around the yard. Cheap plastic chairs, the kind that melt and start to buckle when it gets too hot, sat on the slab front porch. They'd been white, once, but now were green with an algae-like growth on the legs. A dozen damp cigarette butts, kissed with lipstick marks, moldered in a glass ashtray on a side table and a deflated beach ball lay trapped between a chair and the wall. We checked around back, where I found more trophies of suburban bliss: a cracked kiddie pool, a push mower leaning up against the house, a rusting grill with a couple of empty propane tanks lolling around. I sidled up to the back door, which looked into an ugly, if neat, kitchen. Faux cherry cabinets, brass-patina knobs, linoleum floor cut and colored to look like Italian marble, but $1.99 a square foot at your local hardware store. I put my ear to the door and held my breath until my pulse was knocking in my ears. Nothing.

We went around front and walked up to the door again. I told Julie to stand well off to one side, then I knocked. I stepped back and let my hands swing down by my sides. Nonthreatening, but ready to go for my gun in a hurry. It was a wasted precaution: two more authoritative knocks and I was sure no one was home. At least, no one willing to answer the door.

"Singer," Julie called and gestured toward the road, where a postal truck pulled up to the gate with its blinkers on.

I hurried to meet the truck by the mailbox, resisting the urge to rub my hands together in glee. Mailmen, paperboys, and garbage collectors are some of the best informants you can dig up. They know everything about anything that goes on in their neighborhood, often so happy to spill the beans that it's hard to get them to shut up. Behind the wheel was a white guy about sixty, sporting a long, drooping mustache and watery blue eyes. He looked back at me, poker-faced.

"Hi," I said, holding a hand up, trying to look neighborly.

"Hi, yourself," the mailman said.

"Sorry to bother you. We're friends of Michael's, down from DC for the day," I said. "I thought I'd surprise him, but it looks like there's nobody home."

"Michael who?"

"Wheeler," I said, acting surprised. "Michael Wheeler."

The mailman chewed his mustache with his lower lip, a habit he seemed to do often, judging by how stained it was. "Michael Wheeler? Nobody by that name here."

"You sure?" I asked, then patted my pockets. "I'm sure I've got the right address."

"Damn right I'm sure," the mailman said. "I've been doing this route for ten years and Layla's the only one who's ever lived here. She's had some lazy shits you might call boyfriends hang around for a while, but I don't think any of them was named Michael."

"Michael's her brother."

"Well, that ain't it, then," he said. "Besides, none of them stuck around long enough to get their mail delivered here."

"He might've just rolled into town," I said. "Would you have seen him around?"

"Maybe, maybe not. You think you'd notice those kinds of things, but I'm only here for a few minutes a day. The Tates down the road had their parents visiting for three weeks and I didn't know about it until today."

"Is that Layla's van?" I said, waving at the blue monster in the driveway.

"Yeah. Transmission's gone. She's driving a rental now, I think. Girl's hard on cars, doesn't know enough to drop a quart of oil into it every once in a while."

"Any idea when she gets home?" Julie asked. "Maybe she can set us straight about Michael."

"Around five. She works down at AgCon, in the office there. All those girls leave at five on the dot. I get stuck in traffic when the place lets out."

"All right, then," I said, looking at Julie as if conferring. "Maybe we'll try back around five or six, see if she can help us out."

He nodded, a short jab of his head forward and down. "Good luck."

We waved as he pulled away, then I led Julie out of the yard, pulling the fence door behind us and heading for the car.

"Nosy bastard," she said as we got into the car.

"All postmen are," I said, starting the engine and pulling out onto the road. "And ten will get you twenty he'll call us into the local cops if we don't head out like we said we were going to."

"To where?"

"We've got some time to kill. We can grab a late lunch and make it back here long before Layla gets off work."

"Maybe I can look in the cooler again, see what I can find," Julie said. I didn't look at her, but could hear the grin in her voice.

"I won't stop you," I said, and concentrated on driving.

CHAPTER TWENTY-FIVE

We parked near the center of town. I would've headed for the biggest crowd of people to find a good place to sit and eat, but Julie pulled out her phone again and told me where we were going, a bistro called the Blue Arbor. It was a quiet café tucked between a pair of antique shops. We got a table with a white tablecloth, a fresh rose in a small crystal vase, and a view of the street. The waiter brought some bread with soft butter. We ordered and then sat looking at each other.

"So," I said.

"So," she said back. "Why'd you get divorced?"

I sat back. "Don't you want to warm up, start with the small stuff?"

"Why bother?" she said. "Lay it on me."

"I thought I already did," I said.

She smiled sweetly. "Technically, I think I laid it on you."

"Ah, yeah," I said, spinning my spoon on top of my place mat. I cleared my throat. "Her name was Sherry. Married nine years. No kids."

"Didn't want them or no time?"

"Just didn't happen," I said. "Which is all right. They would've been an afterthought. For me, at least."

"Was that the problem? The job?"

"Probably. We were young and tough and thought we could get through anything. Rookie cop gets off at five in the morning, sleeps all day, gets up and does it all again. *We'll work through it, honey. It won't be forever.* Then the promotion to Homicide and getting in at five seems like paradise. And it's not like you can come home and talk about your work if you want a stable home life."

"How bad could it be?"

"Bad."

"Try me," she said.

"No," I said.

"Yes."

I sighed, glanced away, looked back at her. "One time, someone calls in a homicide. Home invasion, guy's been robbed. Gunshot wound to the head. No one found him for a week. We go in there, find he's got a dog that couldn't get out. The dog survived, but not because it knew how to use a can opener. And that was one of the *funny* stories."

Julie took a sip of water. "Where is she now?"

"Not sure. We parted, stayed in touch, fell out of touch. I think she lives in Austin now with some Greek guy, owns a nightclub and a Dairy Queen."

Our food came and we tucked in. Which is to say, I stirred the cream in my coffee and took two bites out of a chicken salad sandwich. Julie ate delicately, taking a small bite from her sandwich and looking at the result before taking another. At that rate, it would take two hours for her to finish, but I was content to watch.

"Are you feeling all right?" she asked, looking at my almost untouched food.

"Yeah. I want to be ready and able if we need to do any heavy sleuthing. Not queasy and sick by the side of the road while the bad guy drives away."

"You need to eat more if you're not going to faint instead."

"I'll get to it, thanks."

She was quiet for a moment, then said, "Sorry. I shouldn't be so bossy."

"You're not."

"My mom had cancer," she said suddenly. Her gaze was turned down, looking at her plate. "I tried to get her to eat all the time, you know, figuring that when you eat, you get energy, and with enough energy you can beat anything. Obviously, that's not how it works, but you don't always act logically under the circumstances."

"It was hard?"

"Breast cancer. Quick. But not quick enough." She made a face. "What the hell am I doing? I shouldn't be talking to you like this."

"Don't sweat it," I said, with more gusto than I felt. "I'm getting good care and great doctors. And I've got a couple reasons to live, now."

I put emphasis on the "now" and she gave me a shy look, then smiled. We ate the rest of our lunch, I paid the bill, and we left with a bounce in our step.

◆ ◆ ◆

The bounce took a hit when I rounded the corner by the visitors' center and saw a Waynesboro City police cruiser parked next to my car. Leaning against the front fender, arms crossed, was a local boy in blue, complete with cowboy hat and mirror shades. We walked up to him. His nameplate said "Hanson."

"This isn't where the country cop tells the big-city dick to get the hell out of his town, is it?" I asked.

Hanson tilted his head. "I don't think so," he said, with none of the Southern twang I was expecting. "I'm from Boston. So, unless you're the country cop, I think you've got the wrong scenario. Though you might be a dick. Not sure about that part, yet."

"Fair enough," I said. "How can I help you?"

"Gary Deaver told me he saw a guy and a gal poking around Layla Green's house earlier today. Gave me your plates, the make and model of your car."

"Who's Gary Deaver?" Julie asked.

"Mailman. Looks like a walrus."

"Damn it," I said.

He seemed amused. "That's Gary. It's his dream to catch a crook or a spy or a terrorist in the act. He'll call me later, dying to know if I locked you up."

"Me, too," I said.

"I didn't think much of it, but you did me a favor and parked down the street from police HQ. I saw your ride when I got back from lunch. You look like a cop, talk like a cop, but you didn't check in at the station. Thought I'd see what your interest was."

I eyed him up. Hanson was playing friendly-like, but he could make my life miserable if he thought I was jerking him around. So I gave him the condensed version, stressing my thirty years as a cop but downplaying the part about him possibly having a murderer lying low in his town. I didn't need him rounding up a posse and storming the house on Catalpa Street before I could get out there and ask some questions.

He chewed it over. "You're retired?"

"Yep."

"And you don't have a license?"

"Only to drive."

"You got a gun?"

I hesitated, but why? He could find out easily enough. "Yes. Registered."

He looked out over the street for a second, then back at me. "That's not a good combination."

"Nope," I admitted. "I wouldn't like it if it were my beat."

"You got your driver's license on you?" I handed it over and he pushed himself away from the car. "Gimme a sec."

He slipped into the driver's side of the cruiser and got on his radio while I tried to look unperturbed. Julie pushed up her sunglasses and stared into space like this happened all the time. A family of four walked by, glancing from the cop car to me and back. The mother snagged her little boy by the collar and pulled him close as they hurried down the sidewalk, but the kid slipped backward glances under her arm until they rounded the corner.

Hanson got out of the car. He handed me my ID. I pocketed it and said, "You know someone in MPDC?"

"Remember Bill Collier?"

"Hell, yes," I said. "Runs the armory. Or used to. Gave me grief every time I went to the range."

He grinned. "Me, too. He's my uncle. The one who got me into law enforcement in the first place."

"What'd he suck you in with? The stories about the money? Or the beautiful women?"

"He says you got him out of a jam once," Hanson said.

"Nothing he couldn't have gotten himself out of," I said. "Bill likes his booze. And his guns. I helped him sort the two out, is all."

"He owes you. Which means I do, too. Though that doesn't mean you can head for Green's house and start shooting the windows out of her place."

"I just need to ask her a couple questions. I'll know in thirty seconds if it was a waste of time. Or if she's not telling me the truth."

"Yeah, but then what?"

"Then I come and get you," I said.

"Uh-huh," he said, and looked at me. "Listen, do me a favor and keep your head on straight. I don't want you lighting the town up to get this guy."

"I didn't come down here to blow people away, Hanson."

"Hey, it's the worst-case scenario, is all," he said. "Ask your questions, get your answers, and get out of there. If I hear about anything else, then we have to come get you. Got it?"

I wasn't entitled to more than that. "Sure."

He reached in a pocket and handed me his card. "And give me a call when you roll out of town. I'd like to know you got what you came for."

"And that I'm out of your hair."

"That, too," he said, a smile stretching wide. "Blame me?"

"Not one bit," I said.

◆ ◆ ◆

Hanson let me go and I drove carefully while still in his view, but mashed the gas once I was out of town. Getting the green light from the local law enforcement had cut into time better spent casing Layla's house before she got back from work.

"The big blue wall came in handy," Julie said as we retraced our steps out of town.

"Once in a great while."

"Do you think he'd arrest you if things got rough?"

"Without a doubt," I said. "He'll swing by later, see if I did anything stupid. He's probably at the station, filling out the paperwork now."

What passes for traffic in Waynesboro had picked up since we'd arrived in town, but a veteran of DC rush hour wouldn't have even noticed it. I spotted a better place to park this time, a notch in the road obscured by a drooping oak tree branch that still gave us a view of the house despite the dying winter light. I turned the car off, knocked the seat back, and waited.

Julie unlatched her seat belt and turned to reach in the backseat. She caught my look. "I really just want something to drink, Singer."

I counted thirteen cars on the road, going both directions, before a pale green Kia appeared out of the dusk, slowed down, then pulled into the driveway, taking up a spot right behind the van. The engine rattled to a stop. A minute later, the driver's side door opened and a woman got out. Mid-thirties. Comparing her to her car door, she was around five and a half feet tall, with a mess of curly blonde hair that she probably hadn't been born with. She was heavyset and ponderous. Her charcoal-gray skirt and jacket combo with ruby-red turtleneck sweater, too tight to be flattering, emphasized rolls rather than curves. One arm hugged a bucket of fried chicken she'd already broken into. A cell phone was tucked between her cheek and shoulder and she carried on a lively conversation from the car to the door. High heels forced her to take short, mincing steps that were comically at odds with the thickness of her upper body. She climbed the steps to her front porch, juggled the chicken and her keys around so she could unlock the door, then went inside. The lights came on, spilling thin, glowing lines through the blinds.

"Let's say you're hiding your semi-fugitive brother," I said to Julie.

"Okay."

"He doesn't leave the house except to drive to our nation's capital to harass graduate students once a week. Do you bring home one bucket of chicken at the end of the day?"

She frowned. "What are you asking?"

"Put another way, let's say you're a single, overweight woman with an appetite. Can you finish a bucket of fried chicken by yourself?"

She thought. "It's either not enough or a lot, depending on how you look at it."

"So the bucket of chicken doesn't tell us anything."

"No."

"Shit," I said.

Fifteen minutes would give her time to change out of her work clothes and maybe grab another drumstick, so we waited. I tapped the steering wheel to some nameless tune, then we got out of the car and strolled down to her gate for the second time that day. I went up to the door and knocked while Julie stood behind me and to the side. It took three solid raps that shook the door and made the porch light shimmy; I was fighting the latest Travis Tritt album with the volume cranked to ten. The music stopped and a shadow approached the door. I took a step back as it opened.

It was the blonde that had gotten out of the car. I smiled. "Hi. Layla Green?"

"Yeah," she said. I watched her face. She was suspicious, but not scared. "Can I help you?"

"Ms. Green, my name's Marty Singer and this is Julie Atwater. I'm a retired police officer and Ms. Atwater is an attorney. We're from Washington, DC. I was hoping I could take a few minutes of your time."

"What about?"

"I wanted to ask you about your brother."

"Terry?" she said, her eyes popping wide and her mouth dropping open. "What's wrong? Is there something wrong?"

"Uh, no," I said, nonplussed. "Not Terry. Michael."

Her face froze in that expression of worry for a split second, then scrunched into a scowl. "Michael? Michael Wheeler? He's my stepbrother."

Stepbrother. That would explain why she hadn't come up on any of our searches. "What can you tell me about Michael? Have you talked to him lately?"

"You said *retired* police officer," she said, eyes narrowing.

"That's right."

"So, you're not here officially?"

"Not yet," I said. "We're in the question-asking phase."

"So you can't make me talk to you."

"That's true," I said. "But all I need is five minutes of your time, Layla, and then you'll never see me again."

Her face took on a deep, reddish color. "I can't understand why you people can't leave Michael alone. After all these years, after dragging him through the mud when he didn't even kill that woman."

"We'll have to disagree on that one, but that's not why I'm here—"

"He told me not to come up to DC for the trial, told me that they'd hound me and stick cameras in my face. He was right. That jury found him innocent and it didn't mean shit, people after him constantly, trying to track him down."

"I'm not here to relive the past, Layla," I said. "But someone is threatening the murdered woman's daughter and all signs point to your stepbrother. I need your help to protect that girl."

"Protect?" she shrieked. Tears welled up on the edges of her lids and spilled over onto her cheeks. "Protect *her*? Who protected Michael? Who the hell protected him? You? You were probably the one that put the cuffs on him. Why didn't you shoot him when you had the chance? Why wait?"

"Now, hold on a second—" I started.

"I can't believe you've got the guts to come here and after what you did."

"Layla, what are you talking about?"

She pointed a long, burgundy-colored nail at me. "Don't call me Layla. You don't know me, you have no idea who I am. Now get the hell off my property before I call the police."

"Look, if you can tell me—"

Her voice went up three octaves and the skin around her lips went bloodless as she bawled, "Get off my property, you son of a bitch!"

I put my hands up and backed away from the door. "All right. Calm down. I'm leaving."

She watched as we back-stepped all the way to the fence. I wasn't as afraid of Wheeler jumping out and shooting me now as I was that Layla might do it instead. We went through the gate and out, walking up the road with long, steady steps. The door slammed shut behind us and I glanced back. She'd gone inside. I thought I saw the blinds move, but couldn't be sure.

We walked back to my car, got in, and sat.

"That went well," Julie said.

"Did you see her face?" I asked. "She wasn't faking any of that."

"You don't think she knows where he is?"

"I don't think so. No one pretends that well. I thought she was going to have a stroke."

"It could be she's angry that we've found her out. Her asshole brother gets her involved in something illegal and now the cops are on her."

I thought about it, then shook my head. "I want to believe that, but there wasn't any panic, no shocked innocence. She went straight into full-on fury."

Fifteen minutes later, we were still sitting there in the dark, trying to make the math work, and suddenly aware that we'd have to either drive back to DC or find a hotel for the night, when the porch light came on. We leaned forward and peered through the windshield. Layla came out of the house, closed and locked the door, and walked to the Kia. On the way, she squinted, giving the yard a hard looking-over, as though I might be crouching behind the plastic deer. She decided the coast was clear and got in the Kia. It wheezed to life, and reverse lights winked white, then red as she backed out of the driveway and headed toward town.

"This could be our break," I said to Julie.

"Or she could be going to Walmart."

"I'll take that chance," I said. I counted to ten, started the car, and followed.

CHAPTER
TWENTY-SIX

It wasn't the hardest tail I've ever done. Traffic was nonexistent and the tadpole-colored car was like a neon light bobbing ahead of me, though Layla drove fast and so recklessly that I had to scoot through two red lights in a row to keep from losing her. She skirted the downtown historic district and drove through several suburban neighborhoods, eventually turning down a wide, tree-lined lane named Abernathy Road.

Julie was quiet, watching the road with an intense stare, but I could guess what she was thinking: maybe a cautious Michael Wheeler— aware that someone might know about Layla and was watching her house—wasn't living with her; he was simply holed up nearby. She could be bringing him food and money once a week. Maybe Julie was right. Maybe the reaction I'd seen from her was anger that she'd been dragged into her brother's mess, and we'd spooked Layla into running straight to him. We might be heading directly for whatever shitty motel or rent-by-the-week apartment Wheeler was using as his base.

Abernathy turned from a sedate suburban boulevard into a true country road with steep dips and sharp curves. The surface twinkled with frost. Pastures and meadows flanked the road, their few remaining cornstalks showing up stark and skeletal against the sky. Cars were scarce and I was forced to give the Kia a quarter-mile lead if I didn't want to blow the tail. I continued to give Layla room until we topped a short rise and I squinted into the dark. There was no sign of Layla's taillights in the distance. I squeezed the steering wheel tight and stepped on the gas.

"Wait," Julie said. "Did you see that?"

"What? See what?"

"There was a sign back there. Maybe a driveway, you were going too fast."

"Shit," I said, slowing down.

Decision time. She could be dead ahead and putting miles between us. Or two hundred yards behind us and fading fast. I came to a stop, made a quick three-point turn, and headed back.

"It's up here," Julie said. "There, across from that tree."

I saw it now, a modest white sign with cramped black lettering. Two weathered pillars and a rusty gate formed an entrance for a driveway. I pulled in slowly so we could read the sign. "Abernathy Memorial Garden."

"Damn it," Julie said. "This isn't it."

"No, wait. Look," I said, pointing in front of the car. Tire tracks cut through the frost and headed up the drive. "Let's take a chance."

The gravel driveway split into three paths after the gate. I followed the tracks down the rightmost path. Lamps lit the drive every hundred feet, so I turned off the headlights and crept forward, glancing left and right among the headstones, crypts, and memorials. A breeze blew through the grounds, tearing the remaining leaves off the oaks and maples and scattering them in front of my car. A man-shaped silhouette, standing at ground level, almost stopped my heart until I saw it was a statue of a mournful Confederate soldier—hat in his hands, rifle at his feet—framed against the night sky. After ten minutes of creeping, Layla's car, parked in the puddle of light emanating from one of the streetlamps, came into view. I stabbed the brakes, then backed up behind a bend and turned the car off.

"Not what I was expecting," I said.

"I'll second that," Julie said.

We got out, careful to close the doors softly. It was cold. Using headstones for cover, we crept toward the Kia, staying in the shadows and scanning the ground to make sure that we didn't slip on decaying flowers or drop-kick the miniature brass urns that decorated some of the headstones. The musty smell of rotting leaves filled my nose. We sidled up to the Kia, but from twenty feet away, I could see it was empty.

Julie sighed, then cut it off suddenly. She leaned toward me to whisper. Her breath billowed in the air. "Do you hear that?"

I held my breath and listened. The wind had picked up and rattled the few remaining leaves on the trees. Then, I heard it.

Crying.

We followed the sound. Fifty or sixty feet from the Kia, we spotted Layla squatting near a headstone. A flashlight on the ground pointed straight up, illuminating her. Her head was bowed, held in one hand, while the other hand rested on the ground, supporting her weight. She swayed in the awkward position, rocking back and forth in time to her sobs.

Julie tugged at my sleeve and we retreated to a nearby tombstone for cover. The marble was cold under my hand. I looked over my shoulder a few times, feeling exposed. We watched while Layla's crying wound down. She wiped her nose with the back of her hand, then got on her hands and knees to clear the headstone of leaves and debris. When it seemed she'd done all she could for the grave, she hauled herself to her feet, brushed at her pants, and headed for the car. I peered over the tombstone as she started the Kia up and pulled away, heading out of the cemetery via the driveway loop, away from my car. She took a left at the gate and I watched her headlights rise and fall with the dips in the road until they faded away completely.

We moved forward, but without a flashlight of our own, we had to use the tiny bit of lamplight and my memory to get me to the headstone she'd knelt in front of. We looked down into blackness. It was impossible to read in the dark. I swore. Had the chemo destroyed all of my brain cells? I had a flashlight in the car and I hadn't thought to grab it.

I turned to go get it when Julie stopped me. "Singer, wait."

She pulled out her cell, which had a large screen, and flicked it on. The light wasn't great, but all I needed to do was make out a name and maybe a date. She turned the weak electronic light on the headstone. Inscribed in brass on the flat headstone were the last words I'd expected to see:

MICHAEL A. WHEELER
1968–1997
BELOVED BROTHER

"Jesus," I said, stunned.

"What the hell is this?" Julie asked, her voice hoarse.

I said nothing.

"Singer?"

I traced the letters with my fingers, feeling light-headed and strange. "I don't know."

"If he's . . . Marty, who's doing all of this? Who's following Amanda?"

"I don't *know*, I said."

I crouched there with my brain racing, trying to reorganize years of memories and assumptions that had been set into solid, inflexible lines while simultaneously trying to assimilate how it changed our situation right now. All the pent-up feelings of guilt and anger now had question marks beside them. Not erased. Put into doubt. If I could believe the writing under my hand, Wheeler had still gotten away with something, but not for very long. And whoever was torturing Amanda now probably knew something about that.

I stood up. "Let's go."

"Where?"

"Back to town," I said, striding back to the car. Julie ran to keep up.

"For what?"

"To see if that really is Wheeler under that rock," I said.

"Who's going to tell us that?"

"We've only got one resource down here, so let's use it."

◆   ◆   ◆

I retraced our drive, heading downtown and parking near the visitors' center. The downtown scene was lively, with the antique and gift shops spilling light onto the sidewalk and street, tempting passersby on their way out to dinner. There was more traffic than there had been during the day and I had to circle the block three times before I found a parking spot outside the police department. It was a small building with a red-brick façade and old-timey globe lights that allowed it to blend in with the other quaint buildings on the street. Julie and I went inside. A petite blonde lady in uniform sat behind a Plexiglas window. I walked up to it and asked for Hanson.

"Officer Doug Hanson?" the duty officer asked.

"Do you have another Hanson?" I asked.

"No."

"That's him, then."

She asked me to wait and picked up the phone. Julie sauntered over to look at the curling "Just Say No" posters, hugging herself, while I stayed by the desk. The receptionist stared at a spot above and to the left of my head while it rang, then her face brightened as someone picked up on the other end. There was a quick exchange, then she turned to me.

"What's your name, sir?"

"Singer," I said. "Tell him we spoke this afternoon."

She relayed the message, then looked up again. "He'll be right out."

Three minutes later, Hanson came through a door and around the counter. The mirrored shades and cowboy hat were gone, making him look ten years younger. He had a half-smile on his face. "Singer. Why am I not surprised?" he asked. "You find your man?"

"You could say that." I filled him in.

He whistled after I'd finished. "So this guy you've been looking for is dead?"

"Maybe."

"Mission accomplished, then, huh?"

"Not quite. I need some background on how he died. A coroner's report, case file, anything."

"You'll only get that if he didn't die a natural death."

"I know this guy. I'm going to bet on unnatural," I said. "Think you could dig any of that up for me?"

His eyebrows shot up to his hairline. "Is that all? Why don't I turn in my badge and gun now and save my boss the trouble of asking? You know, since you're not a cop anymore and if he caught me feeding a civilian police reports it could be my hide."

I tried to look sheepish. "Don't do it if I'm putting you out."

"You're serious?"

"A girl's life might be on the line, Hanson," I said. "And this was our last lead."

He gave me a long, steady look, then sighed heavily. "Damn it. I'll need some time to dig this stuff up. Swing back around in a couple of hours."

I nodded. "Thanks. Uncle Bill would be proud."

The half-smile was sour. "Yeah, yeah."

He shooed us out of there and we walked outside into the dark. Julie looked at me. "So, we've got a couple of hours to kill."

"Looks like it," I said.

"Then let's pretend we're relaxing," she said, taking my arm. "And forget we're waiting to see the coroner's report on a killer that isn't supposed to be dead."

So we strolled the brick streets of Waynesboro, admiring store displays and occasionally ducking into shops to chase the chill away. If the decorations were any indication, Christmas was tomorrow, but the tinsel and plastic elves had probably been up for a month already. I caught myself looking down at Julie and smiling, which stirred a jumble of emotions, both bad and good. It had been a long time since I'd been attracted to someone enough to saunter down a city street, arm in arm, looking at dopey holiday decorations and enjoying it. But the cynic in me asked, how long would it last? I pushed those doubts aside, squeezing them into a hole, and gave myself permission to have a good time.

◆　◆　◆

Two hours later we were sitting in the space opposite Hanson's desk, squeezed into two small plastic chairs. His workspace was neat as a pin, with a computer monitor arranged precisely in one corner of the desk and a day planner open to the correct date in front of him. A slim folder rested on the edge nearest me.

I looked around the open office. "Not worried about your boss?"

"He went home early and I'm the only one on call."

"No crime sprees in Waynesboro?" I asked.

"Just the one in here," he said, tapping the folder. He looked at Julie and stuck out a hand. "You know, we weren't introduced there, out on the street."

"Julie Atwater."

He waited for more. "She was Wheeler's defense attorney at the original trial," I said. "That's what an asshole he is. Even his own lawyer wants to see him put away."

He raised his eyebrows and said, "I think you mean was."

"You're sure?"

"I'll let you be the judge of that," he said. He opened the folder and wet a finger before flipping through the pages. "Michael Anthony Wheeler. Male Caucasian. Age, twenty-eight. Blue eyes, brown hair. Occupation, unknown. Found dead in a Dumpster outside Randy's Roadhouse on Sperryville Pike, February 19, 1997. Cause of death would be the blunt force trauma administered to his head and face by approximately twenty-three blows with a pipe or similar object."

"Jesus," Julie said.

Hanson turned forward a page, then back. "Positive ID on him, though dental identification was delayed because of the, uh, trauma."

"How'd they make the ID?"

"Looks like Wheeler had been living with Green, who'd reported him missing four days prior to the discovery. Somebody at the station made the connection and brought her in to look at the body. She confirmed the clothes he had on were gifts she recognized. Fingerprints came back for one hundred percent confirmation that it was Wheeler. Even with the ID, though, the investigation went nowhere. No witnesses, no murder weapon, no remains other than the body itself. They chased the sister for a while, but she was cleared."

"No possible mistake on the ID?" I asked. "I can't afford to be wrong on this."

"Look for yourself," he said, gesturing at the file. "The paperwork is pretty clear."

"Who contacted MPDC?" I asked.

Hanson licked another finger and rifled through the pages, then shook his head. "No contact was made."

"No contact?" I stared at him. "The guy was a former DC cop."

He shrugged. "It's not in the notes. Let's see. Looks like he hadn't been in town long. Living with Green. No known job. No friends, no associates. Hadn't even been in the Roadhouse the night before, according to bouncers and bartenders. The body was just dumped there."

"And she didn't mention to anyone that he'd been a cop?"

"If she did, no one wrote it down."

"Who ran the investigation?"

"Jay Palmer," Hanson said. "Good detective."

"Where is he? Can I talk to him?"

Hanson shook his head again. "Jay had a stroke five years ago. Died a year into retirement."

I cursed. "Would anybody else know anything? Wasn't this some kind of news around here, for crying out loud?"

"It was before my time, but I remember some of the older cops talking about it when I first transferred. Vicious thing like that, looked like a mob hit from the movies. But Wheeler wasn't a local boy and interest fizzled out once Jay couldn't pin it on anyone. People chalked it up to a big-city payback or a bad drug deal or something like that. The less we had to do with it, the better."

Julie stepped in. "Somebody gets their head beat in so bad you can't figure out who he is and no one's interested?"

"After a couple of months, yeah."

"What was Palmer's excuse? Why didn't he follow up?"

"You know . . ." Hanson started, then closed the folder and smoothed his hands over his desk. "You know, I couldn't tell you. He was a good guy and a good cop. I was going to get all righteous on you, but truth is, this is a tenth of the paperwork we'll get for a hit-and-run, never mind a gangland-style execution. Looks like he dropped the ball on this one."

I gestured to the file. "You mind?"

"Be my guest."

I opened the file and glanced through the reports. I was done with the pages in a minute. Hanson was right—there was nothing in the file. I generated more paperwork filling out a prescription. Palmer might've had a reputation as a solid cop, but you wouldn't know it from this case file. The whole thing stunk. Kransky should've seen Wheeler's murder come up on his radar in the first ten seconds of his search, but there'd been nothing. It made me distinctly uncomfortable, because it took some serious clout to shove something like this under a rug.

"How would you feel if I went and talked to Layla again?" I asked.

He shook his head. "Not good. I don't mind helping you out, but you start bothering her and she calls my department and complains, it'll come out that I knew you were up there once already."

"And Palmer's dead," I said. "He have a partner?"

"No," he said. "We're too small. He might've taken somebody on for a big case, but this was picked up and dropped too quick for that."

I was quiet, out of ideas. I'd go see Layla anyway if I had to, but I doubted it would be worth the potential ill will I might stir up with Hanson and his boys.

"Sorry it didn't help," he said.

I opened my mouth to say something, but my phone rang. I pulled it out and took a look. It was Kransky. I nodded an apology to Hanson and stepped away.

"Kransky," I said. "I'm in the middle of something. What's up?"

"Time to come home, Marty."

The way he said it made the blood drop out of my face and pool somewhere around my knees. "What's wrong?"

"My contact in Records called back," he said. "He cross-checked some payroll files, attendance rolls, bunch of other sources that aren't housed in the same locations as the personnel files. Still didn't find out who deleted the files, but he was able to tell that *two* records were wiped out, not one."

"Two? Whose was the other?"

"Lawrence Ferrin's."

My heart leapt to my throat. "Wheeler's partner."

"That's not all. Something about our search got under my buddy's skin. He dug around on the Internet. Looks like Lawrence quit MPDC a year after the Wheeler trial, kicked around for a while, then got thrown in the can ten years ago on a rape and battery charge somewhere in Indiana. Served his time, paid his dues, and got out. Want to guess when he was released?"

"Tell me," I said.

"Two weeks ago. They're on a mission, Marty."

"Christ," I said. "Wait, 'they'?"

"Wheeler and Ferrin," he said. "Aren't you listening?"

"Shit," I said, wincing. Why hadn't I called Kransky to tell him about Wheeler? I knew the answer, but didn't want to admit it: I'd been waltzing around town with Julie, dreaming of another bout of passion in the car with her. "Maybe not."

"What are you talking about?"

I took a deep breath, then told him what we'd stumbled across, from Wheeler's grave to Hanson's homicide report.

There was a dead silence on the other end.

"Kransky? You there?"

Still nothing.

"Jim?"

"I'm here," he said. But his voice was flat, atonal. I could sense the feeling of disbelief and bitterness. A few more seconds of silence passed, then, "You're sure?"

"Short of exhuming the body. The report this cop Hanson scratched up for me has more holes than I can count, but it's official enough."

He swore. "I've spent the last twelve years thinking he's out in the world. Alive."

"You and me both."

"Where's this leave us?"

"Not sure, though I've got a real desire to look up Lawrence Ferrin," I said.

"It bother you he's the son of an ex-chief of police?"

"Maybe," I said. "And we both know Jim Ferrin was dirty as the day is long."

"Is he in on it, too?"

"I don't know," I said. "If he is, we've got more trouble on our hands than I thought."

VIII.

"I asked you not to interfere."

"Hello, son," the old man said. "Good to hear from you, too."

The other's voice was terse. "Call your idiots off. They were stumbling all over campus yesterday, trying to look like tourists."

"Those two never could do a tail." He coughed, a wet sound. "Tell me, what is it you're trying to do, exactly? What am I supposed to not interfere with? Your note wasn't very specific."

"If I tell you, do I have your promise not to get in my way?"

The old man sighed. "Yes."

He told him.

"And that's going to give you your life back? That's what you've been dreaming of these last twelve years?"

"You don't approve?"

"I do if this is it," the old man said. "If it's over after this. If it isn't, I'll have to bring you in myself. My way."

"It's all I need." A pause. Readying himself for an argument. "Are you going to get in my way?"

The old man paused. "No, son. No, I believe I'm going to help you."

CHAPTER TWENTY-SEVEN

Our conference with Hanson ended quickly. I thanked him for his help, grabbed Julie's hand, and bolted. It would've been nice to have talked to Layla again to answer some questions that Hanson's report had raised. Or tracked down Palmer's widow, try to see if the detective had kept private notes on Wheeler's killing. But Kransky's news about the deleted records balled all those ideas up and dumped them in the shitter. We jumped in my car and headed north. Julie and I hashed and rehashed what Wheeler's apparent death meant. I tried not to say much about the issue that was truly bothering me, but had forgotten Julie was a lawyer: she could sniff out an omission from a mile away.

"Lawrence Ferrin," she said at one point, musing. "Son of Jim Ferrin, right?"

"The one and only," I said. "Hopefully."

"He slipped through some corruption charges, I remember. Pretty bad character."

"Pretty bad," I said, watching the road.

"Are we looking at a father-son thing here?" she asked. "Should we be worried?"

"More worried than we are now? I don't know. If the older Ferrin is involved, probably. He was a scary son of a bitch when he was on the force. Had his own personal cadre of crooked cops in all the departments. Kind of a blue mafia. Though he never got pinned with anything."

"He retired a few years ago?"

"Yeah. Doesn't mean he's less connected, just not as official."

"What's our next step, then?"

"Kransky's going to run the same background checks and searches he did when we thought we were dealing with Wheeler."

She looked out the window into the black. "That didn't help very much."

"We didn't know Wheeler was dead at the time," I said. "Ferrin is almost certainly alive and kicking, so hopefully he's left a fresh trail we can follow. Then we put him away."

"And if his father's involved, too?"

"Then we do the world a favor and put him away, too."

"You make it sound easy."

Anything I would've said would've been a lie, so I didn't say anything. She took my silence for what it was worth and matched it with one of her own. Miles of farmland rolled by, lit occasionally by a lonesome golden rectangle of light coming from a home or the sterile glow of a white light over a barn. Fifteen minutes later, she asked me, "Why would the old man be involved?"

"If his kid and not Wheeler is the one responsible for everything— possibly even Brenda's murder—then it means he's been covering for him for more than a decade. Maybe all the way back to the trial. Though that's speculation. Maybe it's as simple as Lawrence went crazy in stir those ten years. The old man doesn't have to be involved at all."

She nodded, but didn't reply. Her gaze traveled out into the darkness, watching fence posts pass by. I had the sense she wanted to keep talking. But she curled up in the wedge between the seat and the door and fell asleep instead. She woke an hour later when I crossed over a set of train tracks that shook the car like we'd been run off the road.

She took a deep breath, floating to consciousness. A moment later, she said, "Where are you going when we get back?"

I hadn't thought about it. Going back to my place—with its revolving door marked "Bad Guys"—didn't seem like the smartest option right now. "I don't know."

"Stay with me," she said.

I didn't say anything. Maybe I leered. A little.

She gave me a smoky look. "Until we get this thing fixed, Singer. Then you're on your own."

Two hours later, I pulled up beside Julie's car at the Metro station parking lot, exhausted. The bones of my hands were somehow simultaneously numb and aching, and I could still feel the vibration of the car, as though I'd steered by holding on to the engine block instead of the wheel. She got into her car and I followed her to the Great American Extended Stay on Route 50, a place with nice long-term rates, if their billboard was telling the truth. I found a dark corner in the back of the hotel's parking lot to hide my car, then met Julie by the front entrance. She smiled when she saw me, though the corners of her mouth quivered and her expression looked brittle.

"Feeling weird?" I asked.

"A little," she said. "I haven't exactly batted a thousand with my relationships."

"I could sleep on the couch if it'll make you feel any better."

"That's just stupid," she said.

We went inside, toting our day bags that were going to turn into night bags. Instead of plodding down one of the anonymous corridors on the lower levels, however, when we got in the elevator, Julie punched the top floor. We exited into a foyer with four doors. The halls below us had ten or twenty doors for the same space. Julie fished her keys out and unlocked one marked "C." She bounced the door open with a hip and walked in. I followed her into an enormous suite, complete with kitchen, office, and separate bedroom. It smelled of glass cleaner and potpourri. The living room had a fireplace, a flat-screen TV, and a wet bar. A sliding glass door led out to a balcony with a wide-angle view of the Potomac and the Washington Monument.

I turned to look at her, eyebrow raised. "I thought you said Wheeler ruined your career."

She smiled wanly. "I decided if my life was in danger, I'd be damned if I was going to stay in some fleabag motel out on the Beltway. Besides, I'm charging it. If we live through this, I'll worry about it next month."

I dropped my bag and went into the living room, pacing the perimeter, too jittery to sit down. I walked over to the sliding glass door. It whispered open on oiled tracks and I stepped out to look over the city. The Washington Monument gleamed ivory in the night, erupting out of the landscape like a ghostly tusk. The wedding cake outline of the Capitol building was visible to the right, its sculpted dome and fluted walls giving it more architectural heft. But the straight lines and honest corners of George's memorial appealed to me more than the Byzantine stretches of the Capitol.

The door slid open and Julie joined me, near enough that I could feel her body heat. We stood, sharing the silence. The air had a crystalline snap, that strange quality in winter that makes it seem as if ice is hanging in sheets around you and sounds from the far distance are delivered to you like they'd occurred within arm's reach. Julie broke the spell when she gave me an apologetic look and lit a cigarette. I shrugged. It had been a nerve-wracking twenty-four hours; she was allowed her vices.

I went back inside and rooted around the fireplace until I found three good pine logs. Some bark and a balled-up *Washington Post* sports section under the andiron made a decent fire-starter. I lit the bundle with a long match from a box on the mantel and watched as the flames licked upward into a bright orange cone. I sat, mesmerized by the fire until Julie came in, bringing a rush of cold air with her that fanned the flames two feet high. I clambered to my feet with a grunt and turned.

Julie stood in front of me, her eyes diving into mine. I looked back at her, then raised my hands to her shoulders and slid them up to her neck. I cupped her face. She said nothing. I leaned in and kissed her slowly. Her mouth parted. She tasted of smoke, which doesn't normally make my top five turn-ons, but the acrid sensation on my tongue had the opposite effect and my heart tripped into overdrive. We stripped the couch of all its pillows, leaving it shamefully bare, and in a minute so were we. I got up only to turn the lights off and then we made love in front of the fire and under the gaze of the city.

◆ ◆ ◆

I wouldn't have won any awards.

I was tired, worried, sick with a potentially fatal disease. My awareness of those problems curled in on itself and threatened to derail what confidence and energy I had. But Julie was gentle and patient and I think that was where the real lovemaking took place, not in the thunder and lightning of the act, but her acceptance—without pity—of my situation and the way we worked around it. We slept on the floor afterward until the fire had died down into embers both cherry-sized and colored and the chill crept up over our shoulders like a blanket. Julie nudged me and we got up and stumbled to the bed and under the covers, where people over thirty are supposed to sleep.

◆ ◆ ◆

Sometime in the middle of the night, I woke. Eyes open, lucid, wide awake. Not panicked or alarmed, though I must've stirred or made a sound, because Julie's arm reached out in her sleep, slid down my arm, wrapped around my waist. Her warmth joined mine. We stayed that way for long minutes, until I began dropping off again. My thoughts—cohesive a moment ago—fragmented, separated, drifted apart on a sleepy current. I thought about my life, which had seemed a lot like death until recently, and how meeting Amanda had changed it for the better in one way and how meeting Julie again had made it worth living in another. I fought to linger on that thought, to anchor it down and savor it, but it split and flowed through and around my mind, evaporating into nothingness.

I slept.

◆　◆　◆

A few hours later, the angry insect buzz of my phone woke me a third time. I eased out of bed and padded out to the living room where I'd left my pants, hoping to snag the call before it fell through. It was Kransky.

"Singer, where are you?"

"At Julie's," I said, hesitating. "We got back late."

There was a pause, then, "It's that way, huh?"

"It is," I said. "Any problems?"

"Would it matter if there were?"

"Not really."

"Then why ask?"

Something in his tone took my patience between finger and thumb, snapped it in half. "You call me with something important, Jim, or just to punch me in the nuts?"

"I need to drop Amanda off with you or find another place for her. I got a call this morning from IAD. They want me in at eight and I don't know how long I'll be."

"Internal?" I said, surprised. "What about?"

"They're reviewing a case where I potted a meth dealer on a bust two years ago." He let the statement hang in the air.

"Two years ago?"

"Uh-huh."

"Let me guess. The case was reviewed, you were cleared, and no one's mentioned it since then."

"Pretty much."

"Sounds like we poked the bear." I walked over to the window, looked out at a different, less romantic view of Washington. It seemed scuzzy and brittle in the morning winter light. "Can you handle it?"

"This is the warning shot, not the thumbscrews. Someone's going to be checking my computer searches, logging phone calls, maybe tailing me. If it looks like I've gone off the reservation, they'll have the excuse they need."

"Jim Ferrin has that much pull?"

"Maybe not with everyone, not all the time. But he has enough to make life miserable."

Decorative white molding framed the window. I traced one of its ridges with my thumbnail. "You know what I'm going to say next, right?"

"Yeah. And I'm still in. I told you, I'd do whatever had to be done to make things right. But maybe next time don't kick me in the teeth when I ask about you and your new lady while I'm getting fucked by IAD," he said, then hung up.

Julie had gone into the kitchen while I was talking and rummaged around until she found what she needed to make coffee and toast. I explained the situation to her while we ate and sipped coffee out of the anonymous white hotel mugs.

"Where does that leave us?" she asked. Her face was pensive. She made connections quickly. "You said last night we could use Kransky to run Lawrence down, maybe even start a real investigation. If Kransky gets taken away, what do we have left?"

"Jim Ferrin has influence, but he doesn't own the MPDC outright. If the worst he can do is ruin Kransky's day with a couple of meetings, then we'll be all right."

"What if he can do more than that?"

I pinched the bridge of my nose. "I don't know, Julie. Kransky's not the only guy in the MPDC I know. They can't all be on Jim Ferrin's bankroll. We'll have to play it by ear."

She was quiet, then said, "Is Amanda coming here?"

I winced. "I should've asked."

She shook her head. "Don't worry about it. We're running out of options. I'll set up the office for her."

I took a hot shower and dressed quickly, wanting to be downstairs to meet Kransky and escort Amanda into the building. The elevator whisked me to the first floor, where I walked the halls until I found the back door that led to the loading dock. Custodial staff glanced at me as I walked through the bay leading to the dock, but an air of authority and a frown go a long way sometimes. Once I hit the dock, I jogged down the steps to the alley in the back of the hotel. Dumpsters and delivery trucks were lined up in white-lined stalls. An eight-foot-high cyclone fence topped with razor wire separated the hotel from the hillside behind it.

The corner of the building gave me enough cover to case the parking lot. The morning was sharp with cold and overcast like a sheet had been thrown over everything, giving off that kind of ambient, soapy-gray light that makes eight o'clock look the same as four. I flexed my hands and wiggled my fingers to keep the cold away, but my new sensitivity made my stakeout even more miserable than it had been as a beat cop.

Nothing jumped out at me. Traffic on 50 was vicious as usual, a thousand pissed-off people, one to a car, tailing each other into work. The parking lot was placid in comparison, with only two cars either pulling in or out the entire time. The second car was Kransky's, this time in a blue station wagon. He took his time, circling the parking lot at a snail's pace, checking each car out as he passed. I stepped out from my hidey-hole as they came near and let him see me. Kransky stopped, Amanda waved.

They conferred, then she got out and opened the back door to grab her bag. I glanced over the parking lot, then leaned through the passenger's side window. Kransky looked at me with his bladed face. The only evidence of stress he showed at either the guard duty he'd pulled or the impending IAD investigation were light blue smudges under each eye. He probably hadn't slept in the last two or three days.

"How are you going to play it at the hearing?" I asked.

"Cool, calm, and collected," he said. "I don't want to give them any excuses to label me a hard case."

"Call me when you're through. We need to huddle up on strategy."

"You got it."

"Thanks, Jim."

A flicker of a smile crossed his face, then left, as though the current had been turned on by accident, then shut off. "You're welcome, partner."

He took off and Amanda and I went inside. Her face wasn't closed, exactly, but she looked thoughtful on the ride up the elevator.

"What's up?" I asked.

She picked at the stitching on her jacket. "Jim told me what you found in Waynesboro."

"Hard to swallow?"

She nodded. "I'm feeling lost. Michael turns out to be dead. The bogeyman of half my life turns out to be nothing. This guy Ferrin . . . I don't even know who he is, but it turns out he's the one who wants to kill me. Then Jim gets a call this morning and he won't tell me what's happening, just mumbles something about people having connections, making life hard for us. What's going on, Marty?"

I gave her the rundown I'd offered to Julie and intercepted many of the same questions. And, like Julie, she had the same kind of controlled dismay on her face.

"Listen, I know it seems like we're starting over again, but we're not," I said. "We thought we knew who we were dealing with and we were wrong, which is why we were running into walls. Now we know who we're up against. Lawrence has connections. But so do we. I'll get on the horn with some friends of mine, guys in the department and the prosecutor's office who weren't any friends of Jim or Lawrence Ferrin. We'll nail them to the wall. You're not going to have to worry about any of them soon."

She gave me a wan smile, trying to look reassured for my benefit, but it had been another pep talk. And we both knew it.

CHAPTER TWENTY-EIGHT

Once we got up to the apartment, Julie gave Amanda a hug and got her settled in. I camped out in the office and made some calls to find out what I could about Kransky's predicament, Jim Ferrin's current status in the world, and what—if anything—anyone knew about his son. But either the old man's reach was longer than I thought or there just wasn't anything to know, because no one had any answers for me. I sighed in disgust and went back out to the main room. The two were on opposite ends of the couch, talking. I looked in the refrigerator for something to drink but the inside of the thing was white, cold, and empty.

"Since you've been with me for the last day and a half, I think I know the answer to this," I called to Julie, "but you don't have anything to drink, do you?"

She looked over. "I don't cook."

"I . . . never mind," I said. "We still have drinks in the car, right? In the cooler?"

She shot me a look.

"Ah, of course we do. I'll be right back. Lock the door after me."

They waved and I headed downstairs.

◆ ◆ ◆

"You see Singer yet?" Jackson said. "Or Jailbird?"

Taylor held his phone in one hand, a pair of Zeiss binoculars in the other, scanning the parking lot across the street. He spoke without putting them down. "No. And if the old man hears you say Jailbird, he'll cut your balls off."

"Sorry," Jackson said without a hint of apology. He was eating pistachios and Taylor could hear him cracking the shells over the phone. "I was referring to Target One, Sergeant Taylor."

"Don't be an asshole. Okay, there's Singer. He just came out of the building."

"He leaving?"

A pause. "No. Looks like he's screwing around with the car. Anything on your end?"

"Nothing."

They held the line open while Taylor kept the binoculars locked on the parking lot. A minute passed, with nothing but the sounds of chewing filling the line.

"Jackson, could you please put the phone down while you eat? You sound like a fucking cow."

"Yes, SIR. Right away, sir—hey, hey."

"You got something?"

"Hell, yes. Target One pulling up to the loading dock, plain as day. White panel van, red logo on the side."

Taylor tossed the binoculars on the passenger's seat and started the truck. "It's go time. Give me five, then drop the hammer on Jailbird. Let's get done with this shit."

◆ ◆ ◆

I pulled out the cooler full of drinks that I could thank for starting my amorous romp with Julie, then looked around inside. My car was full of the crap that seems to accumulate on any trip: used tissues, crumpled-up receipts, a soda can or two, gum wrappers. I put the cooler down and started scooping the garbage and shoving it in a bag. I wasn't much good as an investigator; the least I could do is keep my car clean.

I was on my knees on the passenger's side, trying to reach a plastic cup that was maddeningly out of reach, when the whole car bucked and shook, accompanied by the scream of metal on metal. My head smacked against the bottom of the dash and stars shot across my vision, but I had my gun halfway out of the holster as I scrambled backward and away from the car.

An old GMC was half in, half out of the space next to mine. The part that was half in was actually *into* the back fender of my car and had lifted it about eight inches off the ground. A guy hopped out of the GMC. Short, trim, close-cropped dark hair sprinkled with gray.

"Shit, man," he said, looking at my fender. "Damn."

I gave him a once-over, then slid the gun back in its holster and came around to the other side. I stared at the side of my car. I was too amazed to say anything at first: I had driven almost three hundred miles the day before without getting hit by so much as a mosquito. I pull into a parking lot in Arlington and someone causes two thousand dollars' worth of bodywork to my car. I looked at the monstrous truck.

"What the hell?" I said. "I know that thing is big, but you weren't even close."

The guy closed his door and bent down to look at the damage, hands in the pockets of his windbreaker. "Don't look too bad. You pull the fender out right there, bet you could still drive the thing. Here, let's give it a shot."

"Hey, don't touch that," I said. "We have to call the insurance company."

"Sorry, friend," the guy said, placid. It looked like his pulse had barely lifted a beat despite having pushed his bumper a foot into my car. "No insurance. I mean, I'm sorry and all, but you can drive it, right?"

I took a closer look at the guy. He had sweat on his upper lip and smelled heavily of the kind of faux aftershave–body spray they sell cheap at the drugstore. The way he held himself, the set of his shoulders, looked familiar and bothered me. "You have any ID?"

He looked surprised. "I'm not going to give you my license, man. I can pay cash, if you want. What do you say?"

"I don't need cash," I said. "I need a name. And you're going to give it to me."

"Fuck that," he said, looking angry. But with a trace of a smile at the same time. The arrogance, the overall look . . . something clicked. I reached for my gun.

Things happened fast. I heard the deep-throated roar of a big engine from across the street and glanced over to see a blue Mustang rocket into the far side of the parking lot. In that second, a fist caught me on the side of the face, above the cheekbone. The guy was carrying brass knuckles, a roll of quarters, something. It felt like a bat wrapped in a blanket. Which is to say, soft but not nearly soft enough. I bounced off the trunk of my car and slid to the ground. I could hear, but things were going black real fast.

I felt, rather than heard, the slim figure crouch next to me. Lips moved close to my ear. "Name's Taylor, asshole."

And then I was out.

◆ ◆ ◆

He hadn't wanted to hit her, but there wasn't much time.

He'd made the big GMC easily, squatting in the parking lot across the street like a tank. But his father would've sent more than one of his flunkies to handle the job. So there was a second car. Probably driven by the guy he'd spotted wandering around GW's campus trying to look like a student or a parent, but looking exactly like what he was: an ex-cop.

So, with Amanda out cold, he put his gun on the older one, the lawyer. She, at least, cooperated, and both were wrapped like Christmas presents in under a minute. He dragged them into the bedroom, then ran back out to the foyer, leaving the front door unlocked. Eyes darting, he scanned the little hall. There was a utility closet to one side of the elevator. The lock was stubborn, but he had the door open in a few seconds and ducked inside. The smell of bleach and orange-scented disinfectant filled his nose as he crouched in the dark, watching through a crack in the door. He heard and felt the rumbling of the shaft gears long before the elevator door opened.

It was the clown from the campus, just like he'd thought, coming out of the elevator holding something in both hands like a gun, but smaller. A Taser. So, his father wanted him alive. He smiled and waited for the idiot to move into the apartment, then slipped his gun into its holster, pulled out a Benchmade folding knife, and followed. Might as well make this one quiet.

I came to feeling like my head was split in half. Cinders and chunks of asphalt ground into my back, so I guessed I was still in the parking lot. One leg was bent underneath me and after a second I could tell I was under the bumper of my own car, so I hadn't been moved.

Weak, I inched my way from underneath the car and unwound my leg from its pretzel shape. The motion made my head wobble painfully, too much, and I puked to the side. I groaned and pawed my way to my feet, using the bumper as a crutch.

The GMC was gone. I held my watch up, trying to move my head as little as possible. Not twenty minutes had passed since I'd come down from Julie's rented condo. A couple quick pats on the way up told me what I didn't want to know. I groaned. Gun, wallet, and keys: all gone. I was dead in the water.

Or maybe just dead, depending on what was waiting for me. I felt stupid and reckless, angry at myself for being taken in the parking lot so easily. I limped to the entrance of the apartment, trying not to panic. There was no one in the lobby and I hurried to the elevator.

It opened at Julie's floor. I hurried across the foyer and listened at her door.

Nothing.

I pushed the door wide and saw nothing in the hall. I took a sniff, hoping not to smell cordite or something worse, then padded down the hall into the living room.

Facedown on the carpet in front of the fireplace where Julie and I had made love just hours ago was a large man, a white guy in a black peacoat. A full moon of blood was spread into the carpet beneath him, originating from his throat, which had been slashed. One arm was bent awkwardly under his body. I searched him quickly, keeping half an eye and ear out for someone coming out of the bedroom or office.

The guy had a .38 stainless Smith & Wesson still in a shoulder rig, a speedloader in a pocket of the windbreaker, fifty-four bucks in a wallet with no ID, and a cell phone. A handful of pistachios rattled around in the other pocket. I filched the money and the phone and felt a hell of a lot better with a gun in my hand. Wincing a little at the blood, I gave his face the once-over, but didn't recognize him at first. White, mid-forties, broad in the face and the gut. Then I thought about how the guy who had slugged me had looked familiar and some things clicked into place.

I left him and headed down the back hallway, feeling sick. The office was clear, but I almost lost it when I saw a body on the bed. Then I saw movement.

It was Julie. A ream of duct tape bound her hands and feet, wrapped around her wrists and ankles sloppily. Another length of it covered her mouth. Her eyes were wide, the whites showing, and she was yelling or screaming behind the tape. I shoved the gun in a back pocket and ripped the tape away.

She gasped and started crying. "Oh, God. Marty."

I worked on the rest of the tape, having to cut it with my teeth to get it started, and ripped it away frantically. I finally got it off her and then wrapped Julie in my arms as she shuddered and cried. I stroked her hair and patted her back until the shaking stopped. She pushed me away. Tears streaked her face, but her voice was steady.

"I'm okay. I'm okay," she said. She grabbed my head with her hands. "You've got to get that bastard."

"Was it Lawrence?"

She closed her eyes, opened them. "It must be. He kicked through the door right after you left. He had Amanda tie me up, then dragged both of us back here, like he was waiting for you. Amanda tried to make a run for it, but he hit her. She looked like she was out cold to me."

"Then someone came in?"

She started to shake again. "I was so scared, Marty. I thought it was you and I tried to scream. He was out in the living room and I heard a fight. He came back a minute later, covered in blood. God, I thought it was yours."

I kissed her. "Not me. I'm right here. Little worse for wear, but alive. He took Amanda?"

She nodded. "He carried her out like a sack."

I grabbed her hand. "Okay, I'm going to need you to keep it together. The guy whose blood was all over Lawrence is out on the living room floor. We're going to head outside and we'll get you someplace safe."

"What about Amanda?" she asked, then her eyes widened as she took a good look at my face. "And, oh my God, what happened to you?"

"It's all wrapped up in the same thing," I said. "We were set up, but so was someone else. They just didn't know it."

"Where's Amanda, then?"

"I'm not sure," I said, pulling her to her feet. "But I think I know someone who has a good idea."

I got Julie outside, shielding her from the body of the guy on the floor of the apartment. She was a tough lady, and as both a prosecutor and public defender had seen more than her share of gruesome crime scenes, but those had been photos. The real thing was different and not an experience she needed half an hour after being assaulted and tied up by a lunatic.

"Now what?" she asked, hugging herself as we stood on the sidewalk outside the complex.

"I need some room to maneuver," I said. I tried to keep my voice steady, but every second that passed we were losing ground on Lawrence . . . and whatever he wanted to do to Amanda. "Call 911. Get them to take care of you and start processing that mess upstairs."

"What are you going to do?"

"I can't get tied up with the questions they're going to want to ask, so I need to be gone by the time Arlington PD gets here. Can you feed them bull enough bull to keep them off my back but not enough to, uh, get in trouble?"

She smiled weakly. "It's what I do for a living, Marty."

"I need one more thing," I said. "Your car. That guy who almost caved in my face took my keys."

She unclipped her Malibu's keys from the ring and handed them over without a word. I kissed her again, then hurried over to her car. I hopped in, wincing as my head felt every inch of the bounce, and then tore out of the parking lot, throwing a wave to Julie on my way.

I didn't have a destination, but I couldn't hang around. I headed for an overpass pull-off I knew about that would put me thirty seconds from about five major highways. Once I knew where I was going.

Five minutes later and I was skidding to a stop on the pull-off. I kept the car running and pulled out the cell phone I'd found on the dead man in Julie's apartment. It was a new smartphone, with all kinds of bells and whistles, but it didn't take much to figure out how to access the call list. In just a few swipes of my thumb, I found the name I'd been hoping to see.

I took a deep breath and hit REDIAL. It picked up on the second ring. I heard heavy breathing, followed by a cough. "Who the hell is this?"

"Chief," I said. "It's your old pal, Marty Singer."

CHAPTER TWENTY-NINE

There was silence on the other end of the line, then Jim Ferrin said, "You've got Jackson's phone."

"Jackson won't be needing it anymore," I said. "And I need a new phone since your man Taylor decided to step things up from breaking and entering to punching me in the head."

Ferrin wheezed a small, short laugh. "Taylor goes overboard sometimes."

"Do I have this right, Jim? Taylor and Jackson were the ones who broke into my place. And they've been tailing me or Kransky the whole time, which didn't make sense until just now."

There was no answer, so I continued.

"Today was a setup. I thought it was because you and Lawrence were working together on whatever it is he's planning to do. But I don't think you're on the same team, not even close. You were hoping I'd lead you to him, that you'd flushed him out by giving up me and the girl. But . . . for what?"

There was a heavy pause, during which the reedy, bronchial breathing came across the line. Then, "They were supposed to pick him up."

"Why?"

"Do I have to spell it out for you, Singer?" Ferrin snapped. "Lawrence is sick. He's insane. He needs to be stopped."

"This is difficult to swallow, coming from you."

"I'm no saint," Ferrin said. "And I could honestly care less if Lawrence shoots you or Kransky or the girl or the fucking mayor. What I do care about is my good name and the fallout that's going to hit if Lawrence goes through with what he's after."

I squeezed the phone. "And what's that?"

There was a wet croaking sound, which I realized after a second was chuckling. "So this is the play, Singer? You got no idea where he is, so I'm supposed to give him up, just like that?"

"You don't have any better idea than I do where he is, Jim, or you would have hung up as soon as you heard my voice. I'm guessing Taylor went inside after sucker punching me and found his buddy Jackson already on the ground. Lawrence took him out. That wasn't according to plan, so now Taylor's driving around in circles, waiting for orders." Another silence. "So, we're both in the woods. And we need each other to stop Lawrence."

"He's still my son, Singer," Ferrin said. "I'm not going to let you put a bullet in him."

I gritted my teeth. "As much as I'd like to, I'm a hell of a lot more worried about Amanda Lane right now. If he gives her up, no one has to get shot. Now, what do you know? You must've talked to him to set me up."

The pause was so long that I thought he'd hung up. I shouted into the phone. "Goddamn it, Ferrin, if you don't give me something, I swear to God—"

"I don't know." His voice was hoarse. "He said something about starting over, about . . . about a plan to get a second chance. Sounded like a bunch of crap to me, the kind of self-help shit you find in books from the supermarket. But he kept saying it over and over."

"You didn't dig any deeper?"

"I didn't think it would get that far," he said. "Taylor and Jackson were supposed to have brought him in by now. I never expected him to slip past those two."

I chewed the inside of my lip. "A chance to start over? That's all he said?"

Ferrin sighed. "That's it. And this girl is the center of whatever chance that is. Seems to think he can go back in time and unfuck his life."

My mind cranked furiously, but I was drawing a blank. I needed a partner to bounce ideas off of. And Jim Ferrin wasn't it. "I'm going to assume you had Kransky yanked this morning. Can you make that right?"

"I can do that. But I'm warning you, Singer: I want my son alive. You know something, you're going to tell me. I can have someone out to pick Lawrence up in a heartbeat. But if you or Kransky end up shooting him, save a bullet for yourself."

"He took her?" Kransky asked, his voice bleak. He was slumped in the passenger's seat. We were sitting at the corner of H and Fourteenth with the engine idling, minds racing . . . and no place to go.

I nodded. "He's got her."

He looked out the window. "What was all this shit with Jim Ferrin?"

"The old man wants to take Lawrence off the street and, I don't know, lock him in his attic or something. The IAD hearing was to keep you busy while Taylor kept me distracted. Jackson was supposed to tranq Lawrence and take him out in a straitjacket, but ended up getting his throat cut instead. The old man thought he was setting up Lawrence, when it was really the other way around."

"If he wanted his fuckup son off the street, why didn't he just say so? I would've been happy to help."

"Not Jim Ferrin's style," I said. "Always in charge, always giving orders. And if he was able to pull it off while leaving us in the dark, all the better."

Kransky swore. "What's our plan?"

"Ferrin said Lawrence is looking for a chance to start over. And that Amanda was the key to getting that second chance."

"God," Kransky said. "What do we have to work with?"

"Just about nothing," I said, feeling myself starting to tip into despair.

We sat in the bright, late-morning sun, trying to pluck an answer out of thin air. We had all the pieces, but they went to different puzzles.

Kransky blew out a breath. "Maybe the words are important," he said. "Ferrin said Lawrence had 'a plan.' If he just meant to kill Amanda, he would've used different words, right? He'd say off her, snuff her, push her into the river."

I liked the idea but said, "It might only be semantics, Jim."

"Is it? Lawrence spends ten years in prison, examining his life. How he ended up where he did. Who was responsible. How he wants to get it all back. Is he going to use just any words to describe that? Or is he going to pick what he says carefully, methodically?"

"Okay, say the words are significant," I said. "What then?"

Kransky slouched in the seat, his eyes half-closed. "A plan implies elaborate thinking. Complicated timing. Something that takes effort to set up. If he wanted to kill Amanda, he would've shot her in the apartment. So there's something special about the place or the time. A ritual."

"And a ritual has to be something significant in his relationship with Amanda. Something from the past." I stared unseeing into the street, thinking. A mob of people were crossing H Street, but I hardly saw them. "Wheeler's a distraction in all of this. You take him and his obsession with Brenda Lane out of the equation and you're left with Lawrence hiding flowers and sprinkling petals on the ground."

"Flowers," Kransky said, musing. "A courtship. He's in love with her."

"No," I said, feeling something come together. "He's in love with the little girl Amanda *was*."

The answer hit me then. It was like walking into a dark room, stumbling, only to put your hand—by accident—right on the thing you were looking for. Kransky sat bolt upright, seeing it at the same time I did. He opened his mouth to tell me to get going, but I was already turning the key in the ignition and hitting the gas, heading for the only place that Lawrence and Amanda could be.

CHAPTER THIRTY

The drive was just like I remembered it.

It had been around midnight, then. The traffic had been lighter and the cars a different make and model, but the streets were the same. A building here or there had been torn down to make way in the name of progress or real estate, but in a minute I was in a section of the city where the structures had stood for decades, and the terrible feeling of having done all this before doubled and trebled. That first night, I'd been on my way to a murder already committed.

This time, I was trying to stop one.

We tore down Connecticut Avenue and then to Reservoir Road, heading for the Palisades at speed, weaving in and out of the lanes of cars like an angry drunk. Until, that is, we got caught in a snarl of traffic just as Reservoir meets Foxhall and came to a complete stop. I laid on the horn, fuming and wishing, not for the first time, that I had a gumball and a siren.

"There's something you need to know," Kransky said in the momentary lull. I glanced over. He was staring straight ahead, the muscles in his jaw bunched.

An elderly gentleman ahead of us put on his right signal, but began wheeling left, blocking the lane. I hit the horn again. "What?"

He took a couple of deep breaths before he answered. "I knew Brenda Lane."

I waited for more. When it didn't follow, I said, "I know that. You told me you and she met—"

"No, I mean I *knew* her," he said, obviously struggling with the words. "We were sleeping together."

For a split second, my sight went dark. "Jesus Christ."

"We did meet at one of Lacey's school things. I wasn't making that up. But things with Beth were rocky. We were already taking turns with Lacey so we didn't need to be near each other. I went to all of the school functions with her by myself. The almost single dad meets the single mom." He shrugged. "After the third or fourth one, I asked her out."

I didn't say anything. My mind was racing through the implications, from the trial to the disaster we were driving to right now.

"I'm the one who told her to report Wheeler when he wouldn't leave her alone," he said, continuing. "I was afraid if I got in his face or reported him myself, word would get back to Beth. Then a divorce would be a sure thing and she'd have everything she needed to take me to the cleaners. Maybe take Lacey away from me."

I cleared my throat. "Were you with her that night?"

"No. I wanted to. But she told me she wanted some alone time." He laughed without humor. "Ironic, huh? I might've been there and taken out Wheeler and Lawrence myself."

I blinked, trying to put things together. "Was that you down in Waynesboro?"

"You mean, did I off Wheeler?"

I nodded.

He looked out the window. "I wish I had. I know I thought about it. A few nights, when the trial started looking like it was going south, I got my gun out and put it on the dining room table. I stared at it. One small thing—a phone call, a noise outside, a stray thought—and I might've been up and out of there. I would've unloaded the whole magazine into him."

"But?"

"There was Beth. Things were bad between us, but they weren't all the way gone. Yet. And Lacey. She was ten. Did I want her to grow up visiting her dad in maximum security because he shot the man who killed the woman he was cheating on her mom with?"

"And?" I asked, sensing more.

He slammed a fist into the armrest. "And the fact that I'd known Brenda for, what? A month? I wasn't in love with her, I was sleeping with her. Was I supposed to shoot Wheeler for that? Throw my life away for her?"

There was a pause.

"You felt like shit for even thinking it," I said. "You still do."

He nodded.

"And you were hoping the trial would take care of Wheeler for you. When it didn't, you thought you'd failed twice. Which is why it's been eating at you for twelve years."

"I promised myself I was going to take him out one of these days," he said. "But when he vanished, I thought I'd screwed up for a third time. We know what happened, now. For years, though, I blamed myself for that night. I kept looking, ready to go after him, to try and make amends. But I never got the chance and never thought I would. Until now."

We were quiet for a minute, then Kransky said, "It was stupid to keep it from you. I'm sorry."

I swallowed the angry reply that came to mind. Now wasn't the time. "Water under the bridge, Jim. Let's get Amanda and talk about the rest over a beer."

The traffic blocking our way finally parted and I stomped on the gas. We took a hard right onto Arizona Avenue and screamed up the hill. The car caught air as we shot across MacArthur Boulevard at seventy. The car slewed around corners, the back end fishtailing, forcing me to slow down near cross streets if I didn't want to kill everyone on the sidewalk.

We entered the Palisades neighborhood proper, passing row upon row of nearly identical Tudor homes. I swore. "Where the hell is it?"

"A block, maybe two," he said. "Near Willow. There, pull over there. We'll have to hoof it if we don't want him to see us."

The car slid on humped piles of rotting leaves, then skidded to a stop. Kransky threw his seat belt off and pulled out his Glock, checking the action. His movements were controlled, but jerky, almost spastic. He had a wide-eyed look I wasn't comfortable with, like he was ready to jump from the car and make a beeline straight for the Lanes' front lawn. I reached over and grabbed his arm.

"Easy," I said. "We can't afford to screw this up. Control is what we need now."

Kransky closed his eyes, opened them. "All right," I said. "Let's go."

We got out of the car and set off at a jog for Willow Avenue. Half a block away from the old Lane house, we cut through a neighbor's backyard and began a crouched, stalking run, taking cover behind fences, water barrels, and jungle gyms. I caught sight of the back of the property through a wooden slat fence they shared with their Willow Avenue neighbor. We eased up to the fence and peeked through the boards. The back porch light was still on, probably forgotten in the morning rush to get to work, but the interior was dark. A midsized maple, skeletal without its leaves and which had probably been a sapling the last time I was here, shielded part of the second floor from view.

Sweat rolled into my eyes and my head and face throbbed from the punch I'd taken. I blinked the sweat away and ignored the pain while I kept watch on the back windows, looking for movement, shadows, anything. After two or three minutes, I took a deep breath and then motioned Kransky to follow me as I stalked to the end of the property to get a different angle. The maple—which did a decent job of hiding us—also blocked our view, leaving us blind.

I looked at Kransky. "We have to go in. You ready?"

With his eyes locked on the back of the house, he nodded, a sharp bob of his head.

My fingers were numb, almost dead at the ends. I shifted my gun to the other hand and rubbed them together, then shook my whole hand to try and get some feeling back. I gave up, took a new grip on the .38, then slipped through the fence and into the backyard, Kransky on my heels.

We kept the maple between us and the house in case Lawrence was looking down from the second floor, but eventually had to break cover. I counted off *one . . . two . . . three*, then crossed the yard at a jog. I got to the house and put my back to the off-white siding. I listened.

Nothing.

The back door was probably locked, the windows were too loud and too noisy, and there was no simple way into the basement. I eased down the side of the house until I could see around the corner. A white panel van sat in the driveway. Its passenger's side window gave me a marred, shadowy reflection of the front door, which hung open. I could see the frame was splintered around the lock.

I froze as a car came up Willow, made the right onto Macomb, and moved on. When my heart slid back down my throat, I peered around the corner again.

Nothing.

I wiped my face, gripped my gun in both hands, and was getting ready to slip up to the porch when Kransky barreled past me like I wasn't there, knocking me off balance, and headed straight for the front of the house.

I squatted there, stunned. He moved through the door before I could say "Kransky!" in a hoarse whisper, my teeth clenched. Ignoring me, he darted through, his gun up and ready. By the time I sprinted after him and got inside—crouched, gun swinging to cover the doorways left and right to the living and dining room—his back was disappearing down the hall toward the steps to the second floor.

I followed, whipping my revolver back and forth, hoping Ferrin wasn't right here on the first floor, ready to lean out from behind a door and take both of us out with double taps to the back of the head. I jumped as a scream tore through the house, coming from the second floor.

I chased down the hall toward the steps, picking up blurred impressions of sleek, modern furniture and bland colors on the walls as I ran. The decorations were different, the smell and feel completely changed, but the general layout had remained the same and I had trouble remembering if it was me, now, or me, twelve years past. I shoved the memories away and hit the steps running, taking them two at a time. There was a long hall at the top, with four doors along its length, two to a side. The first two were shut, the last two open. The one on the right had been Brenda Lane's bedroom. A trail of blood led into it.

Another scream split the air, followed by a sob. Kransky, already at the end of the hall, turned into the bedroom on the right. I followed.

A man, tied and gagged, lay bleeding in the far corner of the room. The trail of blood led directly to his body. A middle-aged woman, also bound with her hands behind her back, lay next to him, screaming, "Jerry!" A piece of duct tape dangled from one cheek, waving crazily as she cried.

The room had been torn apart. It was still a bedroom, but it was obvious the furniture wasn't right. The bed had been shifted so that the headboard was against the far wall, and a chest of drawers had been pushed into its place. A memory tugged at me and in that instant I saw myself standing there, twelve years earlier, with my finger held in front of me like the barrel of a gun. The bed now occupied the same spot as the bed then. The chest of drawers that blocked my view into the room now was in the same spot the stereo had been a dozen years ago.

On the bed, turning the memory to nightmare, was Amanda. She appeared to be alive, but gagged. The right side of her face was bright red where she'd been hit, and a thin line of blood ran from above her cheekbone to her jaw. She was bound in a painfully intricate position, her head falling off the edge of the bed and her arms sprawled across the pillows in an awkward pantomime of sleep or death. The job had been done with clothesline, so much of it that she looked as if she'd been caught in a spider's web. It was an elaborate but sloppy job, done in haste. Yards of it crossed the room and hooked onto doorknobs, furniture, and bedposts, tied so tightly that she couldn't move her head or arms. Only one foot was free to move a few inches and she kicked at the sheets, but it didn't do anything to dispel the illusion: she was bound in exactly the same position as her mother the night she was killed. Dozens of white petals dotted the room, covering the bed, Amanda, the floor.

Kransky was halfway across the room, maybe to help Amanda, maybe to untie the couple, when he stopped and turned, eyes darting, scanning the room. I had started to move as well when it crystallized for me—Amanda, the re-creation of the murder scene, the trail of blood leading conveniently into the room—in the space between heartbeats. At the end of that one-second interval, I began to turn, knowing we'd been had.

And froze when the touch of a gun barrel to the back of my neck—so cold—told me I was too late. Way too late.

"Easy, Marty," a voice said. "Take it easy. There are good ways to die and bad ways to die, right? Don't be stupid."

"Lawrence," I said.

His lips made a wet sound as he spoke. "This whole thing would've been a lot easier, Marty, if you would've just stayed retired."

My heart drummed in my chest. It took everything I had not to go for the gun pressing into my spine. It would've been suicide. Lawrence knew what was in my head as much as I did. Kransky was no help; he'd half-turned when I'd entered the room, but he was stuck, like I was, helpless. "Sorry to disappoint," I said.

"Kransky, too?" Lawrence said. "This is getting better and better. If only Mike was still around, we'd have ourselves a reunion."

I said, "Nice setup, Lawrence. Like Wheeler did it, that night."

"Wheeler?" Lawrence laughed. "I guess you still haven't figured that one out. Still playing at being a detective, Marty? Star of the MPDC? Only now you don't have the badge, just the gun."

"Why don't you fill me in?"

"You've probably guessed most of it." His breathing sped up, moist and hot on the back of my neck. "My tastes are simple. I only wanted Amanda. She's all I ever wanted. Thinking about her, dreaming about her. It's what got me through ten years, hard time. Not easy, being a cop on the inside. But I had something to look forward to, right?"

His voice changed again, dropping to a growl. "But, Mike, now, Mike had a real thing for the mom. Showing up at all times of the day and night. He was as creepy as they come. But, it's funny, for all that attention he paid her, it wasn't Mike she was getting it on with."

"Shut your mouth," Kransky said. His eyes were like pieces of glass.

"See, this is what drove Mike crazy. The bitch obviously had a thing for cops, but she wouldn't give Mike the time of day. It was Kransky that she jumped into bed with. Mike couldn't stand it. He dragged me over there with him that night, talking big like he always did, bigger than he could act. When it came down to it, though, he couldn't do it. So, here's the big secret, the one we've all been waiting for." He leaned forward, so close his lips brushed my ear while his gun rested against my neck, and said, "Mike didn't do it. I did. I killed her. I killed Brenda for him."

Wet lust filled his voice. I could feel the thrill in him, the carnal satisfaction he had both in the killing and in revealing it to me, transferred from his mouth to my ear. I tilted my head away and he laughed, then grabbed my hair with his free hand and twisted it, yanking my head back. "Thing is, Marty, I realized after I got out that loving Amanda is where everything went wrong. I'd always been sick. But it was Amanda that brought the sickness out. I could've lived with it, hidden it, led a normal life. Instead, the whole ugly side of me that I'd been trying to punch down for all those years . . . it blossomed when I saw her. And my life has been nothing but misery because of it. The longing and the frustration and the imprisonment. But if I get rid of her, here and now, I get to set things right. I get to start over. Right . . . where . . . it . . . all . . . began."

I felt, rather than heard, the hammer being cocked on the gun in his hand, the cylinder turning. And I felt his excitement and his expectation of a new life thrumming through him, coming to me by way of the obscene connection of the gun barrel to my skin. I closed my eyes.

But he was so keyed on the scene in front of him, so utterly absorbed with himself and his plans, that he was deaf to everything else. A voice from the hall yelled "Lawrence!" and he shifted his weight, as if to turn. The tip of the gun left my neck.

I was frighteningly lucid. I could feel the indentation in my skin where the barrel had pressed. I could feel my blood pulse through my body, my breath coming in quick gasps, the sweat trickle down my spine. And what became clear to me in that infinite moment is that, ironically, a man with cancer has more options than one that doesn't. Having already stared my own mortality in the face, I couldn't really be threatened with death.

I lunged down and to the left. As I fell, I saw Kransky's arm swing up. I could tell he was calculating, making the minute corrections that would turn a wild snap shot from the hip into something more than a prayer. But the barrel of his gun was only halfway to level when a deafening clap exploded next to my ear and a blood-red rose bloomed in the center of Kransky's chest. His hand spasmed and the gun went off once, twice into the floor as he was knocked backward with a look of sad surprise on his face.

From the ground, I twisted to face Lawrence, trying to bring my gun up. It was incredibly slow, infinitely clumsy. I knew it was futile.

You could be the fastest draw in the West, but there is no way to beat the speed of a finger pulling a trigger. I could almost taste the bullet that surely had to be on its way through my face and out the back of my head, sending me on my descent into darkness right after. But as I swung the barrel around—so slow—I heard a sharp electrical *crack* from the hallway. Lawrence screamed.

Images of his face and body imprinted themselves on my mind, details I would only remember later. His head was shaved bald and his body was thin to the point of emaciation. An indigo prison tattoo of a web ran up the side of his neck and over part of his head. His eyes were wide, the irises a manic blue, the whites bloodshot and veiny. Black jeans and a T-shirt emphasized his pallor; the shirt clung so tightly to his chest that I could see his sternum through the fabric. Two thin wires trailed from his back like marionette strings. He stood there, his face contorted and twisted, hoarse screams coming from his mouth while his body shook like a tree in a storm.

From the ground, I pointed my gun at him. Lawrence's arm twitched at his side and the black barrel of his gun jerked upward. We shot at the same time, the mingled reports sounding like two schoolbooks hitting a classroom floor. My shot took him low center mass, knocking him backward into the hall and out of sight, but pain erupted in my left shoulder like it had exploded from the inside out. The .38 dropped from my hand as I was punched back to the floor by the force of the shot. I contracted into a ball, cupping my shoulder. I gasped, dragging air in through my open mouth and making animal noises while tears flooded my eyes.

The pain was all I had for what seemed a long time, but then I became aware of a shape coming close. I raised my head, expecting to see Lawrence, who had somehow survived the shot. But the image resolved into someone else, a forty- or fifty-something guy with salt-and-pepper hair. Taylor. My mouth opened, trying to form words, to ask for help. Taylor looked at me, his face devoid and as emotionless as a snowbank. He stayed that way for a moment, as if searching for something, then left my field of view.

Time collapsed inward. I thought I heard sirens, once a welcome sound, now unknown. Amanda screamed through her gag—maybe had been screaming the whole time—and distantly I knew that she was experiencing her own personal hell, a sickening rerun of the worst event of her life. The woman on the floor was sobbing words and sounds. The screams and the cries and the wail of the sirens braided together oddly and I felt like someone should be doing something to help them before they both went insane. But Kransky was gone and I was bleeding onto the rug of the nice people who owned the house and there wasn't much I could do for any of them as I went into shock, wondering listlessly how many cancer victims died of a gunshot wound before their disease had a chance to claim them.

CHAPTER
THIRTY-ONE

The house was thirty minutes north of downtown DC in the town of Potomac, the land of newly minted Internet and real estate millionaires. The old money, disturbed by the invasion of the nouveau riches, had left for horse farms and polo grounds in central Virginia, Kentucky, or Tennessee. New money spent as well as the old, though, and my taxi drove past gates and wrought-iron fences so far from the homes they protected that I had to guess that there actually *were* homes somewhere at the end of those long, serpentine driveways.

The precise rows of pines and swards of dead grass rolling by the window had a calming effect on me, though the Demerol I was popping every few hours probably had more to do with my pleasantly fuzzy outlook than the scenery did. The only distractions from the view were my ultimate destination and the fact that my shoulder was held up by one of those metal props so that it stuck straight out from my body, making it hard to get comfortable. The brace was to keep my shoulder immobilized, or so the doctor who had reconstructed it said.

I needed help taking the edge off the memories and the pills helped with that, too. I'd been filled in by the combined stories of the cops on the scene, Julie, and Amanda. A neighbor had seen us skulking around the old Lane house with our guns out and called the MPDC. But Kransky had died before the ambulance had gotten there, his blood pumped out in a pool around his body. I wasn't sure how Amanda was holding herself together. It was too early to tell what the experience might mean for her tomorrow, or the next day, or the rest of her life. And, of course, I wasn't in great shape myself. There was nothing I wanted more than to go home and start the healing process, to apologize to Amanda, to pick things up with Julie, to find my equilibrium. But there were loose ends to deal with that could still wind up killing all of us if I didn't take care of them now.

The driver let me know when we were nearing our target and he slowed down long enough for me to grunt yes or no as we passed more imposing gates and red-brick driveways. On the fourth look, a drive fitting the description I'd been given came into view. I told him to pull in. He pressed the button at the gate. The little box buzzed, then the black iron fence rolled away and we drove up the long asphalt driveway.

The drive threaded through a front lawn that the Redskins could've used as a practice field. With room for the Cowboys to do their drills on the other side. The mansion at the end of the drive had three floors if you didn't count a turret that jutted up above the roof. I could make out three more buildings in the back that constituted the rest of the compound. Stables or garages or shooting ranges, I supposed. The front door was an oak and iron monstrosity that could've been stolen from a Moorish castle and was large enough to drive the taxi through.

As we neared the house, two guys in suits came out and took up positions near the door. They had wide, blocky bodies and watched us as we drove up. As we got closer, I could see the suits, though tailored with impeccable care, were too big even for these gorillas. Meaning they had more than popguns under there. I told the taxi driver to pull up by the door and wait for me. I slid over and got out, then leaned back in, trying not to bump the shoulder cast.

"I, uh, wouldn't get out of the car, if I were you," I said, with what I hoped was an apologetic tone. "Just sit tight."

I approached the door, looking from one guy to the next.

"Mr. Singer?" the one on the left said.

"In the flesh. More or less."

"This way, please," the human block said, gesturing toward the entrance.

Half of the towering front door opened and the guards escorted me into the foyer. We stopped and they motioned for me to put my one good arm up. They did a thorough job frisking me, then ran a wand over and around my body. It went off with a discreet beep when it neared my shoulder.

"It's the prop," I said, gesturing to my shoulder.

"Take it off," the one with the wand said.

I gave him a look. "That and a couple of titanium bolts are all that's holding my shoulder together right now. I couldn't take it off if I wanted to."

The two glanced at each other.

"Look, I'm not here to shoot your boss and he knows that. Call him and ask. Or I get back in my taxi and we'll reschedule. Except you get to tell him that."

A minute later, we crossed the wood-paneled foyer, through a salon that would've made the Sun King proud, and into a drawing room featuring overstuffed furniture and trays with decanters and brandy snifters. On the far wall was a small door, carved with intricate scrollwork featuring a tangle of flowers and vines. The guard knocked once, opened without waiting for an answer, and gestured me through. He held it open, watching as I sidled past, then closed it behind me.

Beyond was an office that was decorated in the spirit of the rest of the house. In other words, like a medieval hall—or a madman's vision of one. There were heavy oak chairs that could pass for thrones. Tapestries of hunting scenes hung on the wall, the hounds and the bleeding deer locked together forever. A leather and wood globe, badly out of date two hundred years ago, sat on a pedestal in one corner. On the far wall, a fancy arrangement of shields and crossed swords hung above a large fireplace, in which burned a log the size of my torso.

But the cheery fire and faux Old World furnishings couldn't mask the smells that reached me from the far side of the room. There was the sharp, sterile tang of disinfectant and the musty odor of bodily fluid, covered up but never totally removed. And the underlying stink of death, which really has no description, but you know it when you smell it.

Sitting in a reclining chair lined with sheets was a small, sticklike man. He was ancient, the skin of his bald head discolored in patches. The few wispy hairs remaining to him were long and white. He was staring into the fire and plucking at the lapels of a flannel robe. In the back of the hand not doing the plucking was a needle with a line running to an IV stand. Next to him was a man dressed in scrubs, fiddling with the valve on one of the lines. Their heads turned as I came in and stopped. The old man, irritated, waved at me to come closer. I crossed the parquet, my footsteps sounding like measured knocks on a door. The nurse dragged over one of the ridiculous wooden chairs for me, then retreated to a corner, out of earshot but not out of the room.

The old man and I examined each other. Close up, he looked and smelled worse than he had from the door. His blue eyes were rheumy and unfocused. His face, which I remembered as being full and florid, sagged in gray folds now. The hand with the IV was heavily veined and I could see small white scars where numerous other needles had been inserted. He seemed to be enveloped by the chair, as if he were fading away into it and it would only be a matter of time before there would just be an empty robe lying there. With a shock, I remembered he was only ten years older than I was. I met his gaze and wondered what he saw from his point of view.

"So," he said. His voice was barely more than a whisper. "Marty Singer."

I said nothing.

"You've caused me a lot of pain," he said.

"Then we're even," I said.

"Really?" he asked. His hand pinched the lapels of his robe, then patted them down. The other hand gripped the arm of the chair, but I could see the tremor. "What the hell do you want?"

"I need to know what's going to happen next."

"I bet you would, Singer. You always wanted answers, but you didn't always ask so nicely."

"I've mellowed."

"Old age?" he said. "And cancer. That'll do it to you. Not the best way to have your clock punched, bleeding out your ass. Then again, there are worse ways to go. Take brain cancer, for instance. You forget things, you start talking funny, you can't move your arms. Then there are the headaches, the fucking headaches that make you want to kill yourself. Danny, over there, had to take my gun away, make sure I didn't self-medicate."

I shifted in the seat. "You want me to feel sorry for you?"

"Now, see, the old Jim Ferrin would've been in *your* face for that," he said. "But, you know what? I don't care. I really don't care at all."

We sat like that for a minute. He looked off into space.

"You shot him," he said suddenly, breaking out of his trance. "You shot my son. I told you I'd kill you for that."

"He didn't give me much choice," I said. "And someone's got to pay for Kransky."

"He's paid," he said. "When you gut-shot Lawrence—besides blowing that hole in him—you nicked his intestine and we all know that's bad news. It won't be long now. He might even go before me. The doctor did what he could, but the wound's septic."

"He's in the hospital?"

"No, he's in the east wing. My doctor swung by this morning, told me I had a few weeks to live, gave the kid a morphine drip."

I sat, looking at him.

"It's not worth lying about, Singer," he said. "Lawrence is dead, I'm dead, you're dead."

"What were you going to do with him? If Taylor and Jackson hadn't screwed up?"

"Do I have to spell it out?" Ferrin asked, leaning forward. His voice gathered strength, becoming clipped and vicious. "I was going to put him away. Forever. Lawrence is a psychopath. Normally, that wouldn't put him out of place on the force or anywhere else in this city, for that matter, but Lawrence liked to . . . possess people. Girls. Lock them up. Do things to them. That girl in Indiana that he took the ten-year rap for. She wasn't his first, just the first one they found. I tried looking the other way, but it was going to catch up with him and, eventually, with me. I couldn't get that through to Lawrence. He was mentally incapable of understanding. Or caring."

As he spoke, Ferrin's face tightened like the head of a drum and I saw him snatch at a small, white box by his side that had a line running up to the IV tube. He pressed the button and a few seconds later his features relaxed. Danny appeared and made a few adjustments, then returned to his spot by the door. Ferrin eased back into the chair, his breathing heavy. He cradled the morphine controller in his hand, but didn't press the button, as if holding it was comfort enough.

"When . . . he was . . . in jail," he said, continuing, "he was under wraps. I could . . . control the situation. No contact, no problems. I tried to protect him. Erased his record. But when he got out, I knew he'd go berserk. It would get back to me, to my family."

The room was quiet, the only sounds the crackling of the fire and the dying man across from me trying to catch his breath. I asked, "What started it all?"

"You want the behind the scenes, huh?"

I said nothing.

Ferrin shrugged. "Wheeler . . . wanted the broad. Nothing more complicated than that."

"What about Lawrence?"

"Tagging along, night after night. When he saw the girl, he lost his mind. I didn't know anything about it until the night they shot the mother."

"Why'd they do it?"

"She was getting ready to press charges. Wheeler thought he was looking at jail time. Lawrence was in his own world, thought somehow that the girl would be his once the mother was out of the way. They drove over there, who knows what they planned. Idiots."

"Then what?"

Ferrin shook himself, sighed. He seemed tired, uninterested. "Lawrence shot her. They called me in a panic. Wheeler was a nutcase, wanted to kill the girl even though he'd already called dispatch and told them he was standing outside her goddamn house. They had that cockamamie story about the break-in, wanted to say some phantom crook shot her. The story would've fallen apart in two seconds. I told Lawrence to get himself together, plant his holdout gun on the body, and just blame it on the bitch."

"But Wheeler took the fall," I said. "Why?"

"I explained a couple things to him. Like how, if Lawrence was the one that got picked up for the shooting, I'd blame Wheeler for it. And doing life in lockup would look like a great option compared to what I'd do to him. That was the stick."

"And the carrot?"

"That I was Jim Ferrin. That I had connections. That I could make the whole thing go away if I wanted to."

I thought about that. "Then I showed up and took the bait," I said. "I keyed in on Wheeler."

"Why wouldn't you? Wheeler was the one always hanging around the house, trying to bang the mother, making an ass out of himself."

"Then it went to trial and you got him off."

He nodded.

"I guess it was easy," I said. "You had an ace."

"A couple of them," he said.

"Landis?"

"I had some dirt on him. People thought Don didn't have any ambitions, but they were wrong. He had his sights set pretty high, in fact. Wanted to be another Giuliani, but what I had would've buried him."

"So he lost the tape?"

Ferrin shrugged. "I didn't tell him how to do it. Just do it."

"That's it? Don took a dive on the trial?"

"He had some insurance. You don't need to know about it."

I thought some more. Something didn't feel right. "Why Atwater for his attorney? You could've gotten anyone."

Ferrin shook his head, impatient with me. "Why the hell do that? Wheeler can't afford shit and out of nowhere some big-time lawyer walks in to defend him? People start following the money and my name comes up? Anyway, I didn't need to have Atwater on the payroll; it was Landis that was the problem and he was already in my back pocket. All I needed her to do was go through the motions. It was just a bonus that it was her third case ever. Landis tossed her softies and she did her part by the numbers."

I sat there, my stomach churning. I'd put most of the story together already, but having it confirmed didn't feel as good as I thought it would. We stared at each other for another minute, then he said, "There it is, Singer. You have it all. Now, what are you going to do with it?"

I blew out a breath and raised my eyes to the coffered ceiling. It was mahogany or some other dark wood, paneled and carved like a Renaissance parlor. It gave a certain monotonous order to the ceiling, like a chessboard above our heads.

"What I *want*," I said, "is to hand all this over to a friend in Homicide and let him go to town on you and your son. I'd be doing myself, the force, and the world a huge favor."

Ferrin said nothing.

"But what I *need*," I said, bringing my gaze down to stare at him, "is to keep Amanda Lane safe. Safe from Lawrence, safe from you. You have no reason to go after her. She doesn't know this side of the story, doesn't know who you are, doesn't know the MPDC like I do."

"What else?"

"I need to make sure Lawrence is dead."

Ferrin shook his head. "You can kill him, Singer, but I'm not going to let you gloat over his body."

"I don't want to gloat, goddamn it," I said. "I want to make sure he can't hurt anybody else."

"He won't," Ferrin said. "He'll be dead in a week. And I don't give a shit about you, Singer. Or the girl. Not if you keep your mouth shut."

"That's it? I take your word for it that Lawrence isn't a threat and you're not coming after me or the girl?"

"And I believe you when you say you're going to keep this whole thing to yourself and let me and my son die in peace."

I ran my good hand along a ridge in the big, wooden chair. "That's flimsy as hell."

"I'm sure we've both taken precautions," he said and nailed me with those eyes. "I know I have."

There wasn't much to say after that. I stood. I didn't want to shake his hand, but it seemed like something I had to do to close the deal. I could feel Danny's eyes on me from the door. Ferrin hesitated, then extended his hand. The skin was cool and smooth, the bones like straws, the knuckles knobby and prominent. We shook.

He looked up at me. "I was a good cop once."

I didn't say anything. I wanted to wipe my hand on my shirt. I walked across the parquet floor, feeling Ferrin's eyes on me the whole way. Danny opened the door and I slid past, trying to fit both my body and the prop through the door. My shoulder was hurting and I needed one of those Demerols badly, but I wanted to be safely back at home before I altered my state of consciousness. One of the suits was waiting for me in the drawing room and guided me back out of the kingpin's palace to the front steps. I breathed out as I walked down the steps and over to the taxi.

Halfway there I couldn't take it anymore and scratched at the armpit of my broken shoulder like a dog going after its fleas. It wasn't the brace and cast that were the problem, though they were bad enough. It was the wad of medical tape holding the digital recorder that was driving me crazy.

CHAPTER THIRTY-TWO

I wouldn't call it a happy ending.

Two days after my encounter with Jim Ferrin, the excitement was over. We sat through endless interviews with MPDC investigators, repeating our statements dozens of times. If I thought I was going to get any preferential treatment because I'd worn a badge until recently, I was wrong. Especially when I wouldn't budge about the missing link in our story, namely that there should've been a third body or at least another shooter at the scene. I hemmed and hawed and stonewalled and made a ton of cops angry at me. I told them everything up to the encounter with Lawrence at the house in the Palisades and then I clammed up. It couldn't have been more obvious that I was hiding something, but that was their problem.

Julie spent the days back at her office trying to resuscitate her practice; there'd been no time to talk about a future, if there was one. Amanda was dealing with a new set of nightmares and coming to grips with the idea that her mother's killer was truly and forever gone. Again. As long as Jim Ferrin had been telling the truth. And some of the things that he'd said continued to bother me. I'd been picking at them like scabs since I'd walked out of that door.

But there wasn't time to brood. I was gearing up for another round of chemo and the fears that went with it. The fact that I was still breathing was a positive sign. But planning for another tangle with the drugs was depressing. It brought the underlying reality of my life—disease—back to me in stark relief and made all the other recent events seem like circus sideshows.

So maybe I should be grateful for the unexpected distraction of blacking out at the oncologist's office. I was told later that things were going swimmingly while Nurse Leah prepped me for some tests. Shortly afterward, I ceased to be conscious. The order of events was simple: I took a seat in the chair, I felt the antiseptic, icy cold swab on the inside of my elbow, and then I pitched headfirst into a yawning hole lined with black velvet. I think I tried to say "Not again!" as I checked out, but I ran out of time. Leave 'em laughing. Or try to.

I woke up in the hospital groggy, covered in sweat, my eyes crusted shut. The titanium brace was still there, keeping my shoulder immobilized, but I was flat on my back in a hospital nightie and my mouth tasted like I'd sucked on a spoon for a week.

Christmas wasn't over yet, that much I could tell from a single dopey glance around me. Green tinsel and glass ornaments were pinned to the wall at uneven intervals and a few candy canes had been hooked over door handles, shelf edges, and curtain rods. Out the window I could see it was dark, but the region's first snowfall was being blown at a steep angle under the sodium-tinted light of a streetlamp. I turned my head. It was dim in the room, but I could see Julie and Amanda hovering at the foot of the bed, talking to a guy in a gray suit, their heads close together as they whispered.

"What's going on?" I tried to ask, but it sounded more like I was trying to spit out my tongue. The girls looked up and their faces brightened simultaneously. The guy glanced over with an appraising look, as though my recovery was unexpected and he wasn't sure what to make of it. Amanda propped me up in the bed and slipped a straw in my mouth that led to a cup of water. I emptied it and sagged back onto the pillow.

"How you feeling, Marty?" Amanda asked. She had dark circles under her eyes and her hair looked lank and greasy, but she smiled at me and reached for my hand.

I said, "Like hell. What happened to me?"

"You had an infection," Julie said.

"An infection?" I asked. "That's it?"

"That's what the doctor said. Quote, 'Chemo kills a lot of blood cells that keep you safe from microscopic threats,'" she said. "'Like the kind you pick up after getting shot.'"

"You passed out at the doctor's," Amanda said. "We didn't know what had happened until the next day."

"What do you mean, 'the next day'?" I said. "What day is it?"

"The doctor's was Tuesday," Julie said. "Today is Friday."

I took that in, then asked, "They mention when I can get out of here?"

"They told us if your fever broke, it wouldn't be long. Probably another day or two," Julie said, then smiled. "You'll need a nurse."

"I'll have to look into that," I said, but my eyes slid away from her face.

The man in gray coughed and took a step closer to the bed. He was slim, with coffee-black hair and a scar over one eyebrow. He had the nervous look of a clerk pushed into a suit or a volunteer picked out of a crowd to be the hypnotist's dummy. I processed the tired face, the wrinkled suit from Marshalls.

"Mr. Singer, I'm Pete Michaels," he said.

"Detective Michaels, I presume," I said.

He smiled. "Yeah. I work under Detective Davidovitch. He wanted to let you know how things were going. Unofficially, of course."

Michaels meant that Dods was involved with, if not in charge of, the shootings at the Lane house. If anyone higher up caught him fraternizing with or, God help us, visiting me in the hospital, he'd be yanked off the case and probably replaced with some hard-ass. If he kept his distance, he could make sure the corners were rounded, the edges smoothed. Especially if Jim Ferrin, despite our agreement, decided to throw his weight around. Of course, if it ever came to that, I had a certain recording on file if I ever needed it.

Michaels made some sympathetic noises about my condition, then let me know—obliquely—what Dods would be doing to shield me from the case. It sounded like I'd get away with skin intact, but I'd probably be dragged in for many more interviews, have to answer many more questions. I nodded. If anyone knew how the drill went, I did.

With his message delivered, Michaels was obviously eager to leave. I told him to get out of there and give my best to Dods. He wished me well and left, promising to come back if he had more to tell me. Distant, tinny Christmas music floated in as he opened the door to leave, then stopped abruptly when it closed.

Julie was right behind him, saying she'd be back in a second. I looked at Amanda. She smiled, looking more weary and jaded than any twenty-four-year-old had a right to be. Her eyes still had that wide-eyed wariness I remember from the night of her mother's murder. She had a scar high on her cheek where Ferrin had hit her. That, and the ones inside, weren't going to go away soon. But there was also resolution and strength there.

"How are you?" I asked.

"I'm better," she said. "I'm still trying to get over how close it was. Real close." She was quiet, then said, "And I have to put the story back together. Again."

"You know what really happened now."

"Yeah," she said. "I told you, part of the way I come to terms with things is accepting what I know—or think I know—as fact. Immutable history. The be-all, end-all of the tragedy. Ferrin came along and took that away. But now I've got what I need to put the whole thing to rest. There won't be any more surprises, no more old faces from the past cropping up. You fixed it, Marty. Thank you."

"You're welcome," I said. "For nothing. I screwed up from the start. I'd make the world's worst bodyguard."

"Not true, and you know it," she said. She looked down. A moment passed. "I feel bad about Jim."

"Me, too," I said. I pushed the bleakness away. No chance for reconciliation. No time to put a friendship back together. We were quiet for a minute, then I said, "What about school?"

She made a face. "The board of directors and the president strongly encouraged me to take some time off."

"Can you fight it?"

"I've got the support of my department, though, and my students, so I may be able to pressure them into reinstating me. Just in time, of course, for the end of the semester and the holidays, so I won't be teaching for another couple of weeks anyway."

I smoothed the edge of the blanket. "You're welcome to stay as long as you want, you know."

She smiled wider. "Thanks, Marty. Maybe until after New Year's, if you don't mind."

"That'd be fine. I don't think Pierre would tolerate anything less."

"Omigod," she said, bringing her hands to her face. "He hasn't been fed all day. I've got to run."

"Don't spoil him too much, okay?" I said. "I'm not going to be able to pick him up with just the one arm, pretty soon."

"Quit worrying, Marty," she said. "I've got him eating out of the palm of my hand."

"That's what I'm afraid of."

She shook her fist at me, then followed it with a peck on the cheek. A quick wave and she was gone.

I lay there, empty-headed. The TV was on, running an endless stream of holiday specials, but the sound was muted, and I watched the flashing images blankly, without comprehension. Julie found me like that ten minutes later, staring at the TV like it was trying to tell me something, but failing.

"What was that about?" I asked.

"I caught up with Detective Michaels, asked him to keep me in the loop," she said. "No way am I going to let them pin anything on you or me or Amanda just for trying to keep ourselves alive."

"Thanks," I said and looked away.

"What's wrong?" she asked, moving closer.

I didn't say anything.

She sat on the edge of the bed. "Are you feeling weird about us? If you are, we can go slow. Once you get out of here, get through chemo . . ." Her voice trailed off as she saw my face.

I cleared my throat. "You know when you run your hand along a smooth piece of wood and you feel a snag but you can't really see it? A little imperfection that you can't ignore? Everything looks good, but there's something wrong and you have to look close to find it."

Julie said nothing.

"When I was out there, talking to Jim Ferrin, sitting in that madhouse, he said something. I was focusing more on what he had to say about the night Brenda was killed, but later I realized something else he'd said didn't add up. He admitted he had Landis in his pocket during the trial. That much I could guess. But then he said that Don was scared, that he wasn't sure he could sandbag the whole trial convincingly. Ferrin said he'd given him some extra insurance, something that would seal the deal. It's bothered me since then, but I wasn't sure why. It was that snag in the wood that I couldn't find. But now I think I know what it was. What Don's insurance was."

I stopped talking and stared at her but it was her turn to look away, out at the night where the wind was whipping the snow in mad flurries past the window. She plucked at the blanket at the foot of my bed. I thought she would stay like that forever.

She started to speak, so softly I could barely hear her. "It was my first real case. I was good and smart and I knew you had nothing solid on Wheeler and that, in the end, it wouldn't matter. Once the jury heard that tape or put the picture together from all the complaints she'd made, it would be over. Who was going to listen to me drone on about burden of proof after they heard that woman screaming into the phone?"

Julie got up, hugging her arms to her chest, and walked over to the window. "I remember thinking to myself that I'd put up a good fight and try to move on to the next one, if there was one. Then Don called. Told me he thought a grave injustice was being done to my client, that he couldn't live with himself if an innocent man went to jail. A real line of bullshit. After the first minute, it was obvious he was scared out of his mind, that someone was leaning on him."

I said nothing.

"He fed me everything. What his strategy would be, how he'd question the witnesses, the gaps he'd leave. But we both knew it wouldn't be enough. I told him he'd have to get rid of that tape or all the cross-examination in the world wasn't going to get Wheeler off."

"So he ditched it," I said.

"I didn't ask. Then the trial came along and I tore him to pieces. With his help. It wasn't easy. I knew Don from my time in the DA's office. It didn't feel good to see him put on a brave face while he waited for the next knife in the gut. While I dismembered his career."

We were both quiet for a moment. I felt hollow inside. "Did you know it was Ferrin pulling the strings?"

"No. Don never told me who it was."

"Were you curious when Don wound up dead?"

She shot me a look. "Of course. But whatever it was that Ferrin had on him was bad enough to break him. Add on the secret that he'd thrown the trial, and the public knowledge that he'd lost a landmark case, and suddenly it's not too hard to imagine Don walking out in front of a train."

"Whatever lets you sleep at night," I said.

She opened her mouth, then shut it. I waited for her to say something, wanted her to say something. When she didn't, I went on.

"Once you knew Wheeler was dead, when you knew that we were up against Ferrin and his son, would that have been a good time, maybe, to tell me you'd figured out who had rigged the trial?"

She shook her head. "What did it matter at that point? You knew who you were up against. Better than I did. And if you're going to hold the trial against me, here's a news flash for you, Marty. Wheeler didn't kill Brenda Lane. So, the fact that I got him off turned out to be the right thing to do. Even if you don't like the way I did it."

She was right. And she was wrong. I wasn't a moralist. I'd seen more shades of gray in my life than most people. I knew how the world worked. But at the end of the day, you have to do the right things for the right reasons. At some gut level, there can't be tolerance for compromises or shortcuts. There was an absolute in there somewhere that I fumbled for, tried to pin down and describe so I could hold it up to her actions like a measuring stick. Nothing came to mind. No easy way to talk the wrongness away. All I know is that, when I looked at her, it wasn't right.

"Get out," I said.

She looked at me, then away, her eyes tearing up. She seemed ready to say something. I think I wanted her to. It came to me that this was the moment, the stark knife's edge when maybe it was time to hold on.

To pull ourselves back, not push us over. A gesture, a look, one word from either of us would've done it.

But it wasn't going to happen. Not now, at least. Maybe not ever. The moment came and went in silence. Julie grabbed her coat, walked to the door, and left. Christmas music wafted in again, then was clipped short. I watched the TV for a second, then turned my head on the pillow and watched the snow fall outside.

IX.

The nurse wheeled the old man by the bed, then left, taking up a spot just outside the door.

The old man looked around. His son's childhood bedroom had been turned into a hospital clinic. There were IV tubes and stacks of bandages and complicated-looking monitoring devices sitting on wheeled carts. He imagined the air was thick with a chemical odor, but his own battle with illness had long since made him unable to smell.

Lawrence was lying on his back. His eyes were slightly opened and glassy; his breathing was hard and his body convulsed after each breath. The old man looked down, then reached out and grabbed his son's hand. It was as much contact as he'd ever had with him.

The eyes opened a fraction. The old man thought of saying something, but his head was empty and he simply stared back. His son's lips moved and he wheeled himself closer to hear what it was he was trying to say. On the third try, he caught it, and when he did, he put his head down and rested it on the two hands clasping his son's.

He had said, "I'm starting over."

PLEASE CONTINUE READING TO
SAMPLE THE NEXT MARTY SINGER
MYSTERY, *BLUEBLOOD*.

CHAPTER ONE

My hands are behind my back. The thumbs have been lashed together with a short length of zip tie, the kind of stuff that gets tighter the more you pull at it, and right now the short strips holding my thumbs and pinkies are so tight that the tips of my fingers feel like they're going to burst like hot grapes. It must be bad, since I lost feeling in the rest of my hands hours ago.

Blood is rolling down my hairline, making a half circuit along the side of my face like a scarlet moon before cutting in and dribbling over a cheek and into one swollen eye. The blood comes from a six-inch trench going from the top of my scalp to just north of my forehead. Someone put it there with a two-foot length of rebar wrapped in electrical tape. The tape wasn't there to soften the blow; it was to give him a better grip. The deep, diamond-shaped cross-hatching that gives rebar a better bond with cement is what laid my scalp open, but it was the force of the blow that cracked my skull. I'm nauseous and can smell my own vomit, which is puddled in front of me. That probably means I'm lying on the floor. I can't tell since my good eye is closest to the ground and any time I move my head, I scream.

The pain doesn't stop at my face. My ribs feel gone, too, half of them snapped like plastic straws. It's hard to breathe, though that may be from the blood running down my throat. The bruises up and down both arms aren't worth mentioning, but my gut is aching and my testicles have ballooned to the size of tennis balls, which is what happens when they've been kicked repeatedly.

The beating, as brutal as it was, wasn't systematic. For what it's worth, this was done in a frenzy; it wasn't an interrogation and it wasn't about payback. Nobody asked questions or took time to gloat. They just wanted to hurt. Small consolation, but the guy with the rebar hadn't done anything a hospital couldn't put back together with enough time and health insurance. No one had lopped off a finger or spooned out an eye. It might take weeks or months or years, even, to heal. But as long as I have a pulse, I have a chance.

I'm still thinking that when he comes back. Quietly, this time, maybe to watch me struggling to take a breath. I don't hear him at first. Blood has pooled in my ear and my pulse is loud. Then a shoe scuffs a wall or a door frame or a piece of furniture and I turn my head toward the sound instinctively. But a small click, like a gear falling into place, tells me my chance is done, and I want to yell, to tell them, no, I need to see my boy and my wife and—

◆ ◆ ◆

"You see it?"

"I see it," I said, putting the last of the crime scene photos down. I was happy to get them out of my hands. A year ago, they would've been nothing special for Marty Singer, homicide cop, especially after thirty years in Washington, DC's police force, the MPDC, but time had given me some distance from that life and I realized I didn't have quite the same perspective on things now that I did then. "This is bad."

"It is," Sam Bloch said. He was a lieutenant with the MPDC Major Narcotics Branch, the catchall division that did most of the city's drug enforcement. Bloch was a slim, tall man with a pinched face and a small, pencil-thin mustache. With his black hair and dark eyes, he could've been Clark Gable's twin, but with a nose so broken that the tip almost touched one cheek, he would've had to have settled for being the stunt double.

"Who was he, again?"

"Danny Garcia," Bloch said. He picked up the photos and slipped them back into a manila envelope, conscious of the people passing our table at the Java Hut. We had a nook in one of the duskier corners of the coffeehouse, but still, no sense risking someone tossing their biscotti just because they happened to see a stack of eight-by-ten glossies of a mutilated body.

"Danny was one of our best undercover guys," Bloch continued. "Hispanic, obviously, so he was a huge help with the Latino gangs, but it was more than that. He was good because he fit in anywhere. Fast talker, knew the street, great instincts on when to step it up or back off. He could put together a buy over in Southeast where even the black cops won't go, for Christ's sake, and the next day be out in Hicksville, picking up a John Deere full of weed from some good old boys spitting Skoal between their last two teeth."

I took a sip of coffee. It picked a fight with the bile Bloch's pictures had brought forth. "Looks like somebody wasn't buying that night."

Bloch lifted the cover of the folder, glanced at the top picture again, then let it fall back shut. "I couldn't believe this when I saw it. We get our share of outrageous shit—more than our share—but Danny was good and this kind of . . . butchery doesn't happen every day. Not anymore. Maybe in a gang war or when people are sending a message about who's boss, but no one was going to mistake Danny for a *chavala*."

I frowned.

"A rival gang leader," Bloch explained. "Danny was going on fifty. The only gangsters that old are either in maximum lockup or dead. Most of today's honchos are in their twenties."

"Maybe someone just made him." I gestured at the folder. "This was vicious enough to be driven by cop hate."

Bloch shrugged, a short roll of the shoulders. "It's possible. Anything is. But, like I said, he was good at what he did. Too good for me to believe he just happened to slip up."

"When he was on a case, did he pose as a junkie? Or a buyer?"

"A little of both," Bloch said, picking up a sugar packet and turning it rhythmically in his hands, corner to corner. I had smelled the cigarette smoke on him when we'd met. Judging by the urgency with which he was spinning that packet, it must've been a while since his last puff. "He'd break in as a user, see who was dealing. Then he'd graduate to hand-to-hand deals. Penny-ante shit, but it gave him an idea on who was willing to play ball. Final stop might be to set up a mid-level buy for a small cut or to get two dealers together, see if they would do business."

"Why such small beans?" I asked. "He was a twenty-year pro."

"For just that reason. If we used Danny once on a big bust, he was burnt. He'd have to sit at a desk for two years before he could go back on the street. Instead, I kept him simmering somewhere in the middle, which worked. We set up three major busts a year without compromising him."

"How'd he like that?"

"Not much," Bloch admitted. "It was blue-collar work. No glory, none of that lining up millions on a kitchen table with a dozen AK-47s and getting on the evening news. He wasn't happy about it, but he knew he was doing good work."

I wondered about that. Cops are people, too, and it can be hard to see the light at the end of the tunnel if you're asked to turn the crank on the same wheel day in, day out. But I kept that to myself. "What was he working on when this happened?"

"I don't know."

I raised my eyebrows.

"Danny demanded a lot of rope," Bloch said. "He kept his own list of snitches, dealers, leads. I got him to agree to weekly updates, but he missed them all the time and even when we did connect, he was cagey about everything."

"So you don't know if this was part of a case or not."

Bloch nodded. "There's no reason to think that it wasn't, but which one? New or old? Was he just fishing, or was this the next-to-last meet before he set up a bust? He left us crap for notes. I've gone over all of them and don't have a clue."

I spun my coffee cup around by the handle. Bloch's fidgeting was contagious. "When you called, you said you had something that made you nervous, something you wanted to talk over. Garcia's killing is bad, really bad, but—no disrespect—it's something you should take up with MPDC Homicide."

"They're on it. In their own way."

"So why me?"

"What do you know about HIDTA?" He pronounced it "hide-uh."

"High Intensity Drug Trafficking Area," I said. "A task force. Feds and locals from all the Metro jurisdictions get together to compare notes on drug traffic, trying to keep the left hand in touch with the right."

"Right. Crack dealers don't pay attention to county and state lines. Dope that winds up in DC didn't magically sprout there; it had to come through Virginia or Maryland. And it didn't start there, either, of course; those are just distribution points along the chain."

"Every city with a population of two or more's got that problem."

"Sure, but we've got two states, a city, and a federal jurisdiction in a ten-mile radius. Dealers know what a headache it is for a DC cop to try and get a warrant in Maryland or set up a wiretap in Virginia. And if they decide to go up to a sunset overlook on the George Washington Parkway to do a deal, well, that's a national park, right? All of a sudden it's a federal case. Then the DEA and Park Service police are in charge, even if every ounce of the dope from that deal winds up on K Street in the District."

"Enter HIDTA," I said.

He nodded. "Virginia cooperates with Maryland cops who work with MPDC who partners up with the DEA. Jurisdictions melt away, everybody shares the work and the glory, bad guys have nowhere to hide."

The wood of the booth popped and creaked as I leaned back. "Must look good on a poster."

"It works better than you'd think. There are a lot of egos, sure, and the higher up you go, the crustier everyone gets. At the soldier level, though, everybody's on the same side."

"It sounds beautiful," I said. "Before I tear up, though, what does this have to do with me?"

"I'm mid-level at HIDTA. Danny worked directly for me. The important point is that, while I might be a DC cop, I'm also dialed in to all the other players. I hear things, I see things I might not get to if I was buried all by myself in Major Narcotics."

"Okay."

Bloch reached into a briefcase resting on the floor and pulled out a thick handful of manila folders identical to the one he'd produced on Danny Garcia. He pushed them across to me.

Inside the top folder was a single photo of another crime scene, another murder. It was a black man in his boxers and a T-shirt. He had a belly and soft, unmuscular arms and legs. Salt-and-pepper hair cropped close. He'd been beaten badly—the bones of his arms and hands were broken and bent out of shape—and shot in the back of the head, apparently with a small-caliber round since there wasn't much of an exit wound to speak of. Blood and probably urine had puddled around the body. It resembled a lot of other scenes I'd seen over the years.

I flipped the photo over, revealing another. A white guy in a tank top and shorts, young and in good shape. Red hair. Pale. Freckles. Or maybe it was blood. Superman tattoo on his left deltoid—a little ironic. Like the first body, he looked like he'd gone through a thresher, with arms out of joint and a lot of bloodletting. The photo had been taken from near his feet, so I couldn't make out details, but two small, quarter-sized black dots in the side of his head testified to more gunshot wounds. His fingers were broken and mangled.

I turned that one over. Beneath, a third scene, a third body. Or fourth, counting Danny Garcia. Like the first, this was a black man, sprawled on a blacktop parking lot or road. There wasn't much context, but comparing him to a nearby car door, he was enormous, maybe six and a half feet tall. Two seventy, two eighty? He was fully dressed, sporting jeans and a University of Maryland polo shirt. Blood was hard to discern against his ink-black skin and the asphalt. Unlike the others, he hadn't been beaten. I couldn't see evidence of a gunshot, but on a body that big, it could be anywhere.

"Bloch, I don't want to look at this," I said. But I cycled through the pictures again. I could feel Bloch's eyes on me as I peered at the glossies, closer this time. Not surprisingly, I'd focused on details at first glance. Looking for setting, characteristics, gunshot wounds. I shuffled back and forth between the three photos several times, then added Danny's, checked, and glanced up. "The beatings. They're crazy. Vicious. Faces broken apart. Arms and hands and feet twisted, pulled."

Bloch nodded.

"Except for that last one," I said. "That one's odd man out."

"Maybe. But for the rest, they're the same. It's the beatings. They were all pre- and postmortem, or so the coroners tell me."

"Coroners? Plural?"

He reached over the table and flipped the stack over so that I was looking at the first body again. "Terrence Witherspoon. MPDC beat cop, First District."

"PSA?"

"One-oh-six."

I grimaced. One of the worst in Southeast DC. "Okay."

He flipped to the next photo. "Brady Torres, Arlington PD." Flip. "Isaac Okonjo. Montgomery County Sheriff's Department, Maryland."

I felt a twist in my gut that had nothing to do with the coffee. "Danny Garcia. MPDC Major Narcotics Bureau."

Bloch nodded, looking at me with eyes like twin lumps of coal. "You see it?"

"I see it," I said, but not liking it. "Someone's killing cops."

Please visit www.matthew-iden.com to find out more about *Blueblood* and the other books in the Marty Singer Mystery series.

ACKNOWLEDGMENTS

As with any debut novel, or any novel for that matter, an enormous number of people helped make the dream a reality.

First and foremost, my wife, Renee, has been patient and supportive from the start, through the middle, and no doubt to the end. I couldn't have even begun this whole shebang without her.

My family—Sally, Gary, and Kris Iden—has been a great source of energy and inspiration for me from the first time I picked up a pencil and started scribbling. Thanks, guys.

Frank Gallivan, Carie Rothenbacher, Amy and Pete Talbot, David Jacobstein, and Eleonora Ibrani were wonderful friends and readers throughout the process, never failing to ask how I was doing or where I stood with all of my mysterious writing endeavors. Karen Cantwell, Misha Crews, Jeff Ziskind, Angie Holtz, Shannon Ryan, Ana Bilik, Tom Scheuren, Erica Mongelli, Jacqui Corcoran, and Lane Stone were patient, meticulous, and incredibly generous with their time and expertise as readers. Karen, especially: thank you for your effort and lending me your ear as a fellow writer.

Thank you to Chip Cochran, Dave Green, and Ray Tarasovic for sharing with me their many years of expertise in law enforcement. A special thank-you to Chip for the many e-mails and late nights chewing the fat.

Eric Cohen and Drucilla Brethwaite of Life with Cancer (www. lifewithcancer.org) were incredibly helpful in describing the process of being diagnosed with cancer, the paths to treatment, and the complex navigation required of patients as they battle their disease. Thank you for taking the time to speak with me. I apologize for any mistakes or exaggerations; all faults rest with me.

Jenny McDowell, Matt McDowell, Bill Way, and Paul Caulfield gave generously of their time to help make sense of the legal processes I pretended to know inside and out.

My original editor, Alison Dasho, was a huge help ironing out the inconsistencies and unrealities I tried to pass off as decent writing. Thank you, Alison; you made the whole much better than the parts.

A heartfelt thank-you to the team at Thomas & Mercer and especially my editor, Kjersti Egerdahl, for giving me the opportunity to introduce Marty to a wider world.

Lastly, thank you to those suffering with cancer, as well as the victims and survivors of violent crime. In my research, I read many accounts of oncology patients going through diagnosis, treatment, and recovery and of the families struggling to cope with a loss borne of violence. The tremendous courage you display in facing your hardships is humbling and inspirational.

ABOUT THE AUTHOR

Photo © 2014 Sally Iden

Matthew Iden writes hard-boiled detective fiction, fantasy, science fiction, horror, thrillers, and contemporary literary fiction with a psychological twist. He is the author of the Marty Singer detective series:

A Reason to Live

Blueblood

One Right Thing

The Spike

The Wicked Flee

Visit www.matthew-iden.com for information on upcoming appearances, new releases, and to receive a free copy of *The Guardian: A Marty Singer Short Story*—not available anywhere else.

IF YOU LIKED *A REASON TO LIVE . . .*

Writers can only survive and flourish with the help of readers. If you like what you've read, please consider reviewing *A Reason to Live* on Amazon.com or your favorite readers' website. Just three or four short sentences are all it takes to make a huge difference. Thank you.

STAY IN TOUCH

Please say hello via e-mail (matt.iden@matthew-iden.com), through Facebook (www.facebook.com/matthew.iden), or Twitter (@CrimeRighter). I also enjoy connecting with readers and writers at my website, www.matthew-iden.com.